Bill Cardoni

About the Author

DIANE MCKINNEY-WHETSTONE is the author of the novels *Tumbling*, a national bestseller; *Tempest Rising*; and *Blues Dancing*. She teaches fiction writing at the University of Pennsylvania and lives in Philadelphia with her husband, Greg, and (from time to time) their college-age twins, a daughter and son, Taiwo and Kehinde.

10659027

Also by
Diane McKinney-Whetstone

Tumbling

Tempest Rising

Blues Dancing

Leaving Cecil Street

A Novel

Diane McKinney-Whetstone

Perennial

An Imprint of HarperCollins*Publishers*

This book is a work of fiction. The characters, incidents, and dialogue are drawn from the author's imagination and are not to be construed as real. Any resemblance to actual events or persons, living or dead, is entirely coincidental.

A hardcover edition of this book was published in 2004 by William Morrow, an imprint of HarperCollins Publishers.

P.S.™ is a trademark of HarperCollins Publishers.

LEAVING CECIL STREET. Copyright © 2004 by Diane McKinney-Whetstone. All rights reserved. Printed in the United States of America. No part of this book may be used or reproduced in any manner whatsoever without written permission except in the case of brief quotations embodied in critical articles and reviews. For information address HarperCollins Publishers Inc., 10 East 53rd Street, New York, NY 10022.

HarperCollins books may be purchased for educational, business, or sales promotional use. For information please write: Special Markets Department, HarperCollins Publishers Inc., 10 East 53rd Street, New York, NY 10022.

FIRST PERENNIAL EDITION PUBLISHED 2005.

Designed by Cassandra J. Pappas

The Library of Congress has catalogued the hardcover edition as follows:

McKinney-Whetstone, Diane.
    Leaving Cecil Street: a novel / Diane McKinney-Whetstone.—1st ed.
    p. cm.
    ISBN 0-688-16385-8
    1. South Philadelphia (Philadelphia, Pa.)—Fiction. 2. African American teenage girls—Fiction. 3. African American families—Fiction. 4. Philadelphia (Pa.)—Fiction. 5. Teenage pregnancy—Fiction. 6. Abortion—Fiction. I. Title.

PS3563.C3825L43 2004
813'.54—dc22

2003055845

ISBN 0-06-072289-4 (pbk.)
05 06 07 08 09 ❖ / RRD 10 9 8 7 6 5 4 3 2 1

In loving memory
Michal Jean Sears
1925—2002

Part One

Chapter 1

ECIL STREET WAS FEELING some kind of way in 1969. Safely tucked away in the heart of West Philadelphia, this had always been a charmed block. A pleasure to walk through the way the trees lined the street from end to end and made arcs when they were in full leaf. The outsides of the houses stayed in good repair, with unchipped banister posts and porches mopped down daily because the people here sat out a lot, their soothing chatter jumping the banisters from end to end about how the numbers had come that day or what had happened on *The Edge of Night*. And even though the block had long ago made the transition from white to colored to Negro to Black Is Beautiful, the city still provided street cleaning twice a week in the summer when the children took to the outside and there was the familiar smack, smack of the double-Dutch rope. The sound was a predictable comfort. Like the sounds of the Corner

Boys, a mildly delinquent lot consumed with pilfering Kool ciga-
rettes or the feel of a virgin girl's behind. But as soon as Walter
Cronkite signed off for the night, the Corner Boys put their voices
together in a cappella harmonies that rushed this stretch of Cecil
and felt like a new religion. They sang nice settling-down tunes
about love and the blues. Sang as the bowls of chicken and
dumplings or pans of corn bread or whatever somebody had cooked
too much of were passed up and down the block. Sang while the
teenagers gathered on steps under the street lamps to plait each
other's hair so that their 'fros would grow out thick and full. Sang
while the women who hadn't yet made the leap to the African bush
put hot combs on the stove to touch up their edges for the next day.
Stirred up a good nighttime mood on the block when they sang.

But now Cecil Street had a new mood working, a fire-in-the-
belly feeling about bad to come. Horrible enough that Martin had
been assassinated last year, but in March the wrong cracker pled
guilty, they believed. The government is the cracker should be on
trial, they maintained as they hosed down their fronts of the dripped
Popsicle juice. Then the undeclared war was threatening to take
down as many of the young black men as the heroin that some swore
was being pushed in their neighborhood by the CIA. Then the milk-
man stopped delivering around here, and Sonny went up on his hoa-
gies by twenty cents. Then Tim, who owned the barbershop on the
corner and the apartment above it that he regularly loaned out for
the pleasure takings of his married men friends, was almost stomped
to death under the el stop when the police mistook him for someone
who'd robbed the PSFS with a water gun. Then BB, who worked in
the shadows of her back bedroom freeing the women who'd gotten

caught when their diaphragms or rhythm methods failed, had her purse snatched on Sixtieth Street; she'd just performed back-to-back procedures and was on her way to buy two hundred dollars' worth of money orders to send to her mother down south who was raising BB's severely retarded child. The market two blocks over started disrespecting the hardworking homeowners around here by keeping dirty floors and wilted lettuce and day-old bread. And now this: the tree in front of Joe and Louise's house died.

It was the summer of '69 and Joe missed that tree. Missed it so much that he put awnings out front to try and duplicate its shade. Generally upbeat, Joe felt sad about the tree right now as he stood on his porch at two in the morning, shocked again by the sight of the stump where the tree should be. Felt sad generally right now even though this was the night that his close-knit block of Cecil Street had opened itself up for the annual block party and Joe had even danced in the street earlier to "Boogaloo Down Broadway." He reasoned he was absorbing what the rest of the block seemed to be feeling lately, edgy and discontented, otherwise he had no explanation for why, now, he was out on his porch at two in the morning lifting up the square of the porch floor that led to his cellar. He hadn't been down in the cellar since the spring, but he pushed through the dust and mold and spiderwebs down there— and the darkness. He'd forgotten about the short in the light. His hand went instinctively to his shirt pocket for matches to give himself a spark to see by. Remembered now no shirt pocket because he was wearing a dashiki. Didn't usually wear dashikis but had worn one for the block party, worn it also hoping to impress the young woman Valadean, up here for the summer visiting relatives across the street. "Who you supposed to be, Super Black Jack?" his wife, Louise, had remarked when she'd seen him in the dashiki.

He stretched his arms through the black air in the cellar, trying to feel his way so that he wouldn't collide full body into what he could not see. Couldn't see, stacked along the wall, the boxes that should have gone to Goodwill the month the light went, couldn't see the milk crates filled with his teenage daughter's outgrown toys; couldn't even see the oil heater that took up a quarter of the wall. Nor could he see the puffy-haired, naked woman making herself go flat against the wall, between the toys and the heater.

Deucie Powell. She wasn't from this part of Philly. She had turned onto Cecil Street earlier looking for her grown daughter's house, wanted to reintroduce herself to her daughter after a gulf of seventeen years. Wanted to reclaim her. But she'd gotten disoriented by the block party and ended up naked in this cellar. She held herself stiffly, almost behind a wooden pony, as Joe walked past. She hoped that if he happened to turn and look down and see her through the darkness that at least she'd have the appearance of one of those life-size walkie-talkie dolls. Being caught down here could land her back in Byberry, the crazy house, she called it, and she was desperate not to die there.

But Joe couldn't see her. Couldn't even feel her naked presence; felt the presence of only one thing as the shapes down here slowly came into view and he was looking at the tall, wide chifforobe, drawn to it. He opened the doors to the chifforobe and was bombarded with the scent of mothballs as he leaned in and riffled through the sweaters and blankets and whatever else was wool and for wintertime use. Tossed things around in there until he felt it, that unmistakable corrugated roughness. Just like he'd packed it away all those years ago in the bottom of this chest.

JOE HAD PLAYED a tenor sax in clubs up and down the Mid-Atlantic before he'd married Louise. When they'd first moved to Cecil Street fifteen years ago, in 1954, the year that Joe quit the club life, he would sometimes stand out on his porch in the mellow warmth of a summer night and blow. People sitting out would even applaud when he was done. One night as he played he thought about a woman he'd spent time with before Louise. C. Not her real name, but the one she went by at Pat's Place, the speakeasy/brothel where the band would go to unwind when they were doing Philly. The first time Joe held C she'd cried on his chest. That melted him for her. He became her regular, looked for opportunities to come to Philly to be with her. Thought he could have fallen in love with her even though he was paying for her time. Some nights, the way she'd occupy his mind, he thought he had fallen for her. Even after he'd married Louise, the feel of her would drift into his consciousness from time to time. Like the night in '54 when he stood on his Cecil Street porch and played "'Round Midnight" with everything in him. Playing was so raw that night. Sweat leaked through his plaid cotton shirt, and though his skin coloring was generally too brown to turn red, it did while he played that night. Afterward he walked down from his house and out into the middle of the street and raised his horn and bowed. Garnered a huge ovation that night because it was Friday and many on the block had just finished a dinner of porgies coated with a cornmeal batter cooked on high in Crisco. The fish tended to put them in a good mood helped along by their Friday-night sips of brown-colored liquid, the comfort of cashed paychecks, the reassurance that their iceboxes contained thick cuts of city dress for Saturday's breakfast, plus Saturday for most was a reprieve from the jungle that was the workweek. They were jovial, celebratory as they leaned over their porch banisters that night congratulating Joe for his significant talent. Asked him when was he cutting a record, why hadn't Steve Allen from the *Tonight* show booked him yet.

He walked back toward his house that night loving this block of Cecil Street, loving his neighbors; loving his beautiful wife; his baby daughter, Shay; his horn. Loved everything in that instant with the sloppy intensity of a nice drunk, endearing and sad. Then he looked at his wife and he froze inside the way she turned her dark eyes on him. Her eyes were beautiful, but when she looked at him dead-on they went from beautiful to severe and her stare could be chilling. "You act like you miss those places where you used to perform," she said. "You act like you ready to go on back out there." He felt as if he'd been caught talking in his sleep. Packed his horn away in the bottom of the chifforobe in the back of the cellar after that. Pulled it out only for rare times because he did miss it. Missed closing his eyes in the blue-colored air of a nightclub and sending his breath and soul oozing through his saxophone. Missed picking a big-legged woman from the crowd to fill him up afterward. Needed filling up the way he sometimes played, the way he'd leave parts of himself hanging in the echoes of the notes he blew. After that night he was afraid to play again with any regularity. Afraid that the playing might whisper in his ear that he had to choose either his life on Cecil Street with Louise and his baby girl and the stability of a good job with the transportation authority, or the jazz musician's life that was irregular and bitter and lush and lovely. Afraid that in the choosing he might end up leaving Cecil Street.

His breaths came faster now as he lifted the case from the bottom of the chifforobe. The case was hard and cool, a tough leather over cork, guaranteed not to let any moisture through. He leaned against the bricked-out cellar wall. Bent one leg back and rested the case along his knee. He thought he should wait until he got back upstairs to open the case but he'd already put his thumbs to the latches. The snapping sound, the cover creaking open, the yawn of air sifting out; the sounds that had been so familiar transported him now and he wasn't even in his cellar. He was on the road in a city like Baltimore and a healthy-lipped woman was telling him how incredibly he'd just played. She was putting a drawl on the end of his name, making it two syllables instead of one the way that Valadean had said his name earlier, had grown his name and made it long and curled her mouth as she did. He had a thing for mouths. A horn player, he would. Looked at the shape of a woman's mouth the way some men looked at the curve of hips. He could have watched Valadean's lips curling all night saying his name, maybe would have if Louise hadn't mashed her fist in the small of his back and said they needed more club soda since he'd insisted on pulling his scotch out, drawing a bunch of people in the house though the party was supposed to be outside. Would maybe watch Valadean's lips close up another night soon since Valadean was here for the summer and had asked Joe if he could suggest things for her to do at night so that she wouldn't get bored listening to her aunt Johnetta go on and on about the private lives of the people on the block. He'd told Valadean he'd welcome the opportunity to show her Philadelphia some Friday or Saturday night. Surprised himself that he'd done that with such ease, loosely made a date with another woman right in his living room with Louise only feet away. Not like he was the running-around type. Married for eighteen years and could count on half a hand how many times he'd strayed—and both of those times were when the marriage was young and he was still in the adjustment phase.

He lifted the mouthpiece from the softness of the velvet lining the case. Always started with the mouthpiece when he'd put his horn together. He'd hold the hard metal between his lips and make whistling sounds while he assembled the other pieces. He couldn't even believe the feeling rising up in him now as he touched the mouthpiece to his lips. Damn. He was crying. He hadn't cried since he was eight. Thirty years since he was eight and though he'd seen enough in his life to bring him to tears, he never cried once he considered himself a man. Considered himself a man at nine when he had to identify his dead father's remains, who he believed had been shot in the head by a racist Pittsburgh cop, he didn't cry then. Saw his best friend beaten to a pulp with a banister post and he didn't cry; saw the twisted metal, still hot to the touch, that had served as his only sister's dying bed when she was eight months pregnant and went for a spin around the block in her husband's brand-new car and he didn't cry; buried his mother within a year of that and he didn't cry. But now the feel of his mouthpiece against his lips was enough to make choking sounds ripple the dusty air down here. His whole body was shaking and he pulled the case to him, sobbed into the case as if the hard case had arms that would reach around him and hold him in an it's-okay-baby pose.

Deucie watched the red and white of Joe's dashiki cave in and out as she listened to him cry. She had to hold herself back from going to him to console him. She loved any excuse to pull a man to her, help a man to release whatever was penned up inside. Drain him. Nothing more honest than a man allowing himself to be drained, she always thought. But she couldn't go to this man, she convinced herself now. She was naked in his cellar. Guilty of breaking and entering. Though without malicious intent. She'd only come down here because she suffered from severe headaches and had felt a headache coming on as she'd moved through the spinning lights and the thumpety, thumpety of the drums from that street carnival. She'd stopped at this house because they had nice awnings hanging from the porch and she needed a square of quiet darkness when a headache was threatening to take her down. She'd intended only to sit under the darkness of the awnings with her head between her legs until the pain thinned. But then she'd realized that she was sitting on top of a latch and that the porch floor was the entranceway to the cellar. She'd gotten excited then, didn't know the houses here in West Philly had cellars that you got to from the outside. Thought it was only that way downtown. She'd lifted the porch floor, could tell that this basement didn't see much human activity by the way her hands were covered with rusted silt from the latch on the door. She'd come down into the cellar's dust and darkness grateful for the respite from the party outside. She'd taken off her red, black, and green tie-dyed dress that was really a big man's T-shirt. But it was dress enough for her since she was short and thin; plus she'd wanted to have on some color for her daughter to see her in after all these years. Once she was out of the T-shirt, she was butt naked because she wore no underwear. Had stopped wearing underwear last month when the headaches had stepped up in intensity. Something about fabric against her skin made the drumming of the headaches more pronounced. She'd curled herself up then on the hard and cool but soothing concrete floor and drifted into unconsciousness. She was just coming to when she'd heard the porch floor lift and the footsteps coming down, had just crawled over to this spot next to the crate of toys and tossed her T-shirt onto the box.

Still, it was taking everything in her to listen to this grown man cry without going to him and whispering to him, Come 'ere, baby, come to me, come on to me. Couldn't remember the last time she'd helped a man like that. But there was the thought of returning to the crazy house. Plus, she knew the sight of her right now would be more a horror than a consolation, so she sat still as a rock and watched the wash of red and white color that was his dashiki quake in and out as he headed for the stairs.

JOE TOOK IN a chestful of air once he was back up on the porch. His sobs had ratcheted down to irregular breaths and the cooled-off night air felt good in his lungs. He unclutched his horn case and held it loosely by the handle and stood there and looked out into the street, took in the remnants of the block party while he finished composing himself. Though the scene out here wasn't helping. The balloons bouncing and dying near the ground, the crepe paper sagging from the porch banisters, the quiet stillness to the air that felt like dreams put on hold threatened to further dampen his mood. He never liked the feel of a place when a party had just ended, could sense that in the leaving, the party had taken away more pleasure than it had brought. And this block party had brought some pleasure as more than three hundred fun seekers crammed the block from end to end. The hot dogs had been free, like the Kool-Aid and the hula hoops and the miniature-size bottles of blowing bubbles. The live band was intense and garnered shouts of "Solid" from the Afro-wearing under-twenty crowd. The old heads though floated from house to house sipping a little cheer at each stop, measuring their worth as they compared themselves with who'd gotten a new French Provincial living-room suite or RCA Victor floor-model color TV. Joe and Louise had amassed both lately, plus the new roll-down awnings out front. Joe downplayed the new purchases to the healthy crowd that had formed in his house to ooh and ah. Resisted measuring his worth by what he had or lacked. Though he did allow himself to beam over his impressive collection of jazz LPs. Did measure his worth that way. Thought that as long as he had some good music on hand he was successful enough.

He walked across the porch headed in. He saw movement on the porch next door and assumed that it was his severely saved next-door neighbor on her way in from an all-night revival. He cleared his throat. "Alberta," he said, glad that his wife wasn't within earshot because he'd have to listen to shit from Louise for speaking to Alberta, since most of Cecil Street ostracized her. The people around here believed that Alberta was in league with the devil after she'd fallen in with a lean-to of a shanty church that operated more like a cult. Though Joe did not.

"Oh, hi, Mr. Joe," came the thin reply, and Joe realized that this was Neet out here, Alberta's seventeen-year-old daughter, his daughter Shay's best friend since they were toddlers together on the porch.

"Neet?" he said. "You okay, sweetheart?" He walked to the banister that separated the houses, about to ask Neet what she was doing out here since he knew that Shay had been in the house for hours and Shay and Neet were generally inseparable. Joe didn't ask it though. Figured he'd let her save her explaining for her mother; better be a hell of an explanation, he thought. Alberta was known for her hardhanded discipline because she expected Neet to be as devout as she herself was. Joe felt for Neet, all of Cecil Street did; as much as the people around here despised Alberta, they loved her daughter, Neet.

"You want me to go rouse Shay?" Joe offered, thinking that Neet could probably use a girlfriend right about now. Only one thing he knew of that would have a young girl out in the streets until two in the morning. Some knucklehead swooning her with bullshit.

"I'm fine, Mr. Joe, really, just looking for my key," Neet whispered.

Neet's eyes were pleading with Joe to be quiet and he realized that she was trying to sneak in. He hoped with everything in him that she would be successful as he nodded and gave her a soft wave good night, then pushed open the door into his vestibule.

LOUISE WAS IN her pink satiny pajamas and turning down the covers on their new queen-size bed as Joe tiptoed into the bedroom. She'd just taken two Anacin and soaked the inside of her mouth with warm, salted water. She was in the advanced stages of gum disease and had already lost two back molars and now all of her teeth were shifting in her pulpy gums, rearranging what had once been a mesmerizing smile. Though she was a licensed practical nurse, she had a horrible phobia about sitting in a dentist's chair. At night when her mouth throbbed, she would resolve that the next day she was making an appointment. But the pain would dull to mild during the day and so she'd put it off until tomorrow. Had been putting it off for months and now she told herself that first thing Monday morning without fail she was taking care of her mouth. She punched the pillow to fluff it when she heard Joe's footsteps creak into the bedroom. Her mood had been strange of late too. Jumping from irritated to anxious to sad. Now she was just angry, so she didn't turn around to look at Joe. Didn't want to look at him because she couldn't get the picture of him from her mind when she'd caught him smiling up at Johnetta's grown country niece earlier. She hated the way Johnetta was always providing a temporary home for her people from down south when they were in between good and bad luck and needed a clean bed and a toilet that flushed. Always young women, but not too young, always over twenty-one with titties and asses that stuck way out, ungirdled. Louise thought that Johnetta went out of her way tonight to parade this latest corn-fed niece through her house though the party was supposed to be in the street. "Come here," Johnetta had called as she'd walked in through Louise's unlocked screen door. "Joe, Louise, y'all come on now and meet my oldest sister's oldest chile, Valadean, up here with me for the summer. Ain't she pretty, look like a colored Elly Mae Clampett, tell the truth."

After that, other people from the block had drifted in, and Joe pulled out his scotch while Louise, trying to be polite, went about setting out olives and cheeses. The lights got lowered, and before she knew it, or could stop it, dancing space had opened up on her just-done living-room floors. That's when she saw Joe in a dark corner by the closet door laughing with Valadean. Joe had a nice laugh, throaty and sexy, as if he was about to go into a moan of baby, you look good. The first time Louise felt the earth move under her feet was when she'd watched Joe laugh. Had already decided before she heard him laugh that first time that he was fine in an unconventional way with his thick sideburns that merged perfectly with his ever-clipped goatee, brown skin, dark lips, nicely shaped forehead that jutted out but not too much, just enough to give him a strong look with eyes set back, thick eyebrows that moved up and down when he laughed, as if he was saying let's get it on. Louise figured he'd given Valadean that let's-get-it-on look as they laughed together in the darkened corner and Valadean showed Joe her perfect teeth.

"Thought you'd be sleep by now," Joe said as he stretched and started coming out of his clothes.

"Well, you thought wrong, I'm not asleep," Louise said, punching the pillow again.

Joe left the bedroom and went into the bathroom to wash off. He'd put his horn in the back of the living-room closet, glad now that he hadn't brought it up here with the irritating mood Louise was wearing. He let the water run hot against his skin now. At least the hot water was soothing. So soothing that he felt a jazzy beat coming together in his head by the time he got back in the bedroom.

Louise was still awake, she was propped against the pillow and her hair was out and fanning back all dark and thick against the pillow. He was surprised that he was aroused by the sight of her now. Hadn't been aroused by the sight of her lately. Felt bad that he hadn't, though he thought it had something to do with the deteriorating condition of her mouth. But right now she looked to him like she had the night they'd first met. She'd been a practical nurse in training at Philadelphia General back then. Joe had rushed Fred, the drummer of his band, to PGH that night for emergency treatment. Fred had been caught with his pants down. He'd been up in a bedroom of Pat's Place. Was in the process of unwinding in that brothel-bedroom when his wife crept in and stabbed him in his ass. Fred didn't even know he'd been stabbed until the woman under him started screaming, still didn't know then, figured he was that good. Pat, the owner of the speakeasy, found Joe, who was being swept away by C right then and not about to tolerate interruption. She told Joe he had to get Fred out of there now or she'd ban them from coming back ever again. Pat's Place didn't allow violence, and as it was, she was going to have to charge them for the cost of cleaning up the blood. Joe peeled himself away from C, kissed her softly, and almost told her he loved her. But that night he saw Louise for the first time and knew he was in love.

Louise was being trained in how to gather patient information at PGH. Joe hadn't been able to take his eyes off Louise as he gave her the account of what had happened to Fred's behind. Her hair was thick and unrestrained behind the nurse's cap; her skin was light and her eyes were black-black, almost severe; but she had the prettiest mouth, a thick and liquid mouth. She gave off such an aura of soft wildness that Joe could hardly contain himself, had to keep jokes going with her about Fred's predicament or he would otherwise have sat up there and gotten serious and sloppy. Said at one point that he was changing Fred's name, from now on he'd be known as Cheeks. Louise had been efficient and professional throughout, but when Joe said that, she'd allowed a smile to turn her mouth. She'd looked directly at Joe when she smiled and he was putty then. Asked

Louise if he got himself stabbed tomorrow night would she be there to take care of him. Tried to laugh when he said it, but by then what he was feeling had already crossed over to serious.

He was feeling warm and loose now as he flashed back on that scene. Louise had recently redone the bedroom in a dusty-rose shade though she used a lot of brown too, she told him, so that he would not feel as though it was too frilly. He really did appreciate that she considered him even down to the small details. He tucked his shirt into his boxers and tiptoed to her side of the bed and sat near the foot and squeezed her toes through the covers. "So, you want to tell me why you still up?" he said.

"I'm up 'cause I'm up," she said, her voice jarring after the low, smooth tone of his. "What's the sense in falling asleep only to be wakened when you decided to finally come to bed."

He knew he was on the losing side when she got like this. Knew the best thing to do was to climb onto his side of the bed and say good night, turn away from her, and go to sleep. But his manhood was fully involved now, its heaviness egging him on to try and scatter her mood. "Sounds to me like you wanted to be awake." He was whispering. "Shit. I could have come up here an hour ago if I'd known you were waiting on me. Were you waiting on me, pretty lady?" He straddled himself over her and leaned down to kiss her.

She wanted him to kiss her, could feel a puddle of desire building deep inside, rising and spreading. But her gums were sore. And worse, she couldn't get the picture of him out of her head from earlier, how happy he'd looked smiling in that dark corner.

"Why? Wasn't Johnetta's greasy-looking country niece waiting on you?"

He thudded onto his back on his side of the bed. "Jesus Christ, Louise," he said, and it came out like a whine, "what in the hell is your problem?"

"My problem? My problem?" She threw the covers over and stomped out of the bed and stood over him, pointing. "You all squirreled up in a dark corner with her fat ass, standing all up on her grinning like a monkey and you ask me what's my problem?"

"Awl damn, Louise. I don't believe this shit." He swung his legs to the floor and just sat on the side of the bed shaking his head. "You know something," he said, talking to the floor. "You accusing me when I'm totally innocent, you gonna be the one responsible when I'm guilty."

"No you don't. Don't try to lay that trip on me." She was back in front of him again, hitting his shoulder so he'd have to look up.

"Come on, Louise, where we going with this? Huh? What reason have I ever given you to be so suspicious, huh? You ever once caught me wrong, huh? I don't mean some innocent smiling at someone. But have you ever really caught me wrong?"

"'Cause you haven't been caught doesn't mean you haven't been wrong." Her tone softened some because she was reacting to the pleading in his eyes. She climbed back onto her side of the bed and Joe barely breathed, afraid to disturb whatever had just happened that had calmed her down.

"Furthermore, I'm getting work done on my mouth," she said once she had settled under the covers and her body was curved away from him.

"Say what?"

"My teeth, my teeth, I'm getting my damned teeth fixed so you gonna have to get up off of some money 'cause it's not gonna be cheap. And I may have to take some time from work while my gums heal, so it's gonna leave a hole in our income."

"I'll come up with the money, Louise," he said, so relieved in fact to hear her say it as he flicked the light switch over his head and the room went dark. "You do what you gotta do. You want to get your teeth fixed, get your teeth fixed. We'll get by."

He was about to reach for her, not as a prelude to anything, just maybe as a pat-on-the-arm good night, a no-hard-feelings type of touch. Didn't want to admit how often their nights ended like this lately. He sighed and rolled away from her. Tried not to think about his horn, embarrassed by the way he'd just cried in the cellar, as if the cellar had a mouth and would tell. Tried to will himself to sleep so he wouldn't think about it.

But right then the bedroom door burst open and their daughter, Shay, ran in crying and jumping up and down. "She's beating her, she's beating her," Shay screamed. "It sounds like they're coming through the wall in my bedroom. We have to go over there. Mommy, Daddy. Please. We have to go make her stop."

Both Joe and Louise jumped out of the bed practically hysterical themselves until they could figure out what Shay was talking about. Realized that she was talking about Neet. Alberta must be over there beating up on Neet.

Chapter 2

EET HAD SLIPPED in and made it upstairs un-
detected by her mother the same way she'd slipped
out earlier, through the back staircase that stopped at
her bedroom door. She freed herself from the tight,
worldly clothes and dressed for bed and stole under the covers still
tingling after her time with Little Freddie. She was lucky tonight.
Her mother, Alberta, hadn't been waiting for her the way she some-
times did. When Neet had crept out, her mother was in the middle of
her prayers. Neet knew that Alberta prayed as if she was in a trance,
sometimes for an hour at a time. So her initial plan had been to sam-
ple the air on the block tonight, the breezy, sugary feel of the block
party with Shay at her side, and then creep back in while her
mother was still on her knees. But she'd overstayed outside to-
night, so she hoped that her mother had fallen into unconscious-
ness the way she sometimes did after she prayed, or else that she

was sitting out on the back steps staring into the night air as if it could do what her prayers could not, make her happy. Neet was content that her mother was either asleep or out back tonight and she considered herself lucky that she'd been able to sneak back in even though Mr. Joe's loud talking on the porch had almost ruined it for her.

She was lying in bed in a half-dream state twirling a LifeSaver around her tongue as she thought about Little Freddie. He sang bass with the Corner Boys, and though Little Freddie probably wasn't headed to a four-year college like Neet was, she'd allowed him to cover her with his tall dark self. Had been allowing him to move all over her, all inside of her, since the spring. Though she and Shay had shared everything since they were babies together on the porch, she hadn't yet brought herself to reveal to Shay what she'd been doing with Little Freddie. It was too tangled up to talk about yet, too complicated and dark.

She tried not to think of the look of confused devastation that had come upon Shay's face when Little Freddie had kissed Neet and then pulled her toward the bedroom that Peedy, who lived in the corner house, rented out when his parents weren't home. She loved Shay so much but she hadn't expected to see Little Freddie at that moment; hadn't expected to have to choose between being with Little Freddie and appalling Shay with the sight of them going into a bedroom. But she couldn't see Little Freddie and resist him, especially not after what he'd done with her name.

Neet had given up the name Bonita when she was eight, after she'd allowed herself to be taken in by the concerned watery eyes of Mr. G. Mr. G was always hanging close to her mother at church and Alberta never dissuaded his company so Neet trusted him.

Trusted his eyes when he'd soft-talked her away from church on a Friday night while the whole congregation was in the midst of a fire-filled revival and they were either frenetic or uncontrollable or in a stupor. He'd promised Neet a candy bar from the store around the corner. She'd ended up in his efficiency apartment instead, where he'd sat her on his lap, tickled her and bounced her on his lap, moved his filth against her until she started crying that he was hurting her. Though the more she cried the harder he moved, splitting her, the whole time calling her by her full name, Bonita, Bonita, a hundred times he must have said her name, perverted her name through the weak line of his mouth. After that, whenever anybody called her Bonita, she'd correct them as politely as she could, ask them to please call her Neet instead. She couldn't stand the way she felt inside when she was called Bonita. She felt dirty and chaffed inside, ruined.

But Little Freddie had erased all of that when he'd called her by her full name. Instead of that chaffed, dirty feeling, she'd felt soft and wavy inside, felt innocent again. Believed now that though on the surface she appeared to be transgressing when she lay with Little Freddie, she was actually being cleansed. Believed that time spent with Little Freddie in that dilapidated room where the wallpaper flaked and the mattress was spring exposed had been ordained by God. Felt forgiven now for allowing herself to be soft-talked away from church those nights by Mr. G. Felt so unbound because Little Freddie had given her back her name.

So right now she was laughing in bed, a giddiness about her as the LifeSaver dissolved on her tongue and she thought about the feel of Little Freddie's fingers against her skin, such a righteous feel. She'd been giddy a lot lately, laughing out loud at nothing in particular. Though she'd been depressed of late too, high and low she'd been the past few weeks. She couldn't explain it, but right now she was grooving on the high, laughing in her bed as if she was being tickled under her chin.

But then she looked up and there was her mother's face. The face just hung there over the bed and at first appeared as if it wasn't even attached to the rest of her mother's body. A Kewpie-doll face her mother had that would have fit on the top of one of those grass-skirted dolls they sell on the boardwalk at Atlantic City, Neet always thought. With those soft brown eyes, almost shy eyes, and her cottony hair that was out now and not pulled back so severely under that hairnet. Her long flannel nightgown was open down a few buttons at the top and her skin glistened in the dark room. Her mother had sensitive skin that Neet would rub down when Alberta came home during the summer months especially sun exposed after a day selling fruit from the roadside stand the church had set up. Alberta would cry when Neet gently spread cream to the areas that were most sore. She would cry and say that all she had in this world was Neet and Jesus, that's all, just Neet and Jesus. Neet would love her mother all over again. Though she never really didn't love her, but often the love was so mingled with despicableness and Neet would get confused and she didn't know what she felt. Like now, as her mother's face appeared over her bed and she snatched the pillow from under her head.

"Get up," Alberta said in that voice that sounded as if she had an infected throat. "Get up, you hell-bound liar, you. Got the nerve to pretend that you've been in here all along. Get up."

Neet scurried to jump out of the bed and Alberta raised her hand

and Neet grabbed her hand in midair. She didn't know what made her do it. She'd never raised a hand to block a face slapping before. Maybe the fact that she'd become a woman made her do it, but the fact that she'd grabbed her mother's hand at all like that frightened her. What next, would she raise her hand to hit her own mother, would that be next since she'd already crossed the line? Would she slap that Kewpie-doll face until welts came up, choke her mother's slender neck until all the veins burst behind her soft brown eyes? In that instant as Neet looked at her mother's face, a mixture of rage and hurt that Neet would dare raise a hand toward her even if it was to keep from being hit, Neet knew that she was capable of picking up the porcelain lamp with the heavy brass base that sat on her nightstand, knew that it was within her constitution to use that lamp and smash her own mother's Kewpie-doll face. Just the knowledge that she was capable of such an act of defilement against her own mother crumbled her. "Oh, Mommy, I'm sorry," she said with a gasp. "As the Lord is my witness, I'm so sorry, Mommy. Please forgive me, Mommy." She dropped her hand and hung her head and collapsed even though she was still standing. In that pivotal moment, when she glimpsed the ugliness that made up the lining of her heart, she did the only thing she could think to do. She got saved.

Alberta watched, petrified at first as Neet raised her arms and her head slowly, with such symmetry, such grace; she looked like a lovely swan taking off in flight. But then her face went contorted and she started shouting Jesus, Jesus, in that drawn-out rhythmic way of the Saints. Alberta realized what was happening to her child as Neet started jumping up and down and running through the small bedroom. She knocked over that porcelain lamp as she ran, and books and the chair at her desk, even tilted the heavy wooden desk. She pounded the walls and she shouted unintelligible phrases as she moved convulsively through the room.

Now Alberta wanted to cry herself because finally, after all her prayers, her counseling sessions with the Reverend Mister and the other Saints, the older, wiser ones who Alberta would confess to that she feared her child was incorrigible, and they'd reiterate in that singsong way that had Alberta hanging on their every word that she must not spare the rod, that she must train up that child, that she herself must be even more diligent in her service to the church, keep herself set apart from the ways of the worldly, that the Lord would stop by to visit her child one day, one day, one day.

So Alberta just got out of Neet's way. She moved what she could so that Neet wouldn't hurt herself, and then she just got out of her way. She sobbed quietly as she stood in a dark corner of Neet's room and Neet stretched out on the bed and let go with a series of uninterrupted shrill cries. Alberta just stood there and sobbed; it was a happy cry as she let the Spirit of the Lord finally come down over her child.

I T S E E M E D T O Joe as if they'd been standing on Alberta's porch for a while now, ringing the bell after polite intervals. Though Louise had tried to talk Shay out of coming over here and getting involved in what should remain between a mother and her child, Shay had refused to relent. And Joe wasn't about to allow Shay to come here by herself, so he'd ignored how Louise darkened her eyes when he told Shay to wait, let him throw on some clothes, he would come too.

"I don't know, Daddy's Girl," he said to Shay. "Sounds like it's quieted down in there. Maybe your mother's right and we got no business doing this, maybe we should go on home."

Shay was about to agree. But right then a sudden burst of a bright light showered down on them from over the top of the door, and they both squinted.

"I didn't even know they had a working light on this porch," Joe whispered. "I don't think I've seen this light come on in years."

He stopped talking then and stood as if being called to attention as the door edged open just a crack, just enough for them to make out the outline of Alberta's face, half hidden behind her hair. Joe thought that she looked like a ghost, or a witch, he couldn't decide, just knew that what he could see of her face was so translucent, like if something touched her face right then it would go on through. He got a chill as she stared at one, then the other of them through the crack in the door, such disdain for them, no, such disdain for him. He was so unused to being looked at in that way. He was used to bringing out a smile in people, a wink, a blush, an expanded face, widened eyes. He couldn't figure it. He was one of the few people on the block who went out of his way to be nice to Alberta. Yet sometimes when Alberta looked at him it would feel as if she'd snagged something inside him, grabbed hold and twisted and made him feel so diminished. He was having a visceral reaction to the way she looked at him now and almost wanted to ask her why. Instead he said, "Evening, Alberta, sorry to ring your bell like this in the middle of the night—"

"What do you want?" She cut him off in that voice that was so dry and cracked.

"Is Neet all right?" Shay spoke up, struggling to keep her

voice clear and unwavering. "I could hear screaming through my walls, we all could. Is she all right? Because we can take her to the hospital—" And then she stopped because she thought she was getting ready to cry and she didn't want to give Alberta the satisfaction of seeing her cry.

"Neet's fine. All you heard was the power of the Lord, though I'm not surprised that you wouldn't recognize it as such. Not surprised that it would scare you either. Should scare you." She closed her door then, right in their faces.

Joe and Shay just stood there. Neither moved at first. They just stood there and looked up at the door as if it was still edged open and they were looking at Alberta's translucent face. Shay pounded the door with her fist then. "You old mean old thing," she shouted at the door. Then she did start to cry.

"Come on, Shay. Come on, Daddy's Girl," Joe said as he reached for Shay's hand. "Let's go back home. Come on. Happens again and we'll do like your mother said. We'll just call the cops, that's all."

LOUISE WAS WAITING by the door when they walked back inside. She'd felt a mix of guilt and anger that on the one hand she had not led their charge as they walked across the porch and climbed over the banister and rang that bell, and on the other that they had totally disregarded her anyhow. But now she just felt relief as they walked through the door. "Awl, Shay," she said as she took Shay's face in her hands.

"She wouldn't even let us in, just slammed the door on us," Shay blurted out. Louise kissed her cheek and Shay started for the stairs saying that she was tired, exhausted, that it better be quiet over there because she just wanted to go to sleep.

Louise and Joe stood in the living room and neither said anything. Louise was so struck by how Joe looked standing there, his face so disassembled, like she'd rarely see it. As if his face had been a perfectly completed jigsaw puzzle but now the pieces were beginning to shift. So needy he looked. She was rushed then with the realization that he was needy, and she'd been so unresponsive lately. Didn't know why his presence made her go tight inside, worried some days that she was beginning to hate him the way she'd heard couples sometimes did when they were together for years. But she knew she wasn't even close to hating him. Just the opposite. Feelings for him ran so deep she was afraid that one day he'd no longer reciprocate, that one day he'd turn his back and walk away from the mostly beautiful life they'd built. Felt sometimes as if that day was already here the way she'd catch a crease on his brow when he looked at her sometimes. She felt old and ugly then. The condition of her mouth didn't help. But right now he looked so vulnerable, as if something inside him was making him want to cry. She opened her arms then. "Come 'ere, Joe," she said. "You were right to go over there with Shay. You were. Come 'ere."

Joe needed Louise's closeness more than anything right then. He felt as if he had been stripped of some vital piece that kept his workings intact, that kept him the good-natured, charming Joe. Felt it with the horn, felt it again under Alberta's diminishing gaze. He squeezed Louise so tightly because he needed her to restore him right then, needed her to help him get his balance back, put his firm foundation securely under his feet again. He buried his head in Louise's chest and she started moving against him, all the while telling him how right he was, and good. "You so damned good, Joe," she said over and over in his ear as they moved upstairs to their bedroom and he kissed her wherever his lips fell, and held on.

Chapter 3

OE WOKE WITH his horn on his mind though he resisted thinking about it right now. He still wasn't ready to process the uprising of emotions when he'd felt the mouthpiece between his lips. Wouldn't even allow himself to picture the horn right now. He rearranged his pillow under his head and pulled the bedspread up around his shoulders because he and Louise had slept snuggled under the chilled-down air of their new Emerson Quiet Kool. Louise had been good to him last night after he'd climbed back over the porch banister debased from the look in Alberta's eyes. Louise had gone loose and open for him last night the way she hadn't in weeks. He felt her hand on his stomach now, making soft circles as he tried to close his eyes on how the sleek metal of his saxophone had gleamed through the black cellar air last night. Thankfully, what Louise was doing to him now helped him clear his mind of the saxophone. Louise was all over him. This was like the old days. He could barely turn all the way around onto his back before she was mashing her fleshy mouth across his chest. He wished he knew what he'd done to have her moving like this so that he could keep on doing it. Like fire she moved now, jumping red and hot from spot to spot until all of him was burning hard and fast, then melting. Crying: awl, awl, awl. Damn, baby, damn.

She got up then and took her time walking to the chair where her robe was. She was still fine, he thought, small waist, with slim hips that she knew how to throw for maximum effect. She turned around and faced him, loosely tying the sash to her robe as she did. Her black, black hair was wild and falling every which way. Her head was tilted and her dark eyes squinted, her lips parted halfway to a smile. She looked like someone he'd just paid to do him from head to toe ready now to go to work on her tip. "Come 'ere, woman," he said. "Come over here and whisper in my ear and name your price. Damn. The hurtin' you just put on me, shit, I know I'ma be paying for this through the nose. Either that or it's my birthday. Shit, if that's the case, come 'ere, baby, and sing happy birthday in my ear."

Louise was laughing out loud now and Joe was grooving to the sound of her laugh. Seemed like such a long time since he'd heard her laugh like that. She went to the nightstand where his cigarettes were. She hit the bottom of the pack and pushed a cigarette out. Put the cigarette between his stunned lips. She generally didn't allow him to smoke in the house because of the way the smoke seemed to settle on her beautiful floors. She leaned over him and flicked his lighter against the tip of the cigarette and he felt drunk from the rush of the smell of lighter fluid mixed with the sweet, musty scent of her womanhood rising up from the robe and now the wave of euphoria that always came with his first cigarette of the day. He closed his eyes to take it all in. When he opened his eyes, she was staring at him. He couldn't read the stare through the blur of smoke that was rising up between them. "So you gonna tell me why I'm so deserving of this fine, fine treatment this morning?" he said as he sat all the way up and she produced an ashtray right where he held his cigarette.

"Why? You done something that makes you undeserving?" she asked, leaning in close to his face, that half smile back, and he actually felt himself beginning to throb again.

"Shit. Me? Baby, you know I walks a straight line that leads only to you. But damn, after what you just whipped on me. I didn't know you had it in you like that for me anymore."

She stood all the way up and her robe fell open when she did. "Bring your ass straight home tonight, Negro, you might find I got more in me than that."

"Ooh," he said. Letting out a slow laugh as he watched her walk away. "You keep talkin' like that, I'm not even going in today, Saturday's optional for me anyhow, overtime, but I could always pull down extra time during the week." He didn't want to mention what she'd said last night about the dentist, about the expense. She might have changed her mind already about getting work done on her mouth and he would be too disappointed if she had. Plus, he didn't want to give the appearance of pushing too hard, she might dig her heels in then and refuse to go to the dentist altogether.

"No way, take your ass to work." She went to her dresser and pulled out underwear and laid it neatly on the arm of the chair.

"Uh," he said, slapping his forehead. "I just remembered, baby, about tonight. I'm supposed to be meeting with Tim and Pinochle Eddie and Wrigley and a few other men from 'round here. I told you we're working on security for the party next month. Didn't I tell you we're having one more block party before the season's over?"

"Johnetta said something 'bout that. Said she thought it would be good since everybody seemed to be in the dumps lately, though I think that's overkill." She had her back to him, riffling through her closet, no doubt to lay out the clothes she would wear today. Always did that before she took her bath. He thought it was her nurse's training that made her so methodical. "Why y'all meeting tonight?" she asked as she unhung a cotton shirt and stretched it over the back of the chair.

"I don't know why tonight, baby. But I'll try and get out of it. Tim's the one pushing it and you know he ain't been right since those white cops kicked him in the ass. I'll stop past and see Tim on my way in, get a quick haircut while I'm there."

He drew hard on his cigarette as she left the room for the bathroom. Wondered if Louise was trying to work a spell on him the way she'd turned into a wild woman between last night and this morning. Trying to pussy-whip him to keep on the straight and narrow. An old cat who used to scat with the band when they'd play Wilmington used to swear that every woman had a little witch in her and could work a spell on a man, and the woman you marry got more witch in her than most, he'd say. Wondered if Louise had worked a spell on him years ago to make him put his horn down and quit his life on the road. Now his mind was sliding back there again and he was suddenly picturing some of the women he'd been with in that other life. Louise had been the only one to get inside his head. Louise and the one who'd worked at Pat's Place, C, though he couldn't picture her face because she'd never allow the lights on when they were together. Had the reddest lips, red and pouty and soft. And damn, could she move, she would move and cry and the feel of her tears on his chest touched him so that when he reached his explosion, he felt it all the way to the bone and the marrow. She'd gotten inside his head for sure. He hadn't thought about her in years and years. Wondered what the fuck was going on with him now: unpacking his horn last night, crying over it; now trying not to think about it; now flooded with memories of some soft, shy hooker from years ago, the memories bothering him now.

Louise was back in the room. She was wrapped in a towel and the sunlight pushing through the window sheers made rainbows of the drops of water that slid down her arms and legs. The sight of her now mixing with the scent of the Camay soap rising off her skin had Joe's manhood converging all over again. He mashed out his stump of a cigarette and went to her and tugged at the towel. Louise slapped at his hands, playfully, said she'd have to take a bath all over again and she had a hair appointment shortly. Joe wasn't playing right now. He thought about wrestling the towel away and pushing into Louise with an intensity that he didn't even understand. And not just for his physical release. He didn't even know what all he was feeling the need to release.

Louise backed away and Joe's hand slid down her arm until all he had left of her were her fingertips. "You know Clara opens the shop at seven for me every other Saturday," she said, at the chair now where she'd laid out her clothes for today. "Like I said earlier, you bring your fine self straight home tonight, we can take our time tonight."

Her back was to him and he could hear the giggle in her voice, and even that bothered him now. He felt as if he needed to cry all over again as the image of his saxophone muscled its way into his head, taking it over. Felt as if he'd lost his footing and was going into a skid, slipping and sliding closer and closer to his past.

D EUCIE HAD WAKENED around the same time as Joe this morning. She'd ended up staying the night in Joe's cellar after all. She'd sat on the steps under the porch floor waiting for Joe to go in, then waiting for the commotion over her head to still, then waiting as two sets of footsteps ran across the porch. Figured by then the D bus had stopped running for the night, so she curled up under the steps, out of view should anyone else come down before she could leave. Now she woke with a fire in her throat and Luther on her mind. Luther was the man who'd saved her when a headache had taken her down in front of his house. He was big and blue-black, with a gash that continued his mouth all the way around to his ear. Kept a loaded gun on his kitchen table, which faced the door. He'd held cool compresses to the base of her neck and cried over her because he said she reminded him of his dead mother. She didn't have the heart to tell Luther that she'd be dead fairly soon herself; her cirrhosis of the liver had moved into an advanced stage according to what the doctors had said. That was last month and she'd been living with Luther ever since. Each morning he'd spoon-feed her buttered grits and she'd try not to vomit them up until she was out of his sight. He was devoted to Deucie, and as she slipped her T-shirt back on she hated right now to think that he might be worried about her. She pushed her feet into her rubber-soled flip-flops where her quarters for her bus fare home were taped to the inside soles.

Her throat was parched and her tongue was sticking to the roof of her mouth as she looked around at where she'd slept. A cellar for sure. Walls half concrete, half bricked out. A drum-shaped oil heater took up half of one side of the wall, boxes and milk crates filled with books and toys and assorted junk from what she could see of it filled the other half. The big closet-looking thing that the crying man had rummaged through last night, doors still open, sweaters hanging out.

She squinted toward the light. A window pleated with cobwebs faced the back of the house and looked up on the yard and alley. Though glory, glory, there was a spigot protruding from the wall under the square of a window. She held on to the wall because her head had that floaty feeling and she knew she was prone to pass out when she felt that way. She managed to inch toward the spigot. The circle handle over the spigot was hard to turn though, so it took some time to get the water to trickle out because after each try she had to be still and catch her breath. She stood there and watched the water trickle down, a single drop at a time. Her thirst was slicing up the inside of her mouth and she felt defeated. But right then a blast of sound moved through the pipe leading to the spigot and beautiful orange-colored water came gushing out. She laughed. "Ain't this just like life," she said as she waited for the water to run clear and then used her hands as a cup and drank for what felt like hours. She imagined as she gulped that this must be how the water would taste after she was dead. Thought herself heaven bound though she'd done wrong in her life: stabbed a woman in the chest with an ice pick; went for her own mother's throat; called a preacher a lying son of a bitch to his face; drank without boundaries; spread herself for more men than she could even remember. Still knew she'd get in because she believed heaven was designed for people like her, people honest enough to live their lives from inside out, so by the time they died they were pure and free, having emptied themselves of their sins. She would be light and floatable on her deathbed, the easier to fly away. Not blubberous, weighted down with a lifetime of repressed desires, rotting and thick and sinkable. Thought about the man she'd watched cry down here last night. Thought he was hell bound if he didn't let go of the shit he was keeping locked way. Felt a dropping inside at not being able to help him. Could have put a hurting on him before she got sick. She laughed at the thought.

Realized now that she was doing everything she could to keep from thinking about her daughter. It had come to her as she'd slept that reclaiming her daughter now wasn't the best thing. Would maybe make her feel better, but it surely wouldn't bring her daughter joy. Not in her current condition, more a horror show than a loving mother the way she looked now. She was grateful there were no mirrors down here. Scared herself some days now when she'd surprise herself in the mirror. The last time she'd seen herself the whites of her eyes were more yellow than white. She felt sorry for people like Luther who had to look at her eyes; she didn't want to put her daughter through that, so she amended her plans now. Decided that she wouldn't try to find her daughter's house after all. If she saw her daughter walking through the block once she left this cellar—she'd know her because she'd marked her when she was an infant—she wouldn't introduce herself. She'd just look at her, that's all. She'd hold herself back from calling out her name. She'd look at her and then she could let herself die.

There was a grate in the back corner of the cellar floor. She went to it hoping that it was a drain because she hated the thought of peeing in the sink. It was a drain. She squatted over it and did her business. Felt bad that this was all she had to leave here, her urine; because whenever she spent the night at somebody's house, she liked to leave a little parting gift. She looked up at the window, at the cobwebs hanging there. Darted her eyes around the cellar for something to use as a step. Fixed on the wooden pony that had been her cover as she'd tried to hide last night. She dragged the pony to the window and stood on top of it. It gave her just enough height to swipe away at the cobwebs. She cleared them completely from the window. Figured her making the way for more sun to get in here was a gift. She started for the stairs. That's when a pain the size and shape of a pool ball ricocheted through her head. Lord Jesus, Luther, she said. They usually didn't start this early in the day. Usually came on with the sunset, usually got some kind of warning in the form of smells too. She sniffed, hoping the pain was just a one-hit jolt; took in the dusty, moldy smell down here. Now she was picking up traces of Niagara spray starch. "Shoot," she said out loud. "Y'all got your days and nights confused in there." She leaned against the wall and slid down it until she was sitting. Nothing she could do but wait it out. Sure couldn't make it to the bus, wasn't even going to make it up these stairs. As if to confirm that, another pool ball crashed through her head, hitting it from front to back. "Gotdamn, Minnesota Fats must be wracking them this morning," she said as she came out of the T-shirt dress, again, and folded it under her head for a thin pillow. She lay under the steps again, out of view should someone come down here this morning. Though by the moldy smell down here, this basement didn't seem to get much human interaction on a daily basis. Still, she kept herself out of view to wait out this episode of a headache.

Felt footsteps walking over her head, on the porch. "Don't you motherfuckers ever sleep up there?" she muttered as she tried to concentrate on Luther again. "I'll be there when I can get there, Luther, don't worry, baby boy, I'll get there by and by."

T HIS TIME IT was Shay walking across the porch. It was just a little past seven and the block was still absent people and felt so deserted to Shay even though the street was filled from end to end with the party's machinery. The rides and the concession booths and the makeshift stages had seemed so magical as the night unfolded amidst the glitter of the lights and blowing bubbles and ha-ha-has, the barbecue smoke and the sweetness of the sugary-coated funnel cakes. The party in the street had held so much potential as Shay and Neet went into the house on the corner through the back alley. They were just supposed to stay down there for a few minutes, laugh at the boys with their hard-ons, whisper about the scampy girls being felt up and lied to. But then to Shay's horror Neet had become one of those girls. Shay had watched at first in disbelief as Neet had appeared to swell last night when Little Freddie had come on the scene in that hallway upstairs in the corner house. Neet had looked suddenly fat to Shay last night. Even Neet's chest that they would joke wasn't in the dictionary because it lacked definition had definition right then, an engorged roundness that Shay had never noticed before. Neet's light-complexioned skin had gone red and flushed and an oily sheen had taken over her face. She looked to Shay like their gray-and-white cat looked when its nature came down. Wanted to ask Neet why didn't she just throw herself down and open her legs and start writhing and meowing in the middle of the hallway floor. Shay's disbelief turned to horror as she watched Neet and Little Freddie go behind the closed bedroom door. She stormed out of the corner house like a tornado leaving. Tried not to cry as she pushed through the heaviness of the crowds that had taken over her block. She'd fallen asleep angry and tight. But then her anger had dissolved when she woke to the sounds of Neet getting beaten over there. Anger became terror that Alberta was really hurting Neet this time.

Shay now went to the banister that separated her house from Neet's and sat. They'd always meet at the banister like this. Maybe once or twice they'd tried tapping on the bedroom wall, but these row houses were old and filled with all kinds of taps and bumps and knocks coming through the pipes or radiators, and it would have been too confusing trying to decipher the nature of a tap on the wall. But for as long as Shay had memory, one or the other of them would come outside to the banister and sit, and the other would just know, as if the one's presence on the banister gave off a beep that only the other could hear even deep inside the house. Within minutes, like magic it seemed, they'd both be at the banister where they'd been relegated anyhow because Shay's mother was always shellacking her hardwood floors and Neet's mother demanded quiet in her house so that she could pray. So they'd straddle the banister separating their houses and laugh at the comics they'd unroll from bubble gum bought with pennies gotten when they redeemed quart-size bottles of Franks orange soda. "You my girl, my mf-ing girl," they'd whisper as they raked wide-tooth combs through each other's hair and planned out things like prom dates and likely careers and the names they'd give their own little girls. The view from the Cecil Street banister had always been filled with possibility because they were smart in school, with four-figure SAT scores and college bound and girlfriends.

Neet's door opened and Shay watched her walk toward the banister. Shay had to use all of her strength to keep herself plastered to the banister because she wanted to run to Neet, hug her or slap her, she wasn't sure which, just wanted to make physical contact to know that this was Neet and not some aberration because she looked almost ghostly now, thin again, almost colorless, still in her pajamas, hair in a messy ponytail, eyes and nose red and swollen. But still beautiful, Shay thought. People would sometimes call one of them by the other's name though they had opposite looks because they were together so much. Shay was short and brown and hippy, cute face with her mother's dark, dark eyes and black bushy hair; but a round face like Joe's that kept her eyes from being too stark, and dimples that came up close to her mouth when she smiled. Neet on the other hand was tall and thin and light. Soft brown hair and eyes, soft curve to her cheekbones, soft shape to her pouty mouth, mouth just like Alberta's mouth, plus she had a cleft in her chin. Soft ways too, endeared people to her so that those who might be tempted to hate her for her beauty loved her instead. Shay would blush inside when someone called her Neet by mistake, flattered.

Neet straddled herself over the banister facing Shay. She leaned in and kissed Shay on the mouth the way they'd always kissed since they were toddlers together on the porch. Shay's anger was back; she wiped her mouth hard, exaggerated it. "Don't even be kissing me," she said. "Last I saw of you, you were going into a bedroom with dumb-ass Little Freddie. So I don't know where your mouth's been."

"Dag, Shay, why are you so cold?" Neet said. Then she started to cry.

Shay just sat there mummified as Neet cried. Neet rarely cried. So Shay was thinking that Alberta must have really hurt Neet last night. Was hoping that's what it was, that Neet was crying because she'd suffered an ass kicking. Because otherwise what Shay had been wrestling with in her stomach and her chest and her throat that was just now edging up to her head, bouncing around in her brain and transforming itself from a feeling to a thought, must be an accurate thought. Shay couldn't handle the accuracy. She watched Neet's legs swinging back and forth as she sat straddling the banister. She was trying to focus on her feet. Trying to see if her feet looked swollen pushed into the flip-flops she wore the way they'd been swollen a couple of days ago. She'd met Neet at her summer job at Connie's Cards 'n Gifts on Sixtieth Street. They were going to a house party near Penn and Shay had Neet's change of clothes the way she kept all of Neet's worldly clothes in her closet until Neet was ready for them. That way Neet could leave the house dressed in her loosely hanging dark and dowdy holy clothes to keep Alberta satisfied. Then once they were away from the block Neet would find a place to change. That day it was the stockroom at Connie's. Neet was taking a long time changing and Shay asked Miss Connie for permission to go back there and hurry Neet along. When she got back there, Neet was red in the face from trying to stuff her feet into the stacked-heel sandal. When Shay asked her what the problem was, Neet told her she must have brought the wrong shoes, was she hiding anybody else's clothes in the back of her closet, because she was sure these weren't hers.

"What you mean not yours? Are you crazy? Who else's would they be?"

"Well, they're not my size; I thought I asked you to bring the black ones anyhow."

"You said white to match your white cutoff Wranglers. Look at the inside strap, aren't they a six and a half, haven't you been wearing a six and a half? You been eating a lot of ham or something."

"Ham?"

"Yeah, ham as in salty and making you hold fluid in your feet. Your feet do look swollen."

"Well, I been standing on them all day, how they supposed to look?"

That had sounded reasonable to Shay. Shay's summer job was softer, a city job that Joe had hooked up through the ward leader, where Shay worked in an air-conditioned office at the Municipal Services Building making sure pencils stayed sharpened. But now as Shay watched Neet crying, swinging her legs back and forth against the porch banister, Shay was also remembering an argument she'd had with her mother the other day. Louise had stunned Shay as she'd helped her mother with dinner. Shay was squeezing lemons into a pitcher for iced tea when Louise asked out of the blue if Neet was okay. She said that Neet's skin seemed to be glowing lately and she knew of only one thing that made a girl's face glow like that. Plus, she said that Johnetta had told her that Neet seemed to be sneaking in and out of that house on the corner. "I better not hear of you being in that house, the way those adults who live there are never home. And I just know you better be keeping yourself sewed up tight. I don't care what other girls are doing or not doing with whomever."

Shay stirred the lemons around in the tea pitcher, hitting the spoon against it with such force that Louise told her to stop before she cracked the pitcher.

Shay yelled at her mother. Told her to stop with her crazy thinking then. Asked her where she came up with these crazy ideas. Did she, like, stay up late or wake up early, had to be one or the other because the remark about Neet's skin was one of her crazier ones. Louise had threatened Shay with a backhand to the mouth for talking to her like that. Shay had stormed out of the room. She'd squeezed lemon in her eye and her eye was on fire and she didn't want Louise to think that she was crying, that she'd hit on something about Neet that was upsetting to Shay. Now she looked at Neet straddled over the banister, crying. Tried to see through Neet's pajama top, a pink cotton fabric. Neet had lifted her hands to wipe at her eyes and Shay could see it now. More pronounced because Neet was so thin, the unmistakable curve starting right where her navel should be.

Neet covered her face with her hands and cried into them. She tried to stop herself from crying, but she couldn't. Couldn't stand it that Shay was just sitting there watching her cry like this. Not consoling her, not even asking her what was wrong. She wasn't even fully aware of what was wrong herself, just felt so insulted that Shay would wipe away her kiss like that. She decided that she was going back in the house. Slipped her leg over the banister and onto her porch. She could hear Shay clearing her throat as she was almost to her door, Neet not even knowing how she'd keep the charade going with Alberta about being saved. Feeling so guilty because her mother seemed so happy and Alberta was rarely happy. Wanted to at least tell Shay about that. Needed Shay to help her process it the way they'd always helped each other process what they couldn't otherwise navigate about life. Until Little Freddie.

She stopped now at the sound of Shay's voice. Shay's voice had an odd, excitable quality to it and at first all Neet heard was the "Why, Neet, why?" She'd expected Shay to demand an explanation about why she'd kept Little Freddie a secret from her. She couldn't explain Little Freddie to Shay though. How could she explain Little Freddie? Would never be able to detail for Shay how Little Freddie had given her back her name, made her feel so innocent when he called her Bonita, without also detailing how her name had gotten corrupted in the first place, how Mr. G had repeated her name over and over until the friction of his voice against her name chaffed her name of its girlhood, made it rough and blistered. She just couldn't tell it. Couldn't let Shay in on the dirtiness of it. Needed to protect Shay from the knowledge that she'd been ruined in that way. Shay was so innocent, so unspoiled. And Neet loved her so much, so she couldn't tell it.

Neet turned around then. She dried her voice out and said, "Look, Shay, I know you're pissed, but I couldn't tell you I was doing it with Little Freddie because I never intended to and I was, like, ashamed, and then I felt so bad 'cause you're my mf-ing girl and I tell you everything, and it was hurting not to tell you—"

Neet stopped in midsentence. Something about Shay's face, what her eyes were doing, stopped her and her words hung unfinished on the porch. Shay had dark, dark eyes and they were squinting at Neet like she'd never seen them before, her round, generous face had lost its cuteness, and even her dimples that came up close to her mouth had vanished in the severe scowl that had taken over Shay's face. Shay was waving her hands in front of her, swiping at the air frantically, as if she could shoo away what she was trying not to see. She was gasping out in whispers, "Oh my God, Neet, Neet, oh God, how could you, Neet?"

Neet suddenly realized what Shay was saying. She stood there facing Shay, trying not to hear what Shay was saying. She reached around and pulled the rubber band from her ponytail. It was suddenly too tight as she realized what Shay was saying. Her hair fell around her face and neck in wispy tousles. Shay was going to wash it later and saturate it with Dippity-Do to thicken it up so that she could then pick it out into a 'fro. She lifted her hair with her fingers, wanted to pull at it in desperation now that she knew what Shay was saying. Neet understood it all now. Understood why she'd been so high and so low lately, giddy, then depressed; why she'd been cramping on and off the past weeks but no period, always been irregular, she'd kept telling herself, not unusual for her to skip a month or two. Understood now why she'd raised her hand to protect herself when Alberta had started to hit her last night. Wasn't protecting herself, was protecting what was growing inside of her. She understood now as Shay tried to utter the words, but Neet wouldn't hear Shay utter the words because as long as Neet didn't hear it from Shay, she could pretend that it wasn't true the way she'd been pretending for weeks now. Shay's face was right at Neet's as Neet tried to cover her ears. Shay wouldn't let her cover her ears. She grabbed Neet's hands and held on to them. Mouthed the words as her breath hit Neet's face, emphasizing the words, "You're pregnant, God, Neet, pregnant."

Neet looked beyond Shay's darkened eyes down onto the street.

The orange-and-red-and-silver-colored merry-go-round horses seemed to be spinning though she knew the carousel was still right now. The sky was a perfect blue this morning. It shouldn't be, she thought. The sky should be a gray, thunderous sky this moment. A baby. The shame of it. The guilt and pride and dread and hope of it. She was allowing the truth of it to settle. Her eyes clouded as she listened to Shay already half into a plan. "We'll go to Miss BB," Shay whispered. "At least we know her. She seems careful and she doesn't talk, all these years she's been doing it you ever hear mention of a name? And living next door to Johnetta, if she had mentioned a name, all of Cecil Street would know. We can talk to Sondra first," Shay said, referring to BB's daughter. "Though I can't stand her with her big-butt self, she'll keep it on the q.t., maybe she can talk her mother's price down for us 'cause Miss BB's probably as expensive as shit. Damn. You know Little Freddie's gonna have to help pay too, you do realize that? So he's gonna have to get his ass up from those corner steps and get a real job at least until we get through this. If you didn't have to go to church so damned much, you could pull down some overtime, between the two of us maybe we could come up with enough. What you think, Neet, huh? What you think about that?"

Neet was hearing and not hearing as she tried to see the other side of Cecil Street through the obstruction of the rides. Miss Johnetta's house was directly across the street, Miss BB's next door to Johnetta's. Miss BB kept a porch filled with flowering begonias this time of year in brightly painted clay pots. Neet couldn't see the flowers now. Shay was right up on her now, face right at her face asking Neet how much money did she have saved. Neet started crying again and Shay hugged Neet and told her that they would work it out, that everything would be okay and they would work it out. Neet cried harder because she wasn't sure if she even wanted to go the Miss BB route. What if she wanted to have it? A baby. The thought would nestle against her lately as she floated off to sleep on her mother's bed where she'd take her afternoon nap. A soft thought that would rise up with the airy line-dried scent of her mother's pillowcase. She hadn't realized until now how often she'd inhaled the thought, made it a part of her. So she cried because she knew that to have a baby right now went against everything that was logical. She'd have to run away for sure given her mother's rigidity over a sin as large as fornicating. Either that or get married to Little Freddie. So she was crying already because she knew she didn't have it in her to do either. Knew Shay would keep the logic of getting rid of the baby right in her face so that she wouldn't waver. And really it was the only logical alternative. Really, what else could she do?

Chapter 4

OUISE PAUSED AS she rushed through the living room. Thought she heard the floor sigh under her feet, as if something was moving around below her, under the house, in the cellar. She got a chill then, was about to yell up to Joe to remind him yet again about the light switch in the cellar. Hated that the lowest level of the house was shrouded in constant darkness, a breeding ground for the mice that she was deathly afraid of, or worse. But then she heard Shay and Neet out on the porch, figured that was the cause of the sounds. She said a quick "Morning, darlings" as she hurried past them, then noticed that Neet was crying. She stopped, said, "Neet, baby, you okay?" Shay scrunched her eyes at Louise though, as if to say she had it under control. Go on.

Louise blew them a kiss and kept moving, relieved. She felt guilty for being relieved, but she wasn't the best when it came to giving consolation. Thought that it had something to do with losing her mother young. She was only ten years old when her mother died. The morning it happened Louise was fixing her mother the tea with lemon that she'd have every morning because it seemed to relieve some of the severe symptoms of her female problems. But that morning Louise was late getting to her mother. The matches wouldn't catch as she tried to light the stove and then the water took forever to boil, the tea leaves longer than usual to steep in the water, and she kept adding more boiling water to rush the tea to the whiskey-brown shade. She was agitated as she hurried into her mother's room, knowing though that her agitation would dissolve in the sound of her mother's voice singing her name. Her mother had a beautiful singing voice and would always trill out Louise's name when she told her good morning. The air had been so soft as Louise stepped from the chilly hallway into her mother's room, soft and warm, as if it was crowded with people though it was just Louise and her mother in the house that morning. Later Louise had described the feel of the room to her sister, Maggie, twelve years Louise's senior, who'd finished raising Louise after their mother's death. Maggie told Louise that the angels who had come to guide their mother to heaven were still in the room, that the angels had waited for Louise to get there so that they could comfort her. "Mama made them wait, Louise. Mama said, 'My Loo's all alone in this house and she needs soft, warm air to comfort her right now.'" Louise would challenge Maggie; she'd say, Then why didn't the angels close their mother's eyes? She'd been so terrified by her mother's dazed, unseeing stare that she'd spilled the hot tea right onto her mother's chest. Worried for months after that morning that her mother could feel the tea scalding her as it ran down her chest. She allowed the worry over burning her mother's dead chest to fill her up. Better to worry that she'd caused her mother pain on her dying bed than to be mired in the inexpressible feelings of abandonment, to have to grapple with what she believed deep down: that her mother just gave up on her and died, that she wasn't lovable enough for her mother to stay alive for. Almost thirty years later and she'd still stiffen amidst other people's emotional upheavals. Felt threatened that in the course of consoling others she might unhinge shades of what she'd never allowed herself to feel. Grief that her mother had died.

She stepped from under the awnings of the porch into the shock of the July sun. The area around her house was once the most splendid stretch of Cecil Street. The fragrant shade the tree provided, the songbirds it housed, tended to put people in a good mood. But now the stump where the tree used to be was a reminder of loss, a call to sadness. Louise looked at the tree's remains as she hurried past and felt sad about Neet. Guessed whatever Neet was crying about right now had everything to do with the noise Shay had heard coming from over there last night. To Louise's way of thinking Neet had a crazy, religious fanatic of a mother and nothing short of Neet's turning eighteen would change that. She hoped that's all it was, Alberta's hardhanded discipline. Hoped Neet hadn't gotten herself in trouble. She was thinking now about how Shay had reacted when she'd hinted at the possibility that Neet might have strayed. Shay had almost broken her good iced tea pitcher, she'd gotten so angry. A good sign, Louise thought. A frozen silence would have confirmed it for Louise, but Shay's outburst meant Shay was in the dark. And as close as those two were, if something was up with the one, the other knew. Louise remembered how touching it was when Shay was a baby and woke crying in the middle of the night;

within minutes she'd hear Neet through the walls over there crying too. The same thing happened in reverse if Shay woke first, according to Alberta back when Louise and Alberta were on speaking terms.

Louise was at Fifty-eighth Street now, where Clara's beauty shop was. She'd been a regular here as long as the shop was on this corner though Joe told her she was crazy to still come here after Clara partially blinded herself in one eye giving herself a lye-based perm. Joe used to tease Louise when she'd return from getting her hair done, tell her one side was cut higher, or curled tighter. "This side looks pretty," he'd say, smoothing her hair, "but I guess she did the other side with her bad eye." Louise felt a laugh coming on as she walked down the three short steps and into the shop. Felt a tingle move through her as she thought about her and Joe together last night, and then again this morning. How urgent he'd seemed, such an intensity to his wanting. She tried to wipe the smile from her face as she pushed open the door on the scent of hair singeing in a hot comb mixed with the heavy sweetness of Dixie Peach. Too late.

"Awl, look who got a grin plastered on her face this morning," said Nathina, as soon as Louise was in the door good. "Haven't seen you grin like that since Shay got her Afro pressed for the junior prom. Joe get a raise?"

"Probably more like Joe got a rise." This from Joyce, who lived near the corner of Cecil, bending her ear out of the way right now as Clara leaned in with the hot comb. "That's no money grin, that's a man grin, a my-man-was-good-to-me-last-night grin."

"Y'all need to hush," Louise said, laughing as she stuck her head around the curtain where the washbowls were. "Johnetta not here yet, Clara?"

"She'll be here directly," Clara said, turning all the way around so she could view Louise with her good eye. "Something, something having to do with that niece staying with her for the summer. So that doesn't leave y'all much time to get it out of your systems."

Louise plopped in the chair next to Nathina, and she and Joyce and Nathina looked at one another and snickered. They always tried to arrange their appointments with Clara on the same day and time because the three had always been close. All were just a few years shy of forty, and regular members at the same Baptist church. They'd always worked outside of their homes even before it was fashionable. Joyce taught third grade, Nathina supervised clerk-typists at the city's department of probation. They were attractive, though in different ways, with looks that went from the soft and pretty of Nathina's, to Joyce's pug-nosed kind of cute, to Louise's exotic, almost severe kind of beauty. They all loved Clara too, revered her as a matriarch since she was on the other side of sixty.

"Don't act like you're not brimming to talk about the chile," Clara said, referring to Johnetta's niece Valadean. She put one hot comb in the stove, taking another out, scattering the smoke as she waved the comb to let it cool. "You know I can sense the conversations swirling around in my shop before they've been spoken."

"We know, Clara," Joyce said, hunching her shoulders as Clara pulled the hot comb through the hair close to Joyce's neck. "You can tell by our hair, right?"

"I can tell your emotional state by your hair, yes I can," Clara said as Louise settled deeper in the chair and took in the waves of smoke. The burning hair and heavy sweetness of the pressing oil reminded her of childhood, of Louise's mother hot-combing her hair every Saturday morning without fail. Even after she'd gotten increasingly sick from her severe female problems that she treated herself because she didn't believe in doctors—the female problems Louise learned years later to be ovarian cancer—she still hot-combed Louise's hair on Saturdays. She'd hum and massage Louise's scalp and cause a layer of contentment to fall over the kitchen table that Louise found no place else. When she was done, Louise's hair would be so black and shiny and her mother's eyes would well up, especially after her health declined, as she'd tell Louise that she was just a beautiful doll, she was. Louise shook off thoughts of her mother now. She was not able to recall those scenes and take comfort in having truly basked in a mother's adoration. She'd feel the loss instead, the abandonment. The sense of loss would expand and stretch even to today. She'd feel vulnerable then. As if she was in the process of losing something but not sure what so that she didn't even know what to cling to, what to try to protect so that it wouldn't leave her. She looked around the shop at the young pretty faces on the full-color posters advertising Ultra Sheen and hair-softening comb-out creams. Their faces so beautiful with their oversize eyes and flawless skin and perfect teeth. Thought now her feelings of loss had to do with going to the dentist next week. Was about to tell them that she was finally getting work done on her mouth, but Nathina and Joyce were already buzzing about Valadean.

Joyce had just asked how old Valadean was. Nathina said she'd put her at about twenty-five, but since she was so country it was hard to say exactly. "They can act younger than they are."

"Right dumb-acting, huh?" Joyce said.

"Dumb like a fox." This from Nathina.

"Why you say that, Nathina?" Louise asked, trying to climb out of her own head and focus in on the conversation. She took the towel from Nathina's hands to dab at the side of Nathina's face, at the auburn-colored dye trying to edge out from under the plastic cap.

"Well, I heard that she's up here trying to leave a man," Nathina said. "Though it seems more to me like she's trying to catch one."

"Say what?" all three said at the same time.

"All I know," Nathina said, taking her voice down, "is that I caught her flopping her titties all in Tim's face. I didn't say anything. But when I saw her go to walk in your kitchen, Louise, I looked at Tim, and after fifteen years of marriage he knows all of my looks. He knew my eyes were telling him that if his black ass got up to follow her in there he was gonna be pulling my foot from his behind for at least the next seven days."

"Cow," Clara said as she moved the clip separating the pressed from the undone portions of Joyce's hair.

"I don't know what part of the South she's from," Nathina went on, "but my people are from Georgia and when the women are built up like that chile's built up, they wear girdles and underwire bras when they go inside of someone's house."

"Well, you know now, I understand what you're saying," Louise said, "but women are burning bras these days, you know, as an expression of liberation."

"Yeah, white women," Nathina said. "Women libbers with rich husbands. I tell you what all that little hussy wants to liberate. I know the type. I supervise young girls eight hours a day and I can pick out the thick-natured ones who like the thrill of being with someone else's man. It's a whole psychology. And honestly, Johnetta's not above encouraging it. I had to step to Johnetta about the last relative she had living with her, gonna have the gall to ring *my* bell for *my* husband to give her a ride to the African store on Sixtieth Street to pick up some statue or some shit."

"Well, that one was really here to see BB," Clara said, concentrating on the strands of Joyce's hair being transformed under the power of her hot comb.

They all got quiet then. Though they acknowledged that aborted secrets lived in the shadows of BB's back bedroom, they never spoke about who procured BB's services. BB never named names. The woman having herself fixed would have to tell it herself for anyone to know, as the last niece staying with Johnetta had done. Started crying under the hair dryer at three o'clock on a Saturday afternoon, peak time when the shop was packed and every chair occupied. Detailed for everyone in the shop her ordeal at BB's hands. Clara had had to take that one in the back and ask her if she wanted to see BB in jail, did she want to go to jail herself, then she better keep that particular experience to herself. "Well, I guess some things about a person we just didn't need to know," Clara said as they all now cringed at the memory of that scene.

Nathina started talking again about Johnetta, and Louise was about to tell them how she'd had to punch Joe in his back when she'd caught him angled in a dark corner with the loose-dressing niece, but then Clara stopped her in midsentence, told her to hush because Johnetta was already halfway in the door, mouth moving fifty miles an hour before she was in the shop.

By the time Johnetta stood in the shop untying the scarf on her head, she was well into her description of the puffy-haired monstrous-looking woman who'd come onto Cecil Street last night. Johnetta was a big woman and her heftiness shook to the rhythm of her words as she tugged at her scarf to loosen where it was knotted under her chin. She'd heard about the woman, she said, from Maryland, whose son was a Corner Boy. Said the Corner Boys had just finished singing "Looking for an Echo," which was the cue for the live band to start, so everybody had turned their attention to the section of the block where the band was. "Maryland said her son said this wild-looking woman walked over to them and said she was looking for her daughter's house, then she asked them what was all the foolishness going on, some kind of night carnival? Then they started sassing her, you know, being the hardheaded boys that they are. Then they said she turned her back to them and lifted her clothes, a red, black, and green tie-dyed something, and exposed herself, wasn't wearing no panties."

Johnetta paused to catch her breath and wipe the perspiration forming at her hairline. She had long hair that fell around her shoulders once she'd gotten her scarf off. "I got Indian in me," she'd say when anyone complimented her hair, pointed also to her red complexion and high cheekbones as confirmation that she was more than just black. She pulled her fingers through her hair now as if the rest of the story was a part of her hair and needed to be teased out. The shop was quiet. Just the rustle of the exhaust fan carrying the smoke outside, and the hiss of the hot comb as it steamed through Joyce's hair.

"Then," Johnetta continued, "the woman had the mighty nerve to tell the Corner Boys that she was old school, told them couldn't none of them handle her. Is that something or what? They tried to follow her to see whose house she was going in, probably too just to sass her some more, those Corner Boys being half raised like they are, but there was too much activity and too many people and they lost sight of her right around your house, Louise. Said they hung out till late trying to find her and they never saw her leave the block by either end."

"Well, whose house was she looking for?" Clara asked.

"Don't know, don't know. Just know what I think."

"And that would be?" This from Nathina, who generally lived at the opposite end of any point of view Johnetta espoused.

"Probably got something to do with that devil worshiper living next door to you, Louise," Johnetta said, ignoring Nathina. "That Alberta. Dollar to a doughnut it's related to her."

"Or it could be that the Corner Boys had just finished their Friday-night jug of Tokay wine," Nathina said.

"Look, Nathina, I know what I know," Johnetta said. "And everybody knows Alberta ain't been right since she joined up with that cult that got her dressing funny and snubbing everybody 'round here."

"Johnetta, it's been over ten years since Alberta fell in with those people, and she kept to herself before that. You need some new sources of conversation," Nathina said. "Now you wanna hear what somebody knows, I can tell you what I know, who I saw trying to make a play for my husband."

Clara tapped the straightening comb against the barrel-shaped countertop stove. "Nathina, go sit at the sink so I can rinse you," Clara said, quick to scatter any contentious air before it could form into a full-blown fight in her shop. "And, Louise, you may as well get settled back there too 'cause BB's Sondra will be walking through the door any minute and she'll get you washed. Got a new leave-in conditioner I'm trying on you today."

Louise did as Clara instructed, yanked Nathina by the hand,

who otherwise was content to spar with Johnetta. Louise was glad she hadn't had the chance to tell them how she'd felt when she'd seen Joe in the dark corner with Valadean. Would have certainly heard it repeated when Nathina finally let loose on Johnetta, which she inevitably would. "Even Louise said she made a move on Joe," Nathina would surely say to push her point had Louise said how she'd felt last night. And Louise was embarrassed now that she'd felt that way, so jealous. Joe was right when he'd said that he'd never given her cause to be so suspicious. She reasoned that her anxiety over the condition of her mouth was affecting her logic. She settled in at the washbowl and thought about what she'd wear for Joe tonight. Thought she'd wear the new silky emerald green robe he'd given her for her birthday. She'd open wine and put something sultry on the hi-fi and offer herself up to dance. She imagined the feel of the silky robe brushing against her nakedness once they were into their slow drag and Joe got going with his hands. She was tingling all over by the time BB's daughter, Sondra, eased Louise's head under the warm sprays of water. Sondra was asking Louise if she'd had fun at the block party last night. Asked her if she'd heard about the monster-woman Miss Johnetta was in there talking about. "Probably nothing to concern ourselves with, Sondra," Louise said, even as she wondered how much of it was true, if there was some crazy woman holed up somewhere on their block. Now she felt chill bumps forming on her arms and legs. She shivered and rubbed her hands up and down her arms and told herself that it was cold back here.

Chapter 5

HE BLACKNESS STARING Deucie in the face told her that it was nighttime again. She'd slept the day away down here and now she sat up thinking that she might never leave this cellar. Had the thought that she should rummage through the boxes and find swatches of clothes that she could spread out for her dying bed. She didn't want to die at Byberry State Hospital. She wasn't crazy anyhow, had never been crazy, just made a spectacle of herself from time to time when a headache came on. And that was her main concern now, that a headache would come on as she was trying to get back downtown, and there she'd be all over again treated to a trip to Byberry with their arm restraints and rubber rooms and hypodermic needles that were supposed to mainline her to sanity.

"Awl, Luther," she whispered, "it might not work out for me to get back to you, baby boy. I'ma try. But it may not happen."

She pulled her frail, naked self to standing. Held on to the wall and inched to the back of the cellar. She used the drain as a toilet, then walked to the spigot and turned it to get the water running. She squatted under the gush of water and let it run down her back, turned then to douse her front, using her hands to rinse where the water didn't flow. The water was neither hot nor cold, so it wasn't shocking against her skin. A placid feel it had and she felt herself coming back to life some. Felt now what she hadn't felt in weeks as she stood there dripping water and looking out into the yard where drizzles of light fell. She watched a gray-and-white cat on the ledge just outside the window above her head. Felt hungry right now as she watched the cat turn its back on a bowl of food and walk into a little wooden cat house. Got to be a man cat, she thought, probably got bowls he eats from all over the place. She'd eaten cat food before. Both the dry kind from a bag and the chunks that came from a can and looked to be covered in slime. It all went down good though when her circumstances dictated that that's what she'd eat. Her trusty step stool of a wooden pony was patient under the window from when she'd cleared the cobwebs earlier. A laugh crackled up from her throat as she climbed onto the pony's back and thought about how she'd swiped away at the cobwebs as a gift for the people who lived here. Now her gift had boomeranged and she would be the primary beneficiary. "Ain't that just like life," she whispered as she braced herself for several tries of pulling at the window latch, thinking the latch, like the spigot, was stuck in place from lack of use. It wasn't though, and the ease with which the window lock turned was so out of proportion to her use of force that the pony almost tipped backward. She steadied herself and hoisted her body all the way onto the ledge in case the window was more stubborn. It was. It took her several tries before she heard the grunt of air and felt the window rising. It was a cool night for July and the air sizzled against her face, wet from a combination of her makeshift shower and the perspiration from working so hard to raise the window. She was tempted to just climb all the way through the window and out of this cellar and head on home to Luther. She reminded herself that she was naked, and wet. Might catch a cold. She laughed at the irony. Her cirrhosis was in the advanced stage; her prognosis a month ago had been that she'd last weeks rather than months, and here she was, worried about catching a cold.

She reached out of the window and retrieved the bowl filled with cat food. Could see from this vantage point that a Cyclone fence surrounded the concrete backyard. Would be too emotionally draining to try to leave through the yard and then discover that the fence had her locked in. She watched the cat slip out of the yard under the space at the bottom of the fence. She was small these days, but not that small, she thought. The smell of fish wafted up from the bowl and pulled her attention to her meal. This was the canned kind. Good. She didn't have to work so hard to chew the kind that came out of a can. She settled in on the ledge and enjoyed the night air flowing in through the opened window. She ate with her fingers, licked them between bites as if she was eating filet mignon and the gravy drippings were that good.

She thought about her childhood now, which had been filled with rich gravies and thick cuts of meat, real satin ribbons for the ends of her plaits.

She grew up the pretty daddy's girl to a hardworking stevedore who made a good living before he started losing toes to sugar. Deucie's heart would drop lower in her chest as the gauze wrapped around his perpetually elevated foot grew thicker, the brown stains seeping through the gauze more intense, the gauze moving higher and higher up his leg until one day there was no leg to elevate. He'd cry out in pain and Deucie, hysterical herself, would ask him what could she do, please let her do something to take away his pain. "Rub Daddy's leg, Deucie," he'd cry, pointing to the empty space where his leg once was, "please, please, rub Daddy's leg." She'd get down on her knees and caress the air, she'd lightly stroke the air and ask him if it was better, was she making his leg all better again.

As much as Deucie was devoted to her father, she despised her own mother. Deucie blamed her mother for her father's demise. Thought that if her mother hadn't always demanded a lace something this, or pearl-studded that, he wouldn't have had to work so many hours at the waterfront, causing him to lose his leg. Had it confirmed when her father was in his last days and Deucie caught her mother swinging hands with a big-shouldered merchant marine up on Broad Street. Deucie went for her mother's throat that night, called her a conniving, murdering bitch. Shortly after the father's death Deucie was sent to live with a distant cousin in New Jersey. Though the mother blamed it on the Depression, explained to Deucie that the war bonds the father had left were worthless and at least the cousin worked a small farm so that Deucie could subsist on corn and tomatoes, but life in Philadelphia would hardly yield even that, Deucie knew that her mother was lying, knew she just wanted Deucie out of the way so that she could lay up with her merchant marine in peace.

Deucie was sixteen by then and she hated Jersey, hated the wide-open spaces and the sounds of crickets at night and the way the air always smelled like horse shit. She hated the cousin too, a poppy-eyed half-white girl who followed Deucie's every move as if Deucie wanted to sleep with her husband. Deucie didn't want the husband, told him so every Friday night when he'd get drunk from moonshine and proposition her. She slept with a switchblade under her pillow should he try to creep in her room at night. Rolled over on the switchblade one night, snapping it open and gashing her lovely face. Decided this was no way to live and ran away from that farm, hitchhiked back to Philly with a red-complexioned man named Jeffery. Jeffery was short but had the most well-defined arms she'd ever seen. And though he didn't seem to be too smart— he'd stare blankly when Deucie made a joke and after a pause his eyes would light up and he'd let go with a gawking laugh and say, "I get it"—he was charming in a boyish way, good looking, with well-cut features, and could move on the dance floor like Bojangles. His stepmother, Pat, ran an all-night speakeasy in South Philly. Deucie got drunk for the first time that night and fell in love with Jeffery. She experienced her first headache that night too, which was preceded by an intense bombardment of smells: the chitterlings and potato salad that Pat sold for fifty cents a plate, the cherries that she'd jam into the flasks of mixed drinks that were more water than alcohol, the sweat pouring from the bodies slapping around on the beds upstairs; Deucie could even smell that right before the headache unrolled itself in thunderclaps that disabled her completely. All she could do was get naked and curl up in a ball and moan out for her father since she wholly hated her mother by then.

S HE EMPTIED THE bowl of cat food and belched. She slid the bowl back out of the window and curled up on the oversize window ledge. She heard the sigh of the floor above her head. Someone had just come in through the front door. Shortly there was the prolonged squeal of water flowing through the pipes and the hot-water heater down here replenishing, which she guessed meant someone was taking a long bath. Then she could hear the faint but recognizable singing voices of the Temptations sifting through the basement ceiling. Later more footsteps, faster, lighter footsteps crunching on the porch. Then much later, heavier stomps on the porch, a hesitation about those. Deucie rightly guessed that it was the wife-mother, the daughter, the father-husband coming home, in that order. Only here twenty-four hours, she thought, and already accustomed to the sounds.

JOE DIDN'T GET home until after eleven though he'd told Louise he'd be straight in when he got off at six. Coming straight in had been his intention at six o'clock when the shift changed at his station at Fifty-sixth and Market where he worked as a commuter engineer. A glorified cashier, he called what he did. Collected fares and hit the button to make the turnstiles move. Made small talk with the regulars about the Phillies or the Black Revolution. "Hey, man, when we taking this shit over," he'd greet the Huey Newton impersonators dressed head to toe in black or the Rap Brown wannabes wearing sunglasses at night. He'd flirt with the women, occasionally allowing one or two to ride for free. "Baby, you go ahead on through, you looking too good to pay," he'd tease. He'd say polite "how do yous" to the elderly and make jokes with the little kids.

This evening he left work in good form, felt so unwound, so

loose and energetic because he had money in his pocket and tomorrow was a day off. Was going to suggest to Louise that maybe they go out for dinner, Chinatown maybe, tonight. He and Louise could walk through Center City after they ate and allow the night air to make them feel young and in love. He headed up Market Street in the direction of the sun hanging in the back of the sky as if it had no intention of setting tonight. People were out and about and Joe called, "Hey now," every so often as he walked. For all of the talk of how the neighborhood was going down, Joe took it as a bright sign that the streets were bustling at six on a Saturday evening. As long as people were getting together outside their houses, talking and relating and bonding, this area would stay desirable. Knew his block of Cecil Street would. Thought his block quicksanded in all that was good about the previous decade because of the way they leaned on one another. The way they'd take up donations for whoever on the block was in the midst of a money crisis, or prepared enough food to serve a two-hundred-person repast when somebody died. They streamed in to visit the hospitalized; fed each other's children bologna and cheese sandwiches and got them started on their homework for whoever was late getting home; crowded auditoriums for school awards nights whether or not their own child was a recipient. They were tight. And though personalities sometimes erupted like a case of German measles, and they'd divide into cliques and stop speaking for a couple of days because somebody's child dripped cherry-water ice and attracted flies to somebody's front that had just been hosed down with bleach and water, Joe thought his block of Cecil Street a storybook of what community meant—of life wrought with the struggles of being black in Philadelphia in 1969. But because they had Cecil Street to greet them at the start and end of each day, it was, in Joe's mind, a good life, a desirable life. He'd chosen well, he told himself now as he turned from Market onto Fifty-seventh.

He'd grown up in Pittsburgh, one of two. Left there as soon as he could because by the time he was seventeen he'd lost everything a young man could. Lost his father, though he couldn't prove it, for being pegged a "smart-ass nigger" by a flat-footed Pittsburgh cop. His father was found in a field a mile from their house with a single bullet to his head a day after he had stepped to the cop for his comments about his wife, ". . . titties looking like they dripping milk. Wish I had me a cup," the flatfoot had said to Joe's mother. Then Joe lost his best friend to a gang war, his older sister in a car wreck, and his mother; he guessed she really died of a broken heart. So he left Pittsburgh at seventeen with the only thing that still mattered. His horn. He'd been given the horn by an old-timer who'd hung with his father, Mr. Tyne. At the repast for Joe's father, Mr. Tyne had pulled Joe outside, away from all the women in his house that day clutching at him, trying to console him, trying to feed him hot buttered yeast rolls or smothered chops. Joe walked under Mr. Tyne's hand as he held Joe's shoulder as if it was the curve of his cane. "Boy, I got something that's gonna help you make it through," he said as he led Joe to his wagon and lifted a blanket and handed him the horn. "I'll show you the basics, and you can add to it 'cause you smart, boy, like your daddy always bragged. This'll help you keep on living when you don't see the sense in life, 'cause as long as you blowing, you breathin'. You keep on breathing and the sense you need to make outta things come to you in the by-and-by."

Joe was seeing that first horn. Now he was back to thinking

about the mass of feelings that had stormed up in his chest when he'd looked at his horn last night, feelings that he hadn't begun to unwrap because of the knife edges they seemed to bear. He told himself now that choosing Louise over life on the road with his horn had been the best choice a man could make. Settling down in Philadelphia on his block of Cecil Street which was almost enchanting to walk through was a treasure-filled choice. He stomped his foot at the corner of Chestnut and Fifty-seventh as if to confirm that, settle it once and for all that he was a happy man, a fulfilled man. And then he saw Valadean.

Actually he didn't see Valadean, he heard her at first as she grew his monosyllabic name to two distinct, perfumed exhalations. "Jo-wo," she called him, right as he was facing Yock's Sandwichville that boasted the world's thickest milk shakes. And that's how her voice sounded right then, milky, and slow moving with that southern drawl. She was right up on him when he turned around, so close that they were breathing in the same inch of air, electrically charged air, Joe thought as he extended his hand and then stepped back half a foot so that it didn't seem as if he was trying to reach out and feel her instead of shake her hand.

"I'm so relieved I ran into you," she said as she allowed Joe to hold on to her hand. "I seem to have gotten myself turned around trying to get to Lit Brothers on Sixty-ninth Street. Aunt Johnetta said the D bus would be easiest but the el would be quickest, and I guess I'm caught between easy and quick right now, might as well have settled for hard and slow 'cause I'm lost sure 'nuff, Jo-wo."

Joe squeezed her hand, then released it. He let his smile take its time forming as he focused in on her lips, what her lips were doing as she added length to his name. He didn't even say anything at first, moved beyond her lips and took in all of her. He liked that she wasn't self-conscious the way some women were when they were being looked at, admired. He thought she was actually guiding him by the way she touched the chocolate, flawless skin of her forehead, then smoothed her hand over her hair, pulled back in an Afro puff behind a hot pink headband, then dusted her off-the-shoulder cotton top, a loose-fitting top but short, so that it barely covered the space where her waistline dented in, where she rested her hand now, her fingers dipping, inviting a glance at the dramatic curve her hips made. She bent her leg to adjust her sandal strap along her heel, showing off her legs, big, like her thighs, big and tight and brown, rendering the pink shorts she wore almost red. When he got to the toenails painted pink like the shorts, there was nowhere else to go so he pulled his eyes back again to her face, her lips. Almost felt as if he should thank her for the guided tour. Laughed instead. Said, "Valadean, consider yourself turned around no more. I'll not only escort you to the el, I'll make sure you ride for free this evening."

She was headed to get stockings for church tomorrow, she told him as they walked. Said that Johnetta had insisted on going with her to the store, but she was emphatic that the only way to learn the area was to strike out on her own. "Though honestly, Jo-wo," she said, "I'm downright suffocating on Aunt Johnetta's stories. When I first got here, all I heard was Alberta is the devil. Now all the talk has to do with some strange woman who came onto the block and never left. You hear tell of her yet, Jo-wo? Aunt Johnetta insists she got something to do with your next-door neighbor."

Joe grimaced. If there was one thing he did not like about Cecil

Street it was the treatment Alberta had suffered from the block once she'd converted to a religion that didn't have a name. Though Joe believed like the rest that Alberta had been emotionally exploited by the suave, good-looking preacher who used to proselytize from his makeshift pulpit outside of the State store at Sixtieth and Locust, he didn't think Alberta hardhearted and evil. Thought just the opposite. He had seen when Neet was a baby how Alberta's face would cloud up after she'd reluctantly peel Neet from her arms to hand her over the porch banister so that Neet and Shay could play together. Alberta would rub her hands up and down her arms, as if she was suddenly chilled. As if she needed her baby's body against her to keep her warm. Needy and soft, he thought Alberta, so he hadn't been as shocked as everyone else when Alberta had fallen for the esoteric religion and begun snubbing them all.

"What do you say about Alberta, Jo-wo?" Valadean asked.

"I say that she's at least bold enough to live the life she chose without conforming to what Cecil Street thinks, that's not the worst trait a person could have. I say like my boys the Isley Brothers, you know, if it's your thing, you gotta do what you gotta do, I'm surely not the one to be trying to tell anybody who to sock it to."

They laughed as they walked up the el steps and Joe pulled Valadean's hand so that they could run because the el was coming into the station. His man in the booth nodded and hit the lever so that Joe and Valadean could push through the turnstiles. Joe hadn't intended getting on the el with Valadean, was his intention just to walk her up to the platform headed west. But the station was somewhat crowded and he allowed himself to be pushed into the car when the train stopped and the swell of people converged around the opening doors. Plus, he considered it the neighborly thing to do. Valadean was obviously confused finding her way around in the city. Was thinking that's how he'd explain it to Louise should word get back that he was riding the el with some fine, well-built dream of a woman. Just being a good neighbor, he convinced himself as he showed Valadean how to grab the poles so that she could make it to a seat without falling, unaccustomed as she was to the jerky motion as the train shook from side to side. He stood rather than sliding in next to her. Looked around the train and whistled, trying not to appear as if he was looking for someone who'd be quick to run to Louise and say, Guess who I saw riding the westbound el at six-fifteen with some young girl? Relaxed when he saw that people on this car were people he knew only vaguely. Chided himself now for even looking around him, reminding himself that he was doing absolutely nothing wrong. Asked himself why he should have to feel the need to explain himself to Louise anyhow. He was her husband, not her kid. He slid into the seat next to Valadean then. Asked Valadean if this was her first time on an el as he settled in and let the side-to-side motion push their bodies closer and closer and by the time they got to Sixty-ninth Street, Joe was inviting her out for a drink.

N EET AND SHAY were in the next car of the el. They didn't get off at Sixty-ninth Street even though it was the end of the line. They were going to ride back down to the eastern end of the line and then back to Sixty-ninth again. BB's daughter, Sondra, told Neet she should ride the el as much as possible between now and a week from now when she'd set up the procedure with her mother. Sondra told Neet that sometimes, if it was early enough, continuous rides on a bumpy el could wash the whole thing down and negate Neet's even having to go through the procedure. Shay said that she thought that was just an old wives' tale. Shay and Sondra had never been fond of each other and were always looking for a reason to disagree. But Neet said what harm could it do and it might even help. So they planned to spend this Saturday evening riding the el back and forth from Sixty-ninth to Frankford, eating soft pretzels and talking about the people getting on and off the el.

The train emptied at Sixty-ninth Street its mixed bag of riders: working-class middle-aged white people trying to get out of Philly before the sun went down; young mothers wrestling with tired children on a Saturday evening, headed to Buster Brown for new shoes for church; long-haired hippies weighted down with peace-sign medallions who'd pretended all day long as they'd grooved in the grass out in Fairmount Park not to be from the suburbs. The sounds of the Fifth Dimension singing "Aquarius" drifted in through the opened doors and ushered in a new wave of commuters, mostly black people loaded down with bags from Lit Brothers and JC Penney, towing children stained with mustard, no doubt from hot dogs that had slipped through the roll. The conductor came through and roused a drunk sitting not far from Neet and Shay, told him to take what was left of his vodka and get off the train, or come up with the fare to ride it back downtown. He didn't bother Neet and Shay though as they sat side by side chattering away, interrupting themselves to say hello as he passed. They had the looks of nice, well-raised girls with their polite smiles and carefully ironed clothes.

Shay's Afro was big, but freshly trimmed and neat looking; Neet wore granny glasses, her semibush barely passing because her hair was so straight. They were talking about whether hippies could be trusted to get involved in black causes. Shay said no way. Said she believed like her dad that a lot of them were CIA meant to thwart any real change to the establishment. Neet said that a half dozen long-haired, raggedy-jean, torn-flag-adorned white boys and girls had come into Connie's Cards 'n Gifts earlier and bought a full fifty dollars' worth of cards and posters and gushed the whole time to her and Connie about how they were down with progress for the people. "So Miss Connie told them that the house next door to her was for sale, why didn't they move on her block and live where she lived and help us progress from inside out. And they were all, like, 'Cool, man, I could dig that.' And after they left, Miss Connie said they were probably high off of acid."

"Probably were tripping," Shay said.

"I don't know," Neet said, turning to look out of the window. "They did spend a lot of money in there. I thought they were sincere."

"Neet, you think everybody's sincere."

Neet was about to go into her routine of you wanna know sincere, I'll tell you about sincere, and detail for Shay the aberrant devotion of the congregation to her mother's pastor and church. From a little girl she would have Shay in stitches when she'd perform one-person skits about the bizarre scenes at her church. Was about to go into one now, feeling the need to make Shay laugh after their devastating time on the porch banister this morning when they both allowed themselves to admit that Neet was pregnant. But right then Neet saw Valadean walking along the platform.

"Look," she said, pointing out the window, "there goes Miss Johnetta's niece. Gosh, she's pretty."

"But she knows it," Shay said, dusting away at the salt falling from the soft pretzel she'd bitten into. "Takes away from the prettiness when somebody's yelling out, 'Look at me, I'm beautiful.' "

"Well, we do it with black is beautiful," Neet said, patting Shay's 'fro.

"That's only 'cause our beauty's been denied, we've been told we're ugly for so long, we have to shout out that it's not true."

"Well, maybe somebody told Miss Johnetta's niece she was ugly growing up, so now she's saying, 'You a lie, I look good.' "

"She does look good," Shay had to agree. "Matching from head to toe too in all that hot pink." Shay was about to go on and say that Valadean probably had every man in her el car ogling her, but right then she saw her father walking along the platform, saw Valadean turn to wait for him to catch up.

"Look, there's your dad," Neet said. "Mr. Joe, Mr. Joe," Neet called but the doors to the el had just closed, so Joe didn't hear her. The el started moving in reverse then, toward Center City, so they were riding backward, which was actually putting them closer and closer to Joe and Valadean. Shay had a clear view of her father's face, his smile, his eyebrows arched as if he'd just asked Valadean a soft and serious question. He reached out then and touched Valadean's back and pointed her toward the revolving wooden slatted doors that were the exit from the platform. His hand seemed to move in slow motion to Shay, seemed not just to lightly touch

Valadean's back but seemed to caress it, and when Valadean turned around to look in Joe's face, to smile back at him, it seemed to Shay as if they had leaned in and kissed.

Neet pushed over Shay to try and tap the window to get Joe's attention. "Aren't you gonna wave to him?" she asked Shay. "Mr. Joe, Mr. Joe," Neet said, hitting the window with her fist.

"Stop it, girl!" Shay said, trying to pull Neet's hand away from the window. "Just stop it. I don't want him to see me."

The el had picked up speed and rounded a curve and left the sight of Joe and Valadean behind.

"What's wrong with him seeing you?" Neet asked as she got up and sat in the seat facing Shay because she said that riding backward made her dizzy these days. "We have our story together, right? We made a bet to see how long it takes to get from here to Frankford, if anybody asks where we're headed, right? So it's not like we'd have any explaining to do, right? So why didn't you want your dad to see you, huh?"

"Just because," Shay said, breaking off another piece of pretzel.

"Why you being all like that?"

"Like what?" Shay asked, needing Neet to help her make sense of the what, the way they'd always done for each other.

"Like you just caught your dad wrong just 'cause he got off of the same el with Valadean?"

"Speaking of caught wrong," Shay said, stuffing her soft pretzel back into the brown paper bag and punching her seat with the bag, "did you tell that dumb-ass Little Freddie yet about your condition?"

"Everything is everything with Little Freddie and me," Neet said, not allowing herself to be baited right now. She stared at Shay, watched Shay's cheeks fill up with air the way they always did when her emotions were tangled. "You should have let your father know you saw him, Shay."

Shay didn't say anything. Just looked out of the window. They were speeding through West Philadelphia and Shay concentrated on the roofs and chimneys of the row houses and stores and row houses again that lined Market Street. A rush of James Brown singing "Say It Loud, I'm Black and I'm Proud" moved through the car when the doors opened at Fifty-sixth Street along with a stream of fried shrimp wafting up from the fish store below. More loud music at Fifty-second Street, this time a little Aretha Franklin, a little Wes Montgomery competing with sirens blaring and a raspy voice shouting, "Jesus saves," through the type of megaphone that politicians made promises through at election time. A tall, slim brother in a Jimi Hendrix T-shirt sat next to Neet, said, "Hello, sister." Neet looked at him and smiled though Shay barely acknowledged him even after Neet tried to introduce them. Neet and the brother engaged in light conversation about whether a man had really landed on the moon the other night. He said he had his doubts. Said the white man was a liar and a thief and would do anything to promote his image of superiority over the entire universe. Shay sucked the air in through her teeth. She was irritated that Neet was so nice, so trusting, so willing to give anybody the time of day, a second chance. Hated having to listen to Neet's polite replies to this wannabe intellectual's comments. So she was relieved when he got off at Thirty-fourth Street, especially since they were underground now and there were no more scenes for her to look out on.

Shay got up then and sat next to Neet, telling herself that it would save her from having to listen to bullshit from the next brother who'd rush to sit there, attracted by Neet's soft prettiness. Once she sat though, she knew that she needed the very thing that irritated her about Neet, her too-trusting nature. "So how do you know my father wasn't wrong back there?" she asked Neet.

"How do you know he was? I just think you should give him the benefit of the doubt. I swear, Shay," Neet said as she put her arm around Shay and squeezed her shoulder. "And I don't have to tell you what the consequences are in my mom's religion if I were to be caught swearing."

Neet went into one of her church routines then. Imitated the Reverend Mister who this time she characterized as a rooster, then the flutter of all the hens who pampered him, mopping his brow and fanning him lest he get overheated even as they themselves were passing out from working overtime laying his eggs. What she did with her face, her arms, even her voice as she cock-a-doodle-dooed had them both laughing so hard that they were doubled over, prompting the occasional comment from some other young black commuter begging, damn, sisters, can I get a hit of what y'all been smoking.

By the time they got to Frankford, the other end of the line, and the train emptied again, Neet had laughed so hard she was crying. She was really crying. She was telling Shay that she was afraid. She didn't know if she could go through with the abortion. She'd gotten attached to the thickening in her stomach, she said. Had even developed the habit of rubbing her stomach softly, trying to soothe it and prepare it for the ensuing void. "Please help me, Shay. Please help me to go through with it, I have to go through with it. But I'm afraid. I'm scared. I'm so scared. I do want to have the baby, but I can't have a baby. How can I even want to have a baby? I want college. You know. I want a future. God. I must be crazy to want a baby. Please help me, Shay."

Shay was terror stricken herself listening to Neet cry that she did want to have the baby, even as she consoled her, told her she would get through it. "I'm here for you, girl. You know that. Don't even let this mess with your mind. This is normal, what you're going through. We'll get through it. Yeah we will. Hell yeah we will."

THEY RODE THE EL until nine o'clock, though Neet said that she didn't feel any different so that she couldn't tell whether or not the jostling motion had done any good. Though it had done her some good just spending time with Shay. She told Shay that now as she stepped into Shay's vestibule so that she could put her long black skirt on to wear into her house. The baggy skirt was actually a relief to her stomach after the Wrangler dungarees she'd had on. They kissed good night, said love you, the way they'd been saying it to each other since they'd first learned to talk.

Shay stood at the door and watched Neet climb over the banister and go into her house. Now she allowed herself to fully realize the panic she'd felt at Neet's admission that she wanted to have the baby. Her breaths were coming fast and tight and she thought she was about to hyperventilate. Suddenly she wanted to talk to her mother. Wanted to ask Louise was it right to coerce somebody into doing something that they didn't want to do even if the thing that they didn't want to do was the best for them. Louise would know what to do. She'd listen with a keen understanding and then direct Shay's path through this ordeal. Her mother would interrogate her for specifics though and Shay couldn't give specifics. Except, she thought now, she could invent a scenario. Somebody from work, she'd tell Louise. Some Irish-Catholic girl who found herself pregnant, a college student, she'd tell Louise. She felt unburdened already just thinking about talking it over with Louise.

She pushed in through the vestibule door and into the living room. The living room smelled sweet, like her mother's Sachet of Roses perfume. The Temptations' *In a Mellow Mood* fizzed softly from the stereo console. They were singing "With These Hands" as Shay called through the house for her mother. "Mommy, Mommy, I need to talk to you," she said. "Mommy, I have to ask you something important."

"Don't Mommy me," Louise said, coming out of the kitchen. Her face was tight and the bones in her slender neck were sticking out. "Don't you dare Mommy me."

"What did I do?" Shay said, retreating inside at the anger shooting from her mother's face, hiding all that was pretty about it.

"You left the washer filled with your wet clothes, for starters," Louise barked.

"Oops, sorry—"

"And you made eggs and didn't even have the decency to soak the pan."

"I was gonna as soon as I got back—"

"And you didn't feed the cat."

"Oh yes I did, I did feed the cat. I fed the cat this afternoon right before I even went out."

"Well, why did he come to the front door crying, he never comes to the front. When I went out into the yard his bowl was completely empty."

"I fed the cat, Mom, don't tell me that I didn't feed the cat."

"When I filled the bowl, he went at that bowl like he hadn't eaten in a week."

"I said I fed the damn cat."

"Who are you using profanity at?" Louise said, coming toward Shay.

Shay wished for her father right now. He had a knack of walking into the middle of an argument between Shay and Louise and with a simple remark or two having them either laughing or instead of going at each other, pitting them both against him. Now the realization pounded her over the head. Her father wasn't home yet. She looked around the living room, the unopened bottle of wine on her mother's good silver tray with two empty wineglasses. Her mother in her silky green robe, her hair so black and freshly pressed twisted in a French roll. Her lipstick red and new. Three hours since she'd seen her father on Sixty-ninth Street. And he hated Sixty-ninth Street. Where the fuck was he? she wondered now. She was seeing again the way he'd smiled at Valadean, the way Valadean had smiled back, her teeth so big and pretty. She was angry with him for not being home yet. Angry with Louise for slamming the window on her need to talk. Angry with Neet for convincing her that her father should get the benefit of the doubt. What kind of judgment did Neet have anyhow, Neet didn't have judgment enough to keep from getting pregnant. She was looking at her mother now. She wished her mother would stop glaring at her like that, she looked like a dog foaming at the mouth. No wonder her father could smile with such open ease at Valadean if this was the face Louise presented when he came home.

"Gosh," Shay said, fighting tears. "I came home really needing to talk to you and you coming at me like a fucking wild woman."

"If I have to tell you one more time about your language," Louise threatened, moving in closer to Shay with her hand opened, ready to go for Shay's mouth.

"Leave me alone." Now Shay was crying. "Just leave me alone and go get your teeth fixed." She ran up the steps then. Stormed into her bedroom and slammed the door behind her.

JOE AND VALADEAN ended up at a small club on the north side where Joe didn't know anyone, and more important, where no one knew him. The club was perfect: so packed and so dark; a nice quartet doing its thing and he and Valadean had to sit so very close. An old cat was on vocals and his voice was so smooth that it melted the air in here. Joe was getting a fine buzz from the Bombay gin and tonic water and he was listening so intently as the old cat sang "Embrace Me." More from instinct than deliberation his fingers went to the space at the back of Valadean's neck. She leaned her neck forward to make it easy. Joe was thinking what he would tell Louise if he was spotted right now, that he'd just popped in there for a drink and hung around for the set, is what he'd tell her. Didn't even realize who in the hell he was sitting next to as dark and crowded as it was in there, he'd insist, he'd just squeezed in right along with everyone else. And then he even started to think about what he would say to his wife if he just went ahead and hung out with Valadean tonight, not too late, just until ten or eleven.

Nothing outrageous either, find another bar where they could sit at a table and face each other, look at her perfect smile and squeeze her fingertips, talk a little jive, tell her the effect she was having on him, and he was, after all, a married man. Follow her cue from there.

He leaned in closer and whispered in her ear that she was such a lovely, lovely lady. "Just lovely," he said. He didn't even consider the rightness or wrongness of his actions as he slipped his hand under her hot pink loose cotton top and rode his fingers up and down her spine. The skin that he caressed ever so lightly was soft and tight, with a hint of an oily wetness to it, and he imagined that's how she would feel all over. "Mnh, Valadean," he whispered. "I hope you wouldn't think I was jiving you if I said that in all of my eighteen years of marriage I have never met a woman who I'd risk it for. But damn, girl, you risky business, you know that."

She sipped her wine. They were sitting so close that he could smell the Bordeaux as she brought her glass down, a perfect lip print on its rim. The tenor sax was soloing now, the notes he blew out swirled around Joe, turning the texture of the melting air in here to cream. This was too large an enticement. A man shouldn't be enticed to this degree. The music and the gin and the creamy air, the oily wetness of the skin on Valadean's back and her lip print on the glass. Her lips moving now, calling him Jo-wo, growing his name until his name was about to burst. Much too much for a man to have on him, he thought as he decided on the Red Moon on Westminster Avenue. Clean and affordable rooms there. He leaned in and brushed Valadean's beautiful lips with his own. Her lips were as soft as they looked, and parted easily for him too, just like he knew they would.

J OE WALKED HOME by himself. He put Valadean in a cab after they left the Red Moon Hotel. He needed to walk off the effects of her, the essence of her womanhood that hung over him fat and heavy, like pea-soup fog. The scent of her Avon perfume and Afro Sheen hairspray had been powerful and he hoped he'd rid himself of it with the sliver of packaged soap in the shower stall. Though all the soap in the city couldn't combine to wash away the memory of the air in the club, thick with whiskey and cigarette smoke and aging men's desires. He felt guilty and sorry right now. Guilty that he'd strayed, sorry that he was a married man anyhow. And sad. Felt the intensity of sadness that he'd felt when he'd put the mouthpiece of his horn between his lips last night. All the breaths he'd wasted over the years talking shit about nothing. Breaths that should have been transformed through his horn, the nothingness of air made into beautiful music. The nothingness of his life given a fine purpose in the notes he blew. He wanted now to resurrect those dead breaths, call them back to life one at a time beginning with the last time he'd played. But that was too big a want, an unhaveable want. So he felt justified now in allowing himself a smaller want. Valadean. She was a minuscule want in comparison to having his breaths back. She was here and now and easy and soft. She was doable, with no history. A willing distraction that he didn't even have to work for. Just take her to a cheap hotel and say distract me, baby, make me forget that I was once young, with dreams.

By the time he got to Cecil Street he had justified his guilt all the way to the edges of his conscious mind. Filled in the spaces left by his retreating guilt with the knowledge that he wasn't going to leave, no intention of breaking up his home, of hurting his wife and daughter. He forced himself to whistle as he stepped into the vestibule and fixed his face for the lie he would tell. Stopped at Tim's for a cut and ended up in Pinochle Eddie's basement caught in a marathon of a tournament. He wouldn't have to worry about Louise checking up on him, that had never been her style. Louise had class, he thought as he pushed open the door into the living room.

She was sitting on the couch, her hair pinned up the way he liked it, dressed in the emerald green silky robe he'd given her for her birthday. He tried not to notice the wine on the tray, the two glasses, the opened hi-fi. High fidelity, isn't that what hi-fi stood for, he asked himself now even as he tried not to remember that she generally didn't turn it on. Her perfume was heavy through the room and he knew how methodical she was, knew she had worked to create this romantic mood. She was looking straight at him with that hard, cold stare she could give so effectively. He wished her stare wasn't so chilling. Wished she hadn't looked at him like that the night he'd played his horn in '54 when all of Cecil Street went wild because his playing had been so ferocious. He went to her now and kissed her cheek. Said, "Whew, sorry I'm late, baby. Got caught in a never-ending game in Eddie's basement."

Louise didn't challenge his explanation of the pinochle game. Knew for a fact that he'd been caught in games like that before. Plus, he appeared so calm as he stood over her. She looked straight into his calmness, at the bright light it generated that had the effect of high beams in her face, blinding her to the heavy bag he dragged into the house that contained the truth of his whereabouts. She got up from the couch and turned off the hi-fi and went upstairs. She shook herself from the robe and dressed her nakedness in cotton pajamas and got under the covers. By the time Joe came upstairs and got into bed, the bag he'd dragged into the house had expanded and took up the space between them. It was like a mountain in the bed between them.

Chapter 6

HAT MONDAY LOUISE had her first tooth pulled. A doctor at work referred her to his brother-in-law, a dentist who saw Louise that afternoon. She shook almost convulsively going into the office, she was so nervous, but determined to go through with it anyhow. Shay had been right the other night when she'd yelled at her to get her teeth fixed. Denying herself denied everyone who loved her, she'd realized then. Shay had come down a few minutes after her outburst, her cheeks puffy with air, and apologized. She'd stood in the middle of the floor and just said, "Sorry, Mommy," over and over and Louise had opened her arms for Shay and patted her back and hoped that whatever else Shay was crying about was dissolving in her tears. Certainly more than sorrow about her outburst since Shay's outbursts were as common as the hydrant on the corner being turned on without a permit. She'd patted Shay's back and didn't pry otherwise about what had Shay crying so hard. She reminded herself that by the time she was Shay's age, seventeen, she'd already gone seven years without a loving mother to pat her back when she cried.

She was bursting with pride now that she'd pushed herself finally through the trauma of walking into the dentist's office. Did it on her strength though Nathina had offered her Valium. She had the tooth wrapped in gauze and she stood in the middle of the living room holding it up as if she was Wilma Rudolph bringing home the gold.

Joe was at the kitchen table reading his *Evening Bulletin*. Shay was in her room. She had found it difficult to tolerate her father's presence since Saturday evening when she'd seen him on the el platform with Valadean. She was listening to Billie Holiday sing "Willow Weep for Me." Accepted even as she listened that this was an old person's song. She should be popping her fingers to Sly or at least James Brown right now. But she was anxious and the song calmed her down. Tomorrow was the day for Neet's abortion. She'd talked Sondra into persuading her mother, BB, into moving up Neet's procedure. She was afraid that Neet would change her mind if she had to wait until Saturday. Now she was afraid generally. Afraid that something might go wrong; afraid about the aftermath, how Neet would be emotionally if she really, really wanted a baby now, the emptiness she'd most likely feel. Just plain afraid right now, so the song that was too old for her calmed her down. She switched the record player off at the sound of Louise's voice and went downstairs.

"Look at the size of that root," Louise said, beaming as she held the tooth up to the afternoon sun pushing in through her window shears. She tried not to spit as she talked because the hole in her mouth was packed with cotton and her lips were swollen and in that uncomfortable place between numb and feeling.

"How many total you got to lose?" Joe asked, thinking that he could already see her face starting to sag, especially the way she was standing in the light, the light magnified things so.

"Well, he's gonna pull a couple each time I go. But he just wanted to start with one today—"

"How many total?" Joe asked again, trying not to look at the blood-encrusted thing she held up as if it were her firstborn.

"Just sixteen," she said matter-of-factly.

"Just sixteen!" Both Shay and Joe said it at the same time. Shay told her that the tooth was disgusting could she please put it away and Joe asked her if she was sure she wanted to go through with it.

"Sure? What do you mean, am I sure? Why wouldn't I be sure?" She dabbed at the side of her mouth to catch the drainage. "What am I supposed to do, walk around with a bunch of rotten teeth in my head and watch you work a room grinning like a Cheshire cat with your perfect-ass smile?"

Joe blew out a sigh and said, "Look, I hope you not doing this for me, Louise. Hell, I've had teeth pulled before and that shit ain't no joke."

"Did it hurt, Mommy?" Shay asked, switching loyalties the way she usually did when they argued.

"No, not really," Louise said, cupping her hand under her mouth. "The worst part was the needle."

"Needle?"

"Yeah, a needle to freeze my gum, you know, to numb it."

"Whew," Joe said, blowing out another long breath of air. "No, that's not the worst part, Shay. The worst part is when the effects of that needle wear off. Later on tonight her gums gonna be throbbing so bad where that hole is—"

"Shut up." Louise cut him off, shouting in spite of the semi-numbness and the feeling in the side of her mouth that a dam was about to break. "If you can't give me some encouragement, just shut the hell up."

"I just think you need to be realistic about what you doing."

"Well, it sounded fine to you the other night when I mentioned it, why didn't you say all of this when I first told you this is what I was going to do?"

"But I didn't know he had to pull sixteen teeth. Sixteen, damn. That's half your mouth, Louise." He shook his head back and forth. "Can't they just fill 'em and, you know, cap 'em or whatever?"

"That is a lot a teeth, Mommy."

"No, that's a lot of years of neglecting myself. I didn't grow up like you did, Shay, twice a year at the dentist without fail. My only sister had to scrape and scuffle after our mother died just to keep me in decent clothes, and to keep a roof over our heads, a dentist was a luxury when I grew up. Furthermore, they say having children is the worst thing for a woman's teeth, leaches all the calcium right out of them."

"Cut the martyrdom crap, Louise." Now Joe was shouting too. "Don't do that, don't try to make Shay feel responsible for the condition of your mouth. That calcium-leaching business is bullshit anyhow. I know women who had ten kids and still got perfect teeth."

"Well, of course you would."

"And furthermore, you grew up better than anybody I know."

"Look, all I'm saying is that I took a big step today to do this, and I was proud of myself because it's something I've been afraid to do. And if you two can't be at least a little sensitive, then just leave me the hell alone."

"Mommy, um, there's, like, blood dripping out of your mouth," Shay said.

Louise ran into the kitchen and spit into the sink. She was crying in the sink because now her gum was starting to throb and she really didn't know if she could go through all that it would take to have the teeth pulled, to adjust to dentures, to restore her smile to the way it used to be. She used to be able to take over a room with her smile. And now not just her smile had lost its appeal but everything about her presence that had once seemed so vibrant and energetic, so young. It was once common for the male patients to joke around with her: Louise, I promise I'll take my medicine if I can have a date with you when I'm out of here, they might say. Or even just the reaction to her from all types of men, the way they'd suddenly pull in their stomachs, or otherwise correct their posture when she approached, or bestow a level of attention on her, rush to offer a pen, or seat, or cigarette. Or the slackened jaw when some of them took her presence in, the glint in the eye from others, the "mnh" disguised in a cleared throat, all of which made her feel so desirable. There it was, she hated to admit it, such a trite, and superficial, notion. This was the sixties after all and women were finding their voices en masse and coming to the recognition that their species was also one of substance, that womanhood had to do with so much more than bearing children and pleasing a man. And here she was crying and spitting into her kitchen sink because she was no longer experiencing those cues that told her that she was pleasing to a man. Her sister, Maggie, had warned her that this would happen. She'd begged Louise not to rush into marrying Joe. Told Louise that she was such an odd kind of beauty and she should take advantage of it while she was young, meet a man this month who'd take her to Coney Island, next month to Hollywood, someone to buy her a fur for Christmas, another to buy her a sapphire for Valentine's Day. There would be time to fall in love, to settle down in the by-and-by, but her look did something to a man so she should use it to her advantage while she was young, while she could. Because guaranteed, the attention would stop one day, so she should create memories that she could curl up with, and if she was also surrounded with palpable things accumulated during those times, well, the more the better. Louise would laugh at her sister and say, Maggie, you'll turn me into a whore. Maggie's response was always, You show me a woman, I'll show you a whore. Joe was nice enough, Maggie would try to persuade Louise, but he was so ordinary. "You deserve extraordinary." But she hadn't been able to talk Louise out of marrying Joe.

And that's what Louise cried over now, Joe. Cried because he'd been so calm when he'd come home five hours late Saturday night. They'd barely spoken, barely touched since then. She spit blood into the kitchen sink, almost gagging.

Joe and Shay were at her back. Joe poured salt into a glass, said he was going to make her a nice warm saltwater mix to rinse her mouth with. Shay said that she would fix dinner, that Louise should just rest, just put her feet up and she'd make soup. "Would you like soup, Mommy?" Shay asked, trying not to cry herself though she believed that was the hardest thing for a child to do, watch her own mother cry.

Louise tried to shoo them away. "Don't be silly, Shay," she said. "I'll cook. I'm fine, really, go on now, if y'all gonna hover over me like I'm an invalid and I just had one little tooth pulled, what you gonna do this time next week when I'm down four? Y'all better save your tending-to skills for when I'll need them most," she said. Composed now. Embarrassed by her outburst the way she'd always been embarrassed by her own displays of emotion. Had even tried not to cry at her mother's funeral. Held her tears in for so long that she peed herself. Then she cried over ruining the beautiful white dress trimmed in black velvet that Maggie had paid a fortune for. Allowed herself to cry over the dress because she could compose herself after that, whereas tears over her mother gone would be unstoppable. Now she told herself that it was the tooth she cried over, not Joe. The rotten, disgusting tooth that should have been pulled from her head years ago. As long as she was crying over the tooth, her tears would be quick and easy to dry. "Go ahead, really, I'm fine. Shay, you might want to check the cat's bowl, he's been eating double his usual the past few days. Go ahead. I'm fine. Just fine."

Shay was about to insist that she'd stay in and cook dinner tonight, but Joe waved her away, told her with his face that he would handle it from here, she could go on out if she wanted to.

———

DEUCIE HAD BEEN down in Joe and Louise's basement for three days now. She hadn't been able to leave because of the headaches that were coming harder and with greater frequency than ever. She didn't know if it was the condition of her liver that was igniting her head to ache, compensating maybe, since other than some swollen tenderness in her upper abdomen she wasn't in much pain from the actual cirrhosis. Still peeing regularly, which meant that her kidneys hadn't started to fail. Though she'd heard that kidney failure was a soft death, since the chemicals backed up to the brain and produced a nice high. Still, she wondered if she was exaggerating the intensity of the headaches, giving her an excuse to stay in this cellar, because the truth of it was she liked it down here. The house above this understory was brimming with life; with music and anger and joys past and to come, jokes and sorrows and disputes and love. Even the sounds of the block when she lay under the steps at the front of the cellar were soothing. Just like her headaches began in her nose, heightening her sense of smell, they left through her ears, enhancing her sensitivity to sound. So she'd come to under the cellar steps hearing the whoosh of the roller skates outside, the little girls chanting in hand-slapping games, the evening song of the ice-cream truck; those other songs, the voices of young men that held over the block and reminded her of going to church with her daddy before he lost his leg. The day-to-day life she heard up there both inside the house and out on the street seemed the perfect balance of treble and bass to fall over her head as she died. So she decided to make up her dying bed right here in Joe and Louise's cellar. She'd made a mattress out of some of the sweaters that Joe had left in disarray half hanging from the chifforobe. Though she enjoyed the bare floor against her naked skin, she thought she should have a little softness under her when she died. Everybody deserved that, she thought.

She was ready to die. Each time a headache would take her down into the sweet numbness of unconsciousness she was sure she wouldn't wake, was sure that she'd be received in her new form light as air and every bit as free. So she was somewhat disappointed that again today she'd come to still alive. She was disappointed and hungry. Didn't understand the sudden revival in her appetite since she'd been in this cellar, hadn't eaten this much in the entire month that she'd been with Luther. She took the hunger as a bad sign, hunger was the body trying to go on living. Told herself that she needed to start refusing food if she really wanted to hurry death. But they kept filling that cat's bowl out in the yard. Made her salivate when she'd venture to the back of the cellar and look up and out of the window and there was the bowl filled to capacity with nuggets of fish or liver or chicken, the juices gleaming. Like now.

She stood on the wooden pony's back and hoisted her small self up to the window ledge. She crowded herself onto the ledge and sat there and caught her breath. She eased the window open and stretched her hand out but pulled it back quickly when she saw motion. It was the cat coming out of his small wooden cat house. He sniffed at the bowl and then turned his back on it. Squeezed under the Cyclone fence and out into the alley. He did this every time. Then started crying when he came back hours later to an empty bowl. She'd hear him on the porch meowing, then in a few minutes a light would go on in the yard. She'd crept back to the window last night and watched him eat, then watched him go into his little house, no doubt to his litter box, then he'd squeezed under the Cyclone fence but this time didn't go out into the alley. He went into the dirt yard next door. Snuggled up against some woman's high-yellow legs as she sat on the steps. That's all Deucie could see of next door, the ground and the bottom rungs of the steps. The cat purred as the woman reached down and played with his gray-and-white fur. Typical man, she thought. Comes home to eat and shit and then creeps next door. She didn't really learn to love men until she understood their need to think they were free. Had her heart broken by Jeffery because she hadn't understood that. But once she understood that, my, my, my, how she could love a man after that. Nothing better in her mind than loving what you didn't also have to own. Possession was a burden and a curse and turned a person into a slave obsessed and working their ass off trying to keep what they never could own. Once she'd come to that realization it was so easy to let a man go. Especially after she'd let go of her baby girl. Could let go of anything after that.

Deucie had gone into labor on a Saturday night, Pat's busiest night. By then she'd taken up residence at Pat's speakeasy bar while she waited for Jeffery to be released from jail. Jeffery had been in and out of jail for robbing places since that night when she'd hitched a ride with him from Jersey and fallen in love. She couldn't stand Pat, hard and mercenary, with the face of a frog. She had even considered going back to live with her mother. She'd tried to have a friendly visit with her mother after she'd learned she was expecting, but her mother was horrified by the fact that Deucie was pregnant, plus Deucie could tell that her mother was afraid of her the way she kept eyeing the vase on the coffee table as if she'd need a weapon against Deucie. Deucie was insulted, said, "You know what, Mother, I don't need this bullshit," and left. So she was stuck living with Pat, waiting for Pat now to go with her to the hospital. It was a soft spring evening and she went outside trying to walk off the intermittent labor pains while Pat poured the first rounds at the bar and otherwise got the night started enough to leave to accompany Deucie to the hospital. Deucie had walked as far as the Christian Street Y where a line of highbrow colored girls were on their way inside for the spring cotillion. They had the appearance of a rainbow in their lime and yellow and pink and sky blue gowns. She paused to watch them, smiled, wishing that if she had a girl, her daughter would stand in such a line at fifteen or so. But right then she was hit with the scent of pressing oils and crinoline slips and patent leather, which meant that a headache was coming on. At the same time a bearing-down pain moved from her chest to her knees, doubling her over. Her water broke then. She stood there as a puddle formed on the ground between her legs and the girls pointed and giggled and then started to scream as Deucie, completely disoriented from the combination of pains, began shedding her clothes and vomiting and running in circles looking for an alley to curl up in.

When she came to in the hospital a nurse placed a baby in her arms. The baby was perfect, the one perfect thing that had come out of her relationship with Jeffery. Deucie had never known such warmth before, such complete and absolute contentment as when her baby snuggled at her breast. The baby was born outside of the sterile conditions of the delivery room and she stayed in the bassinet next to Deucie's bed, though most of the time she was curled up in Deucie's arms because Deucie could hardly bear to put her down. On the morning of her discharge Deucie woke to an entourage of babbling white men hovering over her, but no baby. It took some minutes to understand what they were telling her, that they had taken the baby away just temporarily, they said, until they could do some monitoring, some testing. Deucie panicked, though she tried to remain calm enough to extract from them what was wrong with her child, until she realized that they weren't talking about the baby, they were talking about her, telling her that in their opinion she wasn't up to the immediate task of motherhood. In her own mother's opinion, she wasn't either; her mother had petitioned the court on the baby's behalf and provided a compelling argument for their actions today. But her mother, they said, like they themselves, only wanted what was best for her and the baby.

Deucie realized then that they thought she was crazy. She tried to convince them that she was not. Restrained herself from calling her mother a lying low-down dirty bitch as she set out to persuade them that crazy people had no explanation for why they did what they did. She could explain it all. When her mother would catch her stroking the air where her father's leg should be, asking him if it was better now, was she making it better—her mother had pointed to that as an example of how Deucie had always suffered from hallucinations—Deucie knew she wasn't crazy, that she was in fact taking away her father's pain. When Deucie caught her mother holding hands with another man on Broad Street while her father lay dying and she'd fought her, it was only out of allegiance to her father, she said, trying to counter her mother's claim that Deucie was violent as well as delusional. And when they'd offered as further proof of her unfitness the Jersey cousin's claims that

Deucie had gashed her own face with a switchblade, Deucie's hand went to the poorly healed slash of folded-over skin just below her cheekbone as she tried to explain that yes, she'd done it to herself but it had been an accident. If the cousin would only have put a leash on the husband, kept him from creeping into her room with his dick in his hands, there would have been no need to have a switchblade in her bed for her to roll over on. By the time they got to the police reports, six times in the past year she'd been picked up from some alley completely naked, she tried to make them understand that the headaches told her to do that, then tried to clean that up, stressed that she meant "told" only as a figure of speech, she never heard voices, she swore. She just felt better when a headache came on, she insisted, if she shed her clothes and curled up on the ground.

The more she tried to convince them that she was sane, the faster they wrote on their pages affixed to clipboards, their passive sterilized smiles smelling of wintergreen alcohol as they assured her that her baby would be well cared for until she herself was fit.

She felt dizzy then, felt the inversion of her world from the absolute contentment of her daughter in her arms to the absolute devastation of her absence. She tried to will the room to stop spinning as she weakly asked if she could just kiss the baby good-bye. But once the baby was nestled in her arms again, she knew that she couldn't allow them to take her. How could she go through life knowing she'd let some strange people yank her daughter from her breast—white people at that! But fighter though she was, she also knew that they were too formidable with their arm and leg restraints and hypodermic needles and solitary rubber rooms. It came to her then as she kissed the baby's cheeks and nose and pouty mouth that if she willingly relinquished the child, then they weren't actually taking her baby away.

"Y'all not taking shit," she said then. "I'm releasing her, you receiving her, but make no mistake, and let the record show, y'all didn't take her. Hell no. Hell no." She kissed the baby's forehead one more time as the nurse leaned in to retrieve the infant. But then she was struck suddenly with the need to mark the child so she'd know her when their paths inevitably crossed again. She opened her lips on the baby's forehead and pulled the tender new skin between her teeth. She bit down and held the baby's forehead skin between her teeth even when the blood started spurting and the baby screeched and jerked and the white people started wrestling the baby away. Deucie released the child then, satisfied that she'd marked her so she'd know her again, she willingly let the baby go even as she held on to the puddle of her daughter's blood that had drained into her palm.

She was involuntarily committed then. In the crazy house, as she called it, until she was declared stabilized enough. Out for a couple of years only to be committed again. Tagged as a wild woman after that so whenever she was released and celebrated her freedom with strong drink and big men and loud talking in hard places and ended up arrested for fighting or picked up from some alley curled up naked where a headache had taken her down, she'd end up right back at Byberry again. Then out on the street again for anywhere from a few months to a few years until another explosive episode would have her back in arm restraints all over again. Once in a while she was out during one of Jeffery's rare attempts at life outside a jail cell. Those were the best times. Their drunken episodes were softened by talk of their baby girl. Jeffery would tell her how their child had been placed with a well-to-do black family in Chestnut Hill. And though Deucie was burning to see her daughter, she didn't try to track her down by then because she wanted the child to be well raised first. She had visions of her daughter growing up amidst crinoline slips and lessons at a player piano, a featured soloist on the church's young people's choir, blue-ribbon winner in the school's science fair. Until she learned otherwise. Learned that the child had been placed with Jeffery's stepmother, Pat. Learned that Pat had forced the child into a kind of servitude working that speakeasy and who knew what else. Deucie went into a rage then. She had to stop herself from thinking about that now. Too frail right now to be recalling that level of rage.

She drew her finger across the bottom of the cat bowl, trying to get the last drops of gravy. Beef tonight. Good. She pushed the bowl back outside the window and adjusted herself on the sill. She'd have a couple of hours here before the cat came back crying over his empty food bowl and they rushed into the yard to feed him. She watched as the legs of the woman next door took her seat on the steps, now another set of legs next to hers, same hue, same shape. Must be mother and daughter, she thought as she sat on the sill and closed her eyes hoping that she'd get lucky tonight and meet the Big Man face-to-face.

NEET HAD COME and sat next to Alberta on the back steps. Usually when she'd peep out the kitchen window and see her mother sitting like that on the steps, staring out into the backyard, miles away, she'd get that thrilling jolt that she had time to leave the house through the front, find Shay, and experience for a couple of hours the normal life of a teenage girl growing up in Philadelphia in the sixties. She'd sneak puffs of cigarettes and hang on the corner and listen to the Corner Boys warming their voices to sing. She'd venture to the movies with Shay, or to a Four Tops concert at the Uptown Theater. They'd go roller-skating on Elmwood Avenue, or to the North Side for a poor people's rally, or down to Penn to ogle the smart black boys with their beautiful Afros as they planned how they'd room together in the new dorm on Thirty-fourth Street—they'd already been told by the school counselor that they were excellent candidates for Penn, with their high scores and good grades and well-rounded extracurriculars. She'd slip into blue-lit house parties during the time when her mother was lost on the back steps; she'd slow-drag and giggle at the feel of a boy's hardness coming into its own. And sometimes she'd just sit on the banister with Shay and slurp down cherry-water ice.

But this evening Neet didn't slip out through the front. She went out onto the back steps and sat next to Alberta. It was humid out and the dinner aromas that had crowded the block hung over the backyard now. Mothers' voices drifted into the yard calling the younger children in, three, four times until there was a stream of "Don't let me have to say your name again." Now the Corner Boys were starting up. Their harmonies multiplied over these back steps, like the mounting dinner aromas, and there was a stillness to out-side. Even the mothers who'd yelled and threatened their children over not coming in were quiet as the Corner Boys sang "I Do Love You." Neet laid her head in her mother's lap. Her mother's cotton duster felt good against her face, soft and absorbent, Neet's face clammy from all the moisture in the air. She felt flutters in her stomach then and she eased her hand to her stomach. Now Alberta was running her fingers through Neet's hair. Neet settled her head deeper along her mother's lap and enjoyed the light touches of Alberta's fingers on her scalp. The stomach flutters picked up in intensity and she allowed herself to enjoy that sensation too. Just this once, she told herself, and for the very last time.

Chapter 7

HEY HEADED STRAIGHT to Miss BB's Saturday-morning house, called such because that's when she conducted most of her business, like the number house was called the three-o'clock house because that's usually around the time of day people started at least hearing what number was leading, and like the speakeasy was called the Sunday house because you could buy liquor on a Sunday afternoon, and like the poker house was called the after-seven house because there was usually a game warming up after seven in the evening. So the three headed to Miss BB's Saturday-morning house, on a Tuesday. Shay and Neet had both arranged a day off from their summer jobs; Little Freddie was the third, he'd insisted to Neet that he wanted to be there for support. Sondra had also skipped her job this morning as shampoo girl at Clara's shop. It was Sondra who'd told Shay what time to have Neet there, to come around through the alley and they'd have to climb in through the dining-room window, and to bring the fee of seventy dollars all in one-dollar bills. Shay complied, passed the instruction about the dollar bills on to Little Freddie and was surprised when he said that he wanted to come too. "I mean, she is my lady, I want to be there for some moral support," he said.

Even Sondra was mildly surprised to see him when she edged the dining-room window up as high as it would go and looked at Shay with her eyebrow raised as if asking, What the hell is he doing here?

"Moral support," Shay said in response to Sondra's eyebrows. "Plus, he's paying for the bulk of it. You don't think your mother will mind, do you?"

"Come on in, hurry up, we'll talk inside," Sondra said as she pointed out a soda crate sitting on top of a ten-gallon lidded garbage can and told them to prop the soda crate under the window and use it as a step. Shay went first and then Neet, helped along by Little Freddie from the outside and Shay from within. When Little Freddie had hoisted himself in, Sondra ushered them through the dining room and on into the living room.

The scent of salt pork hung in the living room, which was a jumble of magazines and black-and-white composition books and unsorted mail and a broken-tooth comb sitting right in the center of the coffee table next to an opened jar of Ultra Sheen hair pomade. Shay grimaced inside. Since she and Sondra weren't on friendly terms, she was rarely in here. She had expected immaculateness, thought the furniture would be covered with white sheets, maybe the scent of wintergreen alcohol swirling around, a plate of cookies and a pitcher of juice on the table, and if not that, at least the jar of grease should have been covered, the clumps of hair pulled from the broken-tooth comb, the windows opened to chase away the heaviness of the salt pork. At least that.

She thought then that maybe they should take the disorder as a sign not to go through with it. She looked at Neet, but Neet responded to the hesitation on Shay's face by saying, "Well, come on, let's get this over with before I change my mind." She laughed nervously and then looked down at the floor.

"Only if you're positive, sweetness," Little Freddie said as he put his arm around Neet and kissed the side of her face and Shay thought she saw a moistness around his eyes. She got irritated then, it's not as if he was in any position to be supporting a baby, he should be the most elated out of all of them that he was about to be relieved of a lifetime responsibility that he couldn't shoulder.

"Well, y'all got an envelope for me, right?" Sondra said as she looked from Neet to Little Freddie to Shay.

"Oh yeah," Little Freddie said as he reached into his front pants pocket and pulled out a wad of bills and clumsily pushed it into Sondra's hand. "There's fifty-five there. You can count it if you want to."

"Here's ten more," Neet said as she riffled through her purse, "it's not in ones though, but hell it all spends the same."

"Well, actually it doesn't all spend the same," Sondra said. "If I go into Sonny's trying to buy a sandwich or some bobby socks with a bunch of ten- and twenty-dollar bills, sooner or later he gonna start talking out loud about how am I coming up with all of this money."

"Well, it's not like it's your money," Shay said as she laid the remaining five ones in Sondra's waiting palm. "I mean, your mother's the one and Sonny or nobody got no right questioning her breaking a big bill."

"Well, that may be the case usually, but today I'm the one," Sondra said, not looking at any of them as she said it. Looking instead at the clock as she cleared her throat. "And we best be getting started 'cause we don't have all day."

"Wait a minute, what you mean you're the one, where's your mom?" Shay asked.

"Okay, this is the situation, she's not doing the procedure."

"Not doing it?" the three blurted out in a chorus.

"And can we ask why not?" Neet said.

"She wouldn't do it. She won't do people our age, absolutely refuses, gives them the name of someone in New York, says if something happens to a grown-ass woman, well, she's at least made her own bed, but people our age, generally, she won't touch. Mnh-mnh, doesn't want the responsibility if the procedure were to go bad. Unless of course their mother comes to her. She said if she didn't hear it from your mother, Neet, as far as she was concerned she didn't hear it. So she wouldn't do it. So like I said, I'm the one today. I'm totally capable too."

"Yeah, but we thought we were paying for your mother." This from Little Freddie.

"Well, actually I cut the price way down. But if you willing to pay full price and willing to get Neet's mom to ask my mom to do the procedure on Neet, I could hold on to this seventy as a deposit and then I could set it up for my mother to do, she could probably be ready for y'all this Saturday morning."

The three just stood there looking stunned. "I mean, my feelings won't be hurt. I was only trying to help you, Neet, anyhow, since I didn't think you wanted your mom to know."

"Well, why you bait us, then, acting like your mother was gonna do it, and how do we know that you know what you're doing?" Shay asked, suddenly hating everything about Sondra, her rounded cheeks, her poppy eyes, her bang that was pushed to one side of her forehead, the way her lips curled when she talked, the way she stood with one of her fat hips jutted way out to the side in a gangster lean.

Sondra rolled her eyes up in her head at Shay's questions and let go with an exaggerated sigh. "Number one, I ain't bait a damned soul, okay, Shay. I didn't even know for sure that my mother wasn't going to do it till last night. And number two, I've only helped my mother so many times over the years until I could just about do this thing blindfolded. I even went with her a lot of times, at least twice a month over the past couple of years, when the doctor she helps out does the procedure on rich white women at his office in town."

"Yeah, but that's helping, that's not doing," Shay said.

"Look, it's a simple procedure." Sondra talked to Neet now, ignoring Shay, who was standing directly in front of her. "We use these rod things to get you dilated, then we insert a hoselike contraption and we turn on a little machine. Now, you gonna feel some cramping, I ain't gonna lie and say it don't hurt, it's gonna hurt, 'bout twelve to sixteen minutes' worth of pain that's gonna have you swearing to God and three other white men that you will never ever let no man's exposed privates get within two feet of you in any direction. But then once everything's washed on down, I mean, the pain is the least of it considering what you getting in exchange. In fact, you need to take a few Anacins before you even get started, that is, if you gonna go through with it."

"I'm going through with it," Neet said as she let her purse drop to the floor.

"Well, wait a minute, let's think about this, Neet," Shay said.

"Miss BB's not the only one who does this. I'm sure we can find somebody else."

"They say you can get one on any corner in New York," Little Freddie said as he squeezed Neet's shoulder.

"Well, we not in New York. We're here. So let's get it over with." Neet took off her granny glasses and laid them on the coffee table next to the Ultra Sheen hair grease. "I mean, I been back and forth with this, Shay, you know that I have. I have to admit it. I was, like, you know, a baby's not the worse thing that can happen to a person, okay, so I made a mistake, but is it right to cover up one mistake by making two? I mean, my own mother had me at eighteen and despite what people say behind my back she did okay by me. But I just couldn't close my mind to how I'd be ruining my life, my shot at college, the whole caboodle, okay. You agree with that, right, Shay? If you really think that the best thing for me is to have a baby now, say so." She paused and swallowed and looked directly at Shay. "Say so, Shay, or stay pumped up for me. Don't go getting cold feet on me now."

"Yeah, Neet, but now it's not about me." Shay's voice was shaking. "Forget everything I said up to now. You got to be absolutely sure because right now it's about you opening your legs up for a medical procedure to someone our age. Think about that, Neet."

Little Freddie cleared his throat. "Um, Neet, I never knew you were hesitant, sweetness. I mean, maybe we should talk about this some more, see how we could make it work. Why don't we maybe leave and think about it and talk about it and if we still want to go through with the—the, um, the procedure, we can. But it don't have to be done today."

"It does. It does. Today. I'm ready now, and I might not be

ready tomorrow this time." Neet rubbed her stomach gently, a con-
trast to the way she blasted her words through the living room. She
was wearing an oversize white cotton blouse, one of her church
blouses, had thought about the irony of hiding her sin with such a
pious-looking church blouse as she'd put it on that morning, and
again now. The thought made her dizzy and she sat down along the
edge of the couch. "Plus, I feel it growing bigger by the hour—"

"You ain't felt life yet, I hope," Sondra said, cutting Neet off. "If
so, you too far along. You can't be no further along than twelve
weeks for the procedure to work, and you don't usually feel life till
fourteen or sixteen weeks."

"I'm twelve," Neet said with determination.

"Well, as long as you understand that I ain't pressuring you to
do a damned thing."

Sondra ended her words as a question and Neet nodded. "No
pressure, Sondra, I understand. Now can we just get it over with?"

"All right, well, first we got to get you prepped. Shay, if your
attitude will allow it, I could use some assistance."

Little Freddie started to follow Sondra to the stairs and Neet
grabbed his arm, said, "Baby, I'd feel better if you waited down
here. Really, just knowing that you're this close means so much to
me, but if you're up there it's gonna kill what we got special
between us, please, wait down here."

Shay would have felt a twinge of jealousy if she'd been hearing
right then. She thought herself the most special person in Neet's
life. But Shay wasn't hearing right then, as she just stood there
counting in her head, trying to add up the weeks from the first time
Neet had said she and Little Freddie had done it. She'd just told her
Saturday morning when she'd cried, out on the banister. She'd told

Shay she'd snuck away from church during the monthly revival. Was that March or April? Shay was asking herself now. But she couldn't remember, couldn't even think straight enough to count off the weeks if she could remember. Everything seemed suddenly accelerated, time, life, as if she could feel the motion of the earth moving fast and straight instead of in circles and already they were upstairs in Miss BB's back room.

The wallpaper was a sandy-colored tuxedo stripe and the furniture was faded to a tan that blended in with the beige-toned rug, even the bedclothes were colorless though at least they appeared clean, stainless at least, as Neet's straddled legs made a tent of the top sheet so that the only color it seemed was a blue poly–filled length of wrap that hung along the sides of the bed. Sondra waddled in and out of the room, setting some additional things up on a card table next to the bed, and Shay relaxed some because Sondra did appear to know what she was doing, as if she had a system, as if she'd been totally truthful when she'd said that she had done this hundreds of times.

She wrung a washcloth out in warm water and handed it to Neet and told her to pat herself down and then re-cover herself with the sheet. She turned her head while Neet did this; Shay did too and guessed that someone had told Sondra the way her aunt Maggie had told her that it was bad luck to see another girl's privates. Shay almost laughed right now when she thought about how her aunt used to say that. Shay, she used to say, ain't no way I could be a nurse like your mother and have to look at a grown woman's naked ass. Shit, my luck is hard enough as it is. I already can't hold on to a dollar, next thing I wouldn't be able to hold on to a damn man. Shay let out a giggle at the thought even as she understood that the thought about her aunt was merely a defense mechanism against the extreme nervousness wrapping around her chest for what they were about to do.

Sondra pulled on a pair of plastic gloves. "Good thing you not that far along, my mom turns people away if they're more than three months, some even try to lie and say that they're only eight weeks, but my mom can tell once her hand gets up there, she stops cold, tells them to take their money back, they shouldn't have waited so long to get some help. But thank God you're early."

She slid her hand under the sheet and Neet grimaced. "Just try to stay calm and take deep breaths, I know this isn't an exactly comfortable feeling, but this little contraption makes it so much simpler the way it just suctions everything out. I don't know what they did back in the day. I think they used some kind of twigs. My mom says if a woman want to get rid of a baby, she gonna find a way to do it, so she said by doing what she does she's actually saving them from a dirty coat hanger or knitting needle. You be surprised the extreme measures some people forced to take. Especially poor little colored women who don't have a thousand dollars to pay a legit doctor to do them after hours in his office someplace. But this little contraption here gonna do the job just fine. One of the doctors who was sweet on my mom gave it to her after she helped him out with a procedure."

"Oh God, I know it's gonna hurt," Neet said in whispered moans. "But I'm with you, Sondra. Go ahead, do your thing, I'ma hang in there with you."

"Good. Girl, you gonna do just fine 'cause you got the right attitude. Mama says attitude is ninety percent of getting through it. Okay, now if you want to help yourself some, just feel free to bite down on that teething ring sitting in the dish. It's soaking in a little scotch whiskey to help take the edge off of the pain, that's what Mom does. I got to admit it, my mom's pretty good at this. If you don't cry out too loud, when I'm through I'll tell you who-all my mom helped. Some may not surprise you, but some gonna make you howl."

She spread Neet's legs in a clinical way and again Shay was struck by her appearance of expertise. Shay had moved to the head of the bed so that she could focus on Neet's face rather than the tent her outstretched legs made with the sheet. Sondra continued to chatter on and Shay was surprised that even her incessant chatter seemed a programmed part of the procedure, it was at least distracting and, as such, calming too.

"Yeah, girl, like I said, you gonna be easy to do 'cause you got your head in the right place about this whole thing. I just need to get up in there and start you dilating."

Shay watched Neet's face begin to disassemble and she scrunched her own eyes tightly because she hated to witness the look of torture taking over Neet's face. But then it was as if her ears replaced her eyes and magnified with the sounds in the room what she was trying not to see: Neet's quickening breath, the whoosh of the machine, the air being suctioned out through the tube, the further parting of Neet's legs, Sondra's perspiration sliding down her bang, Shay thought that she could even hear that. There was a second of focused, pointed silence then that opened up and made room for Neet's screams that bounced off the walls and ricocheted through the house. Little Freddie ran to the top of the stairs and stood on the other side of the door trying to ask if Neet was okay, if everything was okay, but his voice couldn't override Neet's screams and he still honored her wish and didn't go in, to keep it special between them, she had said.

Neet's cries were shaping themselves into words as she hollered out for Sondra to stop. "I can't take it, Lord Jesus, we got to stop," she yelled.

"Shh, shh," Sondra whispered. "I wish I had a penny for how many times I've heard those words. Countless times, Neet. By so many women, so many, sneaking in through our back door on Saturday mornings before it's even light outside to have themselves fixed."

"Oh Jesus, please, Sondra, you don't understand, I really can't stand it, stop, just stop." Neet pounded the bed as she hollered out.

"Shh, shh, shh. It's bad, I know, but I can't stop now, Neet. I'm in there now. Please keep still, you messing me up. Please. You know how thin these walls are. If Miss Johnetta next door tells my mother she heard hollering over here this morning—"

"Fuck Miss Johnetta. Fuck the walls," Neet continued to cry out.

"Please, Neet, come on, bite down on the teething ring, please," and then in a sterner voice she said to Shay, "God, Shay, hand her the ring, please, you just standing there like a fucking zombie, the boyfriend would have been more help than you."

Shay jumped at Sondra's words and reached in the dish and was surprised by how rattled she'd become, that her hands were actually shaking, and she knocked the dish over, whiskey and all, but at least she clung to the teething ring that she edged toward Neet's lips.

"If my mom knew what I was doing right now, Lord, you just don't know," Sondra rambled on. "I'll tell you soon as I'm done who our age she turned away. You not passing out on me, Neet, are you?" Sondra asked.

Neet wished that she could go unconscious right now as she writhed on the towel-covered bed and jammed the teething ring in her mouth and almost took Shay's hand off when she bit down on the ring. She gritted her teeth into the ring and nodded that she was okay to Shay's persistent strings of "How you doing, Neet, you holding up?" She tried to concentrate on the yellow-and-blue Mother Goose wallpaper so that she could stop herself from crying out. Except that this wallpaper was tan, tuxedo striped, wasn't it? Where was the Mother Goose? Was that up in that bedroom in the corner house where she and Little Freddie had done it, when he whispered out her name, gave her back her whole name, Bonita, Bonita, and he was tender and clumsy and warm as he wrapped himself around all of her. But that bedroom barely had paper on the walls. No, she remembered now, as the instrument funneled inside her, reaching for her adolescent cervix, the Mother Goose was on that other wall, Mr. G's efficiency apartment over top of the candy store where he'd take her, Neet, on Friday nights when she was only eight, when the whole church was in a frenzy and seeing God, and when they got all frenetic like that no one paid any attention to her and even her own mother didn't miss her when Mr. G took her hand and led her across the street. "We're going to get candy," he'd say. "If your mother asks you where we were, we were getting candy." He'd repeat this to her as they climbed the musty stairwell up to his efficiency apartment. That first time he'd turned on the television that had a hanger as an antenna that didn't work right because there wasn't a clear picture and only static for sound that was so loud she could barely hear him as he continued to repeat over and over that if anybody asked, they went for candy. He sat her on his lap and bounced her on it and tickled her under her chin at first and she giggled even as she asked him to please take her back to the church, she wanted to go back to the church, please. "But we're going to get candy in just a minute, we'll go downstairs and get you candy." By then the tickling had turned ugly and she felt herself being torn apart on the inside as he bounced her up and down on his lap. She focused on the Mother Goose wallpaper that was yellow and blue. There was the old woman who lived in the shoe, how mean the old woman looked to Neet as he bounced her on his lap, all those children in that shoe and that woman with her hand on her hips pondering, not knowing what to do with all of her children, she looked like a witch to Neet, staring out from the wallpaper, maybe she was a witch, like maybe her own mother was a witch for not knowing what Mr. G was doing to her own child. Shouldn't have children and then not know what to do with them. How unclean she'd felt. How chafed and raw inside she was when they'd returned to church. Stiff and sore so that she had to walk wide legged, and her mother didn't even notice that she was walking strangely. And Mr. G said, "I hope you don't mind, Alberta, but Neet was getting very restless so I walked her across the street for candy." Her mother had just smiled up at him and said isn't that sweet, God will bless you because you're such a good soul. Neet stared at her mother, begging her to look at her, to see that she was unclean and raw, that he had made her so. Why couldn't her mother see it? Witch. Witch. She was hollering as the wallpaper went back to its dull tuxedo-striped sandy shade and she realized where she was, not in Mr. G's efficiency apartment but here in Miss BB's Saturday house, straddle legged while Sondra took care of things down there and Shay brushed her bang off her forehead.

Shay's hands were sweaty and cold against her forehead, but still they were a comfort against the cramps that were steady and hard just like Sondra had said they'd be. But then she felt a flash of a searing pain, as if an acid-dipped spear was pushing, pushing, separating her insides, ripping. She felt her womb ricocheting from back to front and then crashing in on itself, falling, with a pull, as if her insides were being snatched out of her the way her mother yanked gizzards from a chicken before roasting it. And now she was going to pass out except that she also had to vomit, she didn't want to pass out in her vomit, knew of a boy on the other block of Cecil Street who'd drunk too much and passed out and then died because he'd choked on his vomit. She started gagging then, as she fought to stay conscious just long enough to spit up, to save her own life, she told herself. Then she felt cold metal against her chin and she realized Shay had the pan there waiting to catch her vomit. God, Shay, she thought. You always been there for me. My girl, my motherfucking girl. She tried to say this, to make Shay laugh the way she'd always laugh when they'd say that to each other, so proud they were to be the other's girl. She tried to force the words out so that she could see Shay beam, knew how tormented Shay must be watching her right now. But then she heard Sondra say Oh my God, shit. And Shay ask What, what, something's wrong isn't it, Sondra, she shouldn't be bleeding that much should she? Look, it's gushing out all over the place. Something's wrong, isn't it, Sondra, no, no, please God, no. Neet. She's passing out, Sondra. Something's wrong. No. No. No. And now it was Shay's wails bouncing off the sandy-tuxedo-striped walls in the back bedroom of Miss BB's Saturday-morning house even as Neet tried to tell

Shay not to cry, that it was okay, it didn't hurt anymore and they were still girls and it was okay. But she couldn't get the words out and anyhow the room was going dark and now she couldn't even hear.

Little Freddie could no longer contain himself on the other side of the bedroom door. His bowels had threatened to break as he listened to Neet crying out like that. But then when he heard Shay screaming that something was wrong he burst through the door, collided with Sondra, who barreled against him with the force of an army tank. "Ice. I got to get ice," she said as she pushed him from against her. "Got to pack her with ice. Dial o. Dial o right now while I go get ice to pack her with."

"What? Dial o?" he called behind her, but she was halfway down the stairs and now he crossed the threshold into the bedroom and now it was no longer his bowels but his throat, as the contents of everything he'd eaten for the past week it seemed was trying to push up his throat and he hadn't even gotten beyond the blood on the floor that was forming itself into a small pond as it dripped from the fringes of the towels that hung down the side of the bed. Shay was yelling into the phone No, she's not conscious, please hurry, please. Little Freddie just stood there, immobilized, looking at the blood and then higher up at the towel where the thicker clots took their time sliding down the length of the towel, and he had the thought to pick up the blood, scoop it up with his hands and put it back inside Neet where it belonged. He was crying now, for Neet and all that spilled blood and the pieces of him that were mixed with that blood, sobbing now as he willed himself not to vomit and went to the foot of the bed and folded Neet's legs together so that the emergency people wouldn't find her in such an undignified position. He rubbed his hand up and down her calf and whispered out her name between his sobs, "Bonita, Bonita, my sweet, sweet love. My Bonita."

Shay had given the address to the operator and was back at the head of the bed. She cradled Neet's head. "I'm sorry, Neet, oh my God, sweet, sweet Jesus, I'm so sorry."

And then Sondra was back in the room, ice cubes falling out of a hand towel as she ran to the foot of the bed and told Little Freddie to move the fuck out of the way. "Come on, you little pussy, I'm trying to save her life, get out of here if all you gonna do is stand there and cry. Should have thought about this when you decided to screw her without covering up your dick. Shit, somebody please open her legs back up or take this ice so I can. Lord have mercy, we all going to jail. Shit. My mom's gonna kick my ass to boot. Wider, Shay, open her all the way, damn. Come on, Neet, hang in there, baby. This ice gonna hold that bleeding at bay. Shit. Please, Lord, let this work. Boy, get the fuck outta here with that got-damned wailing. How long they say they'd be? You tole them she was hemorrhaging, right? God. Is that sirens I hear? Lord, let that be sirens. Damn, we going to jail. Boy, go get a towel and cover that machine and get it out of here. Hang in there, Neet. Come on, baby, you gonna pull through this, just hang on in."

The sirens got closer, in circles, as Sondra continued to push the ice cubes into Neet's womb. Little Freddie had left the bedroom and was now jogging back and forth across the porch trying to calm himself down, and Shay thought that she should run across and get Neet's mother. Neet might be hemorrhaging to death right now, Alberta should know.

Except that Johnetta had already beat Shay to it. She had already put it together as she did her turtle walk up the street, returning home from picking up her *Daily News*. She'd paused in front of BB's house, knowing the aborted secrets that lived there, and knowing also that Neet and Little Freddie had been keeping company in that corner house, and then seeing Little Freddie in near hysterics running up and down the length of the porch, and hearing the sirens come to a slower song as they rounded the corner, Johnetta had moved with uncharacteristic speed across the street to Alberta's house and had already knocked on Alberta's door, interrupted her praying, as she yelled, Alberta, it's Johnetta, I come to tell you that you best get across the street right this instant and make sure your child's okay.

So by the time Shay ran out of the door and onto the porch, Alberta was already meeting her on the porch, grabbing her by her collar and asking her what she'd done to her child, calling her the devil, imp, liar and thief, she called her, and then not able to hold it, called her a bitch. You evil little bitch, what did you do to my child? You fucking little Satan, where is she, Lord have mercy, Jesus, where is she?

Little Freddy was urging the paramedics on, telling them she was hemorrhaging, she was pregnant and something went wrong and now she was hemorrhaging; don't let her die, he was crying now in spite of himself, I never seen so much blood, please, please don't let her die.

Alberta cried out then, No, no, please, Jesus, no. Her voice reverberated up and down the street so that a somber crowd had gathered in front of BB's Saturday-morning house, and some even cried themselves because they all loved Shay and Neet so, Cecil Street's brightest flowers.

Alberta was punching Shay in the chest, and then punching her own chest and pulling her own hair, and grabbing the shirt of one of the paramedics as she rushed to the front door to beat them into the house, up the stairs to where Neet was, to pray over her child, touch her forehead with her hand, to save her, to heal her, restore her to herself. Oh sweet Jesus, she called out. No. Let me. She's my child. Me and Jesus, me and Jesus can fix it. Let me.

Chapter 8

HAY DIDN'T KNOW how she ended up in Miss Clara's shop. Didn't remember walking down the street and around the corner to get here. The last thing she remembered, Alberta was beating her on her chest, calling her profane names. She didn't even remember the stretcher carrying Neet out of the house, but she was sure it must have. Miss Clara was holding a cup of something hot and dark to her lips. "Here, baby, sip, tea. Come on, you gonna be okay."

Johnetta pushed into the shop then. She had Sondra by the hand, Sondra looking as stunned as Shay felt. Johnetta carried a brown shopping bag with a towel hanging from the top. Clara motioned her toward the washroom. "Just push it in under the sink back there," she said, and Shay realized by the tone of Clara's voice that the bag contained BB's machine. Sondra was gasping for air and Clara stooped in front of her now, told her she had to pull herself together. Told her and Shay both to listen good to what she was about to say. "You been here all morning, Sondra. You were helping me arrange the wig displays and Shay came in and you were fixing to shampoo her when whatever happened, happened. You hear me, Sondra? You hear me, Shay? You came in here to get your hair pressed out, Shay. That's all. That's all."

Shay nodded. Then Sondra asked Clara what about her mother, what was going to happen to her mother.

"Was your mother home, Sondra?" Clara asked. "What did your mother do wrong? Your mother doesn't have a thing to do with this."

Sondra nodded again, she nodded and started crying and Shay sat there feeling like a tattered remnant of a deflated balloon that had just taken a pin point to its latex facade and had burst, sending pieces of itself scattering.

Johnetta walked back through. She said she was going to try to find Little Freddie. Shay stood to follow Johnetta out of the door and Clara asked her where did she think she was going.

"To Neet. Did they take her to Misericordia?" Shay asked now. "I have to get over there, is that where they took her, Miss Clara?"

"Shay, I think you need to sit right back down," Clara said. "The police lined up and down Cecil Street right now. I just reached your mother at work, she'll be here directly. I think you need to stay put. I just hope Johnetta'll find Little Freddie before they get to him. He needs to understand what happened in that bedroom. He needs to know he and Neet snuck in there to screw, she started having a miscarriage then."

"No, you don't understand, Miss Clara, I have to find out about Neet. I have to. It's Neet, Miss Clara, Neet." Shay was crying then, repeating Neet's name on her sobs.

Clara fought her own tears as she waved Shay on. "Go on, then. Just remember what I said. You were sitting right here with Sondra getting ready to shampoo you when whatever happened, happened. Go ahead now. Tell Neet we're pulling for her, tell her we got her name lifted up to Jesus. Go on. Go now so you can get on back."

J OE HAD HIS transistor radio going in his cage, the name he gave the booth at Fifty-sixth and Market where he worked. Rush hour was over and he settled in to read, had had his appetite whetted in the past few years for black literature. He looked up and there was Valadean standing there. He sat up with a jerk. He hadn't seen her since their time together Saturday night, though he'd seen every inch of her when he allowed his mind to go back to the room at the Red Moon Hotel.

"Ooh, Valadean, how you today? Mnh, my day just got brighter." He smiled all over himself. He'd told himself that the prudent thing to do was to be cool, not make any more moves in Valadean's direction since she was living right across the street. Too close. Plus, he'd been so affected watching Louise cry in the sink after getting her tooth pulled yesterday. Knew that Louise was crying over more than the tooth. Running around was more complicated than he'd remembered. But now seeing Valadean standing in front of him all in yellow today, from the headband to the sundress to the strappy sandals, and he was already thinking of how he could work it out so that he could be with her tonight.

"Uh, Joe," she said, and the hesitation in her voice told him something was wrong. "I hate to have to tell you this, Joe." He looked at her face, her face unsmiling, serious, and his first thought was that they'd been found out, that newsy-ass Johnetta knew about them, which meant it was only a matter of time before Louise knew too. His fault, he was thinking now, his indiscretion was unforgivable, as he listened to Valadean stammering on and on and then he realized that she wasn't talking about them being found out, she was saying something about Neet and Shay, ambulance, hospital. "Neet or Shay, I'm so sorry, Joe, I have the names confused, one of them was trying to have an abortion, and it's awful. I hate to God to have to tell you, Joe."

Joe was out of his booth, he had his hands on Valadean's shoulders asking her which one was it, was it Neet, or Shay? What did she look like? Was she light or brown? How could she not know the difference between them. He radioed his supervisor, said that he was putting things on automatic, they'd better get a replacement for him because he had a family emergency and he had to go.

SHAY RUSHED IN through the main door of Misericordia Hospital and before she could even maneuver through the oversize corridors to get to the emergency room, there Alberta sat, stuporlike, in a straight-back chair facing pillars that flanked a cast-stone Virgin Mary high up on a pedestal. Shay ran right toward her, disregarding that Alberta had pummeled her chest just a while ago. "Miss Alberta, how is she? Please tell me she's okay." She stopped short then, as if at that instant Alberta had caused an invisible force field to spring up that Shay couldn't get around.

"Happy now?" Alberta said, not even turning to look at Shay.

Her voice was taken up by the volume of air in here and then sent back in an echo that sounded eerie to Shay, as if Alberta's voice was coming from a record player set on a too-low speed.

"Huh?" Shay asked, trying not to cry.

"What you mean, 'Huh?'"

"I uh—I didn't understand what you just said—" Shay's words caught in her throat, Alberta's mocking of her was so unexpected, so vicious at that moment.

"They're in there right now, scraping her out. Hope to God they can leave her intact enough so she can have children," Alberta went on, throwing her voice into the air so that its reverberations were that much more pronounced, lower, off tempo. "So I hope you're happy now."

"Happy? Miss Alber—"

"Yeah, happy. You were always jealous of her anyhow 'cause she's prettier than you, and smarter, and got the Holy Ghost. You're probably real happy right now."

"That's not true, Miss Alberta, you know that's not true. She's my best friend and you know it."

"Your mother hasn't been half the mother to you that I been to Neet. Lets you run the streets however you feel like. Your father just as bad, all he wants to do is hang on Fifty-second Street and turn out some other man's wife."

"My mother and father don't have a thing to do with this," Shay said, a defiance taking over her voice, as if suddenly all the anger she'd ever felt toward Alberta over the years because of her ill treatment of Neet, because of her snubbing of the entire block, was seeping out. She walked around the pillar, all the way into the entrance hall where Alberta sat. "And anyhow, I don't know why you hate me so much, I never did anything to you, my parents never did either. All I ever wanted was to be a good friend to Neet, that's all. And I am too. And you know it's the truth."

Shay looked at all of the hate pouring from Alberta's face but it wasn't her face right now that was terrorizing. She had a nice face, a Kewpie-doll face as Neet used to always say when she was feeling softly toward her mother and spouting off all that was good about her. It was Alberta's voice that made fine bumps come up on Shay's arms and back, because even her skin recoiled at the cracked hacking sound of Alberta's voice so filled with venom toward Shay, broken up by unintelligible words though the words she spoke were horrible enough. "I hope I'm there—to see it—to see it—when—when the Lord my God takes his vengeance out on you—and—uh, your—sor-sorry soul. I hope your mother can feel like I feel right now. If I didn't trust the Lord to dole out his own vengeance I'd do it myself, I'd grab you right where you standing and, and— Oh Lord, my child might end up barren, because of you."

Shay started backing out of the room, fixed her eyes on the Virgin Mary cast in stone, she wasn't Catholic but she sent up a prayer to the statue anyhow that this was all a dream, that she would wake and be where she should be at this moment, at work at her summer job at the Municipal Services Building where she answered the phones and watered the windowsill plants and made sure that everybody had sharpened pencils and rubber bands and paper clips. Please, please, let me wake up and be at work where I should be right now, she mouthed to the statue as Alberta sat zombielike in the straight-back chair. She turned to run then. To go where? she asked herself. Home? To do what? Watch *The Edge of Night*, or cover her head with her pillow, or vomit, cry hysterically, pull out her hair, curse God, pray. What would she do when she got there? What would she say to her own mother, how would she even walk through her block again? Everybody must know by now. She felt as if she was sinking. How could she go back home? She turned to run anyhow, at least to get away from Alberta's spite, to deafen her ears to Alberta's unintelligible ramblings that Shay guessed were attempting to summon all the forces of hell to rise up against her right now. And just the sound of Alberta's voice so filled with hate propelled her to run, and as soon as she had sufficiently distanced herself from Alberta's presence, the reality of what had happened at BB's came crashing down over her head with much too much weight. She was ready to just drop right there on the highly waxed marbleized floor. That's when she felt arms reaching out for her, catching her, familiar arms. Wonderful arms. Her father's arms.

JOE ALMOST CRIED now when he saw Shay, so relieved, so grateful that Shay wasn't the one to leave BB's on the stretcher. Almost cried too realizing that Neet had. Though he wasn't a religious man, he prayed with everything in him that Neet would be okay. ·

"It's okay, Daddy's Girl, it's okay," he said as he almost smothered Shay, he held her so tightly. "Whatever has happened, it's okay. Let's get you home, come on, let's get you home."

Shay collapsed into her father's arms. She cried, "Daddy, Daddy, I'm so sorry, Daddy, Neet, Daddy, Neet's hurt, and it's all my fault, I talked her into going to Miss BB's Saturday-morning house and things went wrong, and Miss Alberta said she might end up sterile and it's all my fault." She inhaled the sweet remnants of the Niagara spray starch clinging to her father's shirt. She didn't want to let him go. Though she'd barely spoken to him since seeing him on the el platform with Valadean, he was holy to her right now. She cried into his shirt that she couldn't go home, Neet almost died because of her, how could she ever walk down Cecil Street again? "Please don't make me go home, Daddy, please. Maybe we could go to Aunt Maggie's instead, anywhere but home."

Joe allowed Shay to rail on. He squeezed her neck some more, patted her back, smoothed her 'fro, then he put his finger to her lips to quiet her. "Listen to what I'ma tell you," he said. "Listen good so you'll understand and never forget this. Nothing on God's earth should ever keep you from going home. I don't care what you did or didn't do, who you helped or never meant to hurt, what the people in the street say to your face or behind your back or around the corner, nothing, and I mean absolutely nothing, Shay, should ever keep you from going home. Now, I'm gonna take your hand in my hand, and we gonna put one foot in front of the other, and we going home. Okay, Shay? We not even gonna hesitate when we come to the bottom of Cecil Street. We gonna round that corner like we got every right to, we gonna keep on stepping. No jive. We going home."

Shay felt closer to her father than she ever had as they walked the half mile to get home. She felt simultaneously protected and exposed. She knew that her father would buffer any glares at her, halt any questions, even curtail expressions of concern that would likely spill over the banisters as they walked. She realized that she and her father had always been closest when she was in pain. With her mother it was the laughter, the silliness, that fused the two. Her mother had always seemed so ill equipped to walk into the middle of her daughter's hurt and rearrange her thinking so that her emotions could settle down. She'd wring her hands herself, and go stiff and quiet. But Joe had mastered the steps to heal his daughter's broken heart as he talked to her in his most soothing voice while they walked. He talked about understanding how sliced up she must feel on the inside, but that she'd have to learn how not to be so hard on herself. He told her how he'd seen his best friend get beat into a vegetable with a banister post all because Joe had stopped to talk jive to a young lady on his way to warn his buddy that a rival gang was after him so he'd better lay low. And when Shay could dry her voice out enough to ask him how did he get over it, he told her that he hadn't gotten over it. That if he chose to he could pick at that scab right now and be oozing all over the street. "I just had to accept my part in it, Shay. I didn't wield the banister against him, and if I'd gotten to him that day, what about the next day and the next? I had to get it through my own head that it wasn't entirely my fault, some of it, but not the whole thing. Just like with Neet, you didn't cause her to get pregnant, right? And you didn't put a gun to her head and make her go up to BB's after she did get pregnant. Right? So that's what I'm talking about. Be sad 'cause your best friend is going through a trauma right now, that's a clean, honest sadness. Don't dirty it up with a bunch of guilt that you choosing to feel. Though I know that you think you have no choice but to feel guilty, how you just supposed to switch your feelings on and off like they're coming out of a water faucet, I know that's what you saying to yourself, but you got to keep talking to yourself, every time your sadness over

Neet gets clouded with guilt, stop yourself from circling that drain 'cause I know from experience you'll be spinning out into the ocean in no time and it'll be darn near impossible to bring yourself back. Just stop yourself, say, 'I'm sad because of what happened to Neet.' Just sad."

"I am sad," she said, starting to cry again. "Daddy, I'm so sad."

They were at the foot of Cecil Street. The dinner smells that usually met Shay when she turned onto the block this time of day were absent now. No aromas from stewed tomatoes, or sautéed pepper steak, or apples boiling for homemade applesauce to accompany the baked pork chops. Shay had always taken comfort in the smells; no matter what, when she turned onto the block this time of day she got confirmation that life did have a predictable normalcy, a beautiful simplicity, like dinnertime smells mixing in the air above her head. Right now though, whispers of "It's gonna be all right, baby," "You gonna get through this, Shay," fluttered from the porches like crepe-paper banners rolled out to welcome home an injured soldier. She felt injured right now. Felt as if her right leg and arm had been lobbed off because she didn't have Neet to walk with; felt at that moment that she and Neet would never again walk through Cecil Street like they used to, side by side, girlfriends. That thought swirled around her now, covered her like the absence of the dinnertime smells; made her dizzy. She moved even closer under her father's arm, trying to hold herself up. And that's how she was as she stumbled in through the front door of her home.

Louise grabbed Shay, holding on to her, saying, "Awl, Shay, Mommy's sorry. I'm so sorry. My poor baby. Poor Neet, oh Jesus, how is Neet? Have mercy, Jesus, poor Shay and Neet." And even as she gave in to her mother's hug and nestled her face against the skin on her neck that was loose and cool and smelled of the Charles Revson dusting powder the two shared, she tried to tell herself that she could keep the guilt at bay, even as Alberta's spiteful words swam around in her head, she told herself she was just sad, that's all, just sad.

A ND HER PARENTS even tried to banish the just-sad part. Louise and Joe insisted that Shay stay home from work for a few days; they just wanted to keep her close. They felt Shay's devastation over Neet refusing all visitors. Shay would walk over to the hospital every day to see Neet, and every day she'd come home, her visits declined. She'd just sit in the chair by the window and stare outside. Louise guessed that she was reliving the scene over at BB's. Louise and Nathina and Joyce had gone over to BB's. They'd stripped the bed and shampooed the blood from the carpet. They'd quickly, efficiently turned the bedroom from a crime scene where an illegal abortion had just occurred to a normal back bedroom where a teenage couple had crept to have sex. No crime in that. All of Cecil Street agreed because this block was tight, tight-lipped when necessary to protect their own. "Neet and Little Freddie crept in there to screw and poor Neet must have miscarried during," they'd say to anyone who wasn't from here. Even Nathina and Johnetta put their differences aside to make sure that that was the story that was told. But when Louise went in there to clean, she viewed the scene not with her clinical nurse's eye that was accustomed to pools of blood, but with the eye of a mother whose daughter had witnessed the scene. She shuddered then on Shay's behalf. Knew that Shay was having a time of it if she kept going back to the scene in that room. So she worked to distract Shay, tried to entice her into a rerun of *I Love Lucy* or *Andy Griffith* or *Father Knows Best*. Shay would sigh. She sighed so much that it was actually a relief for Louise when she'd hear Shay crying. Crying was at least healthy, she thought.

Joe came home with a new gift for Shay every evening for the next week. Charms for her bracelet, hoop earrings, strings of love beads. Louise went out and bought yards and yards of the most expensive fabric from New York Bargain House on Sixtieth Street and told Shay she could pick out her patterns over the weekend. And when Shay reminded her mother that Neet would be home on the weekend, could her mother bake a cake for Neet, could they take it over there then to welcome Neet home on Saturday, Louise even agreed to that. Though she abhorred the thought of setting foot inside Alberta's house, she promised Shay that yes, of course she'd bake a wonderful cake and the two of them could take it over on Saturday when Neet got home. Louise, just glad that Shay could formulate a full sentence without her words going to suds the way they'd done the whole week since Neet had been carried from BB's on a stretcher, even agreed to go into Alberta's house with Shay.

T HE WHOLE OF the block of Cecil Street was in a state of mourning. And in the midst of feeling sorry they did the inevitable, started splashing blame around.

Johnetta said that Little Freddie should have protected himself so that Neet wouldn't have gotten caught in the first place. Sondra said that Neet was too far along, that she knew once she got up

there that something wasn't right. Louise maintained that the after-
math, Neet's inability to come back emotionally, her refusal to see
even Shay, was all Alberta's fault, said that if Alberta had raised
Neet in a real church, a religion with a name at least, then Neet
would have had something to cling to when tragedy struck. "She
never stood a chance of coming through this thing with her head on
right," she'd say to Joe when they worried openly about the effect
Neet's sudden hard-heartedness was having on Shay. Joe blamed
the hospital, said he'd believe to his dying day that if Neet did end
up unable to have children, it was the hospital's fault. Said they
would have taken every measure to make sure a white girl left the
operating table with her womb intact. He swore that they looked at
little Neet and even if they didn't let it pass through their lips, they
let it fester in their hearts, he said as he banged the table or wall or
mantelpiece, that any children she might have gonna just end up on
welfare anyhow, so why we gonna go to extra pains to spare her
womanhood? He'd shake his fist then and say he knew that's how it
went down. "Hell, yeah, they were able to save her life and her
uterus."

Louise couldn't entirely disagree, since she worked in a hospital
and knew the discrepancy in the level of care. And not just between
the races, had seen it also when it came down to being between men
and women. So even though Louise would maintain that Joe's views
were extreme, she did agree that Neet was at the bottom of the hier-
archy, black, female, child. "Furthermore, the child should have
been able to go someplace to get a clean, safe procedure anyhow
without being made out to be a criminal. Should be legal anyhow,"
she'd say.

After they blamed everyone from Little Freddie's father for not explaining well enough the facts of life, to the courts that wouldn't hurry and make abortion legal, to the hygiene classes at school that showed a lot of pictures of naked people and kept the teenagers all hot and bothered; after they blamed Sondra for even attempting such a thing, her mother, BB, for setting a bad example on the one hand, refusing to do the procedures on teenagers on the other hand, because who needed the procedure more than some young unmarried, unemployed emotionally underdeveloped teen; after they blamed the people who lived in the house on the corner for running off to cater on weekends and leaving the house essentially unsupervised, and whoever gave BB the instruments Sondra used that might have been defective in the first place; after they blamed Alberta and her church and even Neet's father for walking out when Neet was six, they'd whisper and lower their heads and make sure that Joe and Louise weren't anywhere near, and mouth the name. Shay. They had to mouth Shay's name because they all loved her too and it would hurt too much to give the name sound. But Shay had influenced Neet so, they said; Shay was there, helping Sondra all the way, Shay talked Neet into it anyhow, Shay. They even blamed Shay. Blamed everyone, everything even remotely associated except for Neet herself. Because they couldn't fault Neet, because perhaps if Neet had been a privileged child, do-good parents, private school, sleepover summer camps, clothes from the upper floors at the department stores in town, perfect in the way she carried herself that was too thick and syrupy, if she'd been that type of child she would have been easy to blame. But she wasn't that type of child. Her life was so full of blemishes: crazy mother that she had, always dragging her off to that farce of a church, back-handing her to the mouth every other minute, forcing her to sneak and lie; abandoned by her father when she was six, broke her heart when her mother forced her father, Brownie, out. No, they couldn't blame Neet. Because in some ways Neet was a fill-in for them and all that was unfixable about their own lives, their own feelings of having been abandoned by the likes of a Brownie, of having struggled against their personal tyrannies, their own dour-faced Alberta who tried so hard to keep them bound. So they wouldn't, couldn't blame Neet. One of Cecil Street's brightest flowers. All they could do for Neet was grieve. And that's what the whole of Cecil Street did. After they stopped splashing blame around from their silver ten-gallon buckets, their hearts ached so on Neet's behalf and they lowered their heads and grieved.

Little Freddie went back to occupy his space on the steps of that house on the corner where the Corner Boys still made magic. Every evening as the sun dropped behind the basketball court at Sayre Junior High, the Corner Boys blended their untrained voices that rose over this little block of Cecil Street and made an arc of sound and then hung there. They teased the approaching night with their songs, Little Freddie's voice prominent, a newness about it now, a grief-tinged strength that enriched his vibrato, so that he was able to sustain his highest note, and even when his voice sounded like a plaintive wail as he took the lead in "Tracks of My Tears," or "Sitting in the Park," or "Misty," it was masterful and so controlled.

There was an air now between Shay and Sondra and Little Freddie. Though they hardly shared conversation, they'd maybe pass each other on the street and say hello, carefully, in quiet voices, as if they were tiptoeing around in a room where a relative had just died.

They'd lower their heads out of respect and go on their own disparate ways. But it was there between them anyhow. A sameness that only they could recognize in each other, as if what they had gone through at BB's together that day had accumulated itself into air that covered them like a loose drape.

Part Two

Chapter 9

EUCIE HAD BEEN affected by all the commotion in the street. The sirens and the people crowding onto the block. The noise. The sadness. The sadness had even sifted down here to her dark, dusty home. This felt like home now and she even had a routine working. She'd clean during the day when the slant of light through the window and her strength and a break in the headaches allowed. Had folded the clothes that Joe had left all over the place neatly back into the chifforobe. Found a cracked vase in one of the crates that she was able to use to rinse her leavings down the drain in the cellar floor, leavings nice and soft from the cat food. Even lucked out on a washcloth and a plastic bottle of doll-baby shampoo taped inside the box with the Tiny Tears doll. Bathed herself as best as she could using the shampoo for a liquid soap. Smelled nice and sweet when she was done, smelled like strawberry taffy.

But still she'd been affected by the commotion in the street. The one woman's screams that had gone right to her chest when she heard her crying out No, no, she's my child, no. Let me fix it, let me. So sad.

Deucie knew what that felt like. A mother's drive to get to her child in the midst of trauma, believing that if she could just get to her, just kiss her forehead, like magic she could make it all okay. She'd felt that maternal drive during one of her releases from the mental hospital. When she'd left the hospital that time, seventeen years ago now, she set out to see her child. She'd purposely not tried to locate her during other periods when she'd been released. She wanted her daughter to grow up in a secure home with her sense of self intact before knowing who her natural mother was. She'd stopped drinking during that stay at Byberry and felt somewhat worthy now of meeting the child face-to-face. She went immediately to Jeffery, who was, as expected, doing a stint in the Holmesburg prison. She went into a rage at what he told her. That their daughter hadn't been placed with a well-to-do black family who lived in a three-story single home in Chestnut Hill, as he'd led her to believe. He'd led her to believe it, he swore, because he was afraid of what Deucie might do to Pat, might try to kill Pat. "Talk about evil stepmother," he said, "that bitch won't even make my bail anymore. So you do what you gotta do, Deucie. That woman's got our daughter slinging whiskey bottles and who knows what else at that house of ill repute."

Deucie knew what else. Knew how Pat had looked at her when Jeffery had first taken her there to live. Pat had looked her up and down the way a farmer sizes up a pig and knows immediately how many dollars' worth of ham she's carrying on her ass. Knew also that Pat was a little afraid of her because of the gash on her face and her reputation for being crazy. So Pat never propositioned Deucie to be one of her girls. But Deucie knew what Pat had forced her daughter to do. She could feel it in her bones. She stood up then in the visiting room at Holmesburg and cried out the way she'd heard that mother crying outside the other day in the midst of the commotion in the street. "No, no, not my chile, I got to get to her, got to save her life, got to fix it, I can fix it. Let me. Let me. Me and Jesus can fix it."

D EUCIE CAUGHT PAT by surprise that night. Snuck up on the house at three A.M., when the bars had closed and the speakeasy/brothel business was booming. She was let right in since she looked like someone badly needing a drink. She knew where Pat would be in the house, having lived there herself when she and Jeffery were a couple. She knew Pat would be in the shed off her kitchen checking her inventory to see how much watering down she'd have to do to make it through the night.

"Pat, you a filthy bitch for turning my daughter out," she said. Then she went for Pat's chest with the ice pick. Wanted to see Pat dead for spoiling the only perfect thing she had produced in this life. That baby girl. "Shit," she said when she felt the ice pick hit bone and she knew she hadn't stabbed her in the heart. But right then Pat wasn't even worth the energy it would take to kill her. Needed that energy to find her child. She left Pat dazed and bleeding and ran down to the basement where the card games were, where the men playing would pay Pat's girls to sit on their laps and bring them luck. She checked their foreheads, looking for her daughter's mark. Then she ran through the house, unstoppable. She hit every bedroom on the second floor, turning on lights and star-

tling the occupants as she got up close to check for the mark. Then
to the third floor, just one bedroom up here. She stopped in the hall-
way to slow her breathing, then eased to the door and put her ear to
it, heard quiet inside. She turned the handle and opened the door an
inch at a time. Heard the bedsprings creaking and a thin voice say-
ing No lights, no damn lights.

Deucie walked into the dark bedroom transfixed by the figure in
the bed. Thank God, Deucie thought, she's alone. Still, she hadn't
expected the reunion with her daughter to be in a place like this. Had
visions of waiting in a grand parlor while the day help went to fetch
her, or at least meeting her in a living room of a nice row house
where they kept a Bible on the coffee table and her high school
graduation picture in an ornate frame on the mantelpiece. She took
a deep breath. "Baby," she said, then she clicked on the light. She
melted then, fell down, though she was still standing as she looked
at her daughter, started with her forehead, the mark was there,
indentations that were lighter than the rest of her skin. The rest of
her skin looked so soft. She looked soft with her pretty brown eyes
and her brown hair that was pulled up in a roll on top of her head.
She was dressed in an emerald green silky nightgown that didn't
even look like something a whore would wear. At least not to Deu-
cie, not right now, because as far as Deucie was concerned, this was
an angel propped up in this bed.

"Don't be afraid," Deucie said, reacting to the look of confused
terror that came up on her daughter's face. "I wouldn't hurt you.
You mine. I marked you so I'd know you. You mine. I just wanted
you to know that." She was all the way to the bed now and her
daughter was so still she seemed not to be breathing as she stared at
Deucie, eyes not leaving Deucie's face. "You pretty as you wanna

be too. And you mine. And you were perfect too. The only perfect thing I ever did. You need to know that. You need to get up from this bed and calmly walk away from this house and never look back here again." She reached out and touched her daughter's forehead. The child gasped, though she didn't scream. Deucie could tell that she was trying hard not to scream. Nice, she thought. What a nice girl I birthed. Don't want to hurt my feelings by screaming right now. Now the daughter was crying. The softest tears Deucie had ever seen as she put her hand on her daughter's forehead and held it there.

She could hear them out back now, filling the cat's bowl. She didn't go to the window though. Stayed under the steps where she'd laid out her dying bed. She didn't have an appetite right now. Took that as a good sign as she thought about the feel of her daughter's mark. It was deeper than she'd expected it would be. And softer too.

Chapter 10

OUISE BAKED THE cake for Neet's homecoming just like she'd promised Shay that she would. Though she pressed her eyes shut and swallowed hard and even said a little prayer that Shay might change her mind about going over there so soon. But Shay hadn't changed her mind and Louise was reluctantly prepared to hold up her end of the deal and go with Shay to welcome Neet back home.

The cake though was perfect, German chocolate, Neet's favorite. Shay had sampled a slice from the extra layer while it was still warm and tears had welled up in her eyes when her mother asked her how it was. "It's delicious, Mommy," she said. "Thank you, Mommy."

"I just hope that crazy-ass Alberta lets us through the door, you know how funny she is, she's probably the one who restricted Neet's visitors," Louise said as Shay arranged long-stemmed carnations in one of her mother's good vases. Shay was excited and afraid as she added baby's breath to the bouquet. She hadn't told her mother about the scene with Alberta on BB's porch or the one later at the hospital in front of the cast-stone Virgin Mary. She reasoned that Alberta was so devastated, so traumatized that day that she had momentarily snapped, and that her good sense, such as it was, had returned by now.

"She's back, Mommy, she's back, come on," Shay yelled as she pressed herself against the radiator and watched the yellow cab pull up.

"Well, let's give her time to get settled, at least a couple of hours," Louise called from upstairs, Louise dreading the visit the closer it got. She'd been to the dentist yesterday and had two more teeth pulled. Down four now. Last thing she needed was the stress of going next door, stress seemed to go right to the empty pockets in her gums. She tried to concentrate on what she was doing at the moment, right now going through her closet separating out clothes that she'd probably not wear again. She'd start a box later, get Joe to take it down to the cellar. Though as trifling as he was when it came to anything having to do with the cellar, she was thinking she'd do bags instead so the weight would be manageable enough for her to carry herself. But he hadn't even fixed the light switch like she'd asked him to do this spring. She sure as hell wasn't going down to the cellar in the dark.

Shay was calling upstairs again, asking Louise for a specific time when they could go next door. Louise blew out a long breath, "Seven o'clock, Shay," she said, trying not to let the irritation show, Shay might think it was directed against her, though it was really directed at the idea of going over there. She pushed hard at a group of blouses and the hangers made a screeching sound as they moved along the metal pole. That sound went right through her as she flashed back on all the overtures she'd made toward Alberta in their early years of living here. Thought at first that Alberta was just excessively shy. She would even defend Alberta when the people on the block talked about her, whispered that she was stuck-up or worse, uncharitable was worse. "She's just quiet," Louise would say. Though soon enough she concluded that Alberta wasn't just quiet; she was just mean.

ALBERTA WAS MARRIED then to a strapping, good-natured, good-looking semiprofessional boxer, middleweight division; Brownie, everybody called him. On Sunday evenings in the space of time between dessert and *Lassie*, the two families would sit on their porches and laugh as Neet and Shay half walked and half crawled, drooling excitedly as they rushed to greet each other at the banister that separated the two houses. One or the other of the parents would hoist either Neet or Shay over the railing so that they could play together on the same porch. Louise would snap Polaroids of the two babies hugging or falling over on top of each other or pointing at each other with smiles on their faces that were so enchanting everybody who walked by the porches would stop, even trot up the steps and have a seat, so drawn in by the baby girls' laughter and the cozy feel to the porches under the splendor of the tree.

Sooner or later, Eddie, the king of the pinochle table, would walk down and say to Brownie and Joe that there was a game starting up, or if not Eddie, then Frank would say he needed help hooking up his new stereo system, or Will, who was always working on one of his immobile Chevys, would ask if they wanted to help, translated, watch him load a transmission. Or some other man on the block would come and break up the two gathered couples, they'd steal Brownie and Joe away to go do whatever men do when they all disappear together after a meal, as if it was a sin that men and women remain in each other's company for too long.

After Brownie and Joe would kiss their wives good-bye and walk on off the porch, trying to take their time so as not to appear too eager to leave, an awkwardness would fall between Louise and Alberta. They'd carry on polite conversations about the price of butter that week, or fabric specials on Sixtieth Street, or upping or decreasing the number of quart bottles for the milkman to leave. They'd focus in on Neet and Shay, comment about their sleeping habits and eating and wetting. And then one or the other would yawn, mention that *Lassie* must be on now, and they'd say a civil good evening and retreat with their daughters back into their own little houses.

The two women never really connected in a girlfriends sort of way, partially because Alberta was younger than Louise, fresh and inexperienced, not even to her twenties yet. Louise appeared so self-assured to Alberta, which magnified Alberta's own feelings of inadequacy, ill preparedness. She felt so unknowledgeable about things a young woman setting up house should know. She hadn't been raised by her natural mother and that was a great embarrassment to her, so she'd stifle any conversations where she might have to talk about her past. Would get agitated by people who probed directly, so Alberta was often agitated with Louise as they sat on the porch on Sunday evenings, having been abandoned by their good-natured buffers, Brownie and Joe.

"Your mother live close by?" Louise might ask.

And Alberta's expression would freeze. "No," she'd say, and then find some excuse for having to run into the house.

"What Neet's grandparents say about her, I know they just love her to death, huh?" Louise might try again.

"'Bout how you'd expect any grandparent to be;" Alberta would say, and suddenly something about Neet would need her attention, maybe her barrette was crooked, or a snap had come undone, but suddenly it was urgent enough for Alberta to tend to that instant and in so doing redirect the conversation.

Louise stopped asking soon enough, even complained to Johnetta that her new neighbor seemed nice enough, but she had some funny ways. "Acts like she can't half talk sometimes, or like she's getting mad at you when you do. And don't try to ask her any-thing about where she's from, you know, basic conversation starters, she'll look at you like you asked her who'd she slept with before Brownie, or some similarly insulting question, then she'll grab her child and run on into her house."

Louise was getting her hair done at Clara's shortly after she'd complained about Alberta to Johnetta. Clara said through the smoke, "I hear from Joyce, who heard from Johnetta, that that young girl next door to you told you to mind your fucking business. She got some nerve, huh, Louise."

Louise tried to clean it up, insisted that of course Alberta hadn't said such a thing, never even hinted at such a thing, that she was a sweet child, really, just a little on the quiet side. "You know how Johnetta will make a mound of manure out of a speck of shit," Louise said, borrowing one of her sister Maggie's favorite sayings.

When next Louise and Alberta were on their side-by-side

porches together, a soft Sunday evening this happened to be, no children playing loud rhyming games in the street or hopscotch or double Dutch because this neighborhood had strong southern roots and they still respected the Sabbath, Louise cleared her throat and decided to move beyond the superficial with Alberta. The way Neet and Shay gurgled back and forth and pretended to carry on a conversation, spurting out their unintelligible words, then laughing, one grabbing the other's arm or foot for emphasis, and then leaning in as if they were whispering, loosened Louise up some. She told herself that it was downright sinful to withhold herself from Alberta just because Alberta had the tendency to go stiff in the middle of a conversation. Louise let go with a flood of sentences then about her own upbringing. Said she hadn't been raised by her mother after the age of ten, raised instead by her sister, Maggie, who still lived downtown. "My mother went quietly in her sleep," Louise said in a hushed voice. "Female problems, though I've since discovered that it was cancer of the ovaries that killed her. Like a lot of colored women back then she tried to be her own doctor. Guess that's why I went into nursing. I was the one who found her, you know, the morning, uh, it happened. I had just turned ten. And you talking 'bout something traumatic. Lord have mercy, girl, Alberta. I thought I'd never laugh again, or recognize when the sun was out, that thing hurt me so bad. But my sister, Maggie, twelve years my senior, took me in. And though Joe complains about her, even though I'll admit too the woman is a bit of a loudmouth, curses, you know, loves her Four Roses whiskey, she still did all right by me, really. She gave me a good life."

Louise glanced up at Alberta, noticed that Alberta's smooth light complexion had gone to a brownish red and she looked as if she was about to cry. Feeling for me, Louise thought, congratulating herself as she watched Alberta appear to settle deeper into the porch glider.

"Yeah, girl," Louise continued, not even looking at Alberta anymore, looking at the remnants of daylight falling over Cecil Street in softened sheets of gray and pink and blue. "I think that's why I hurried and married Joe, I had, like, this opening in my heart that never really closed up, and at the same time it was like I had no feelings in that opening, you know? I thought a man's love could close it up, but truth be told my sister did a better job of helping me heal. Such as I've healed," Louise went on, saying things she'd not planned on saying, telling Alberta now how she had never really cried over her mother's death, cried over other things but not over losing her mother. She began feeling an upwelling of emotion then that frightened her. Movement deep down, she felt as if the ground was shifting and about to release all the gasses trapped there in a huge explosion. She stopped herself. She hadn't cried over her mother yet, certainly wasn't going to now, sitting out on this porch. She'd only started talking about it in the first place to loosen Alberta some any. "Mnh," she said, taking a deep breath, switching the direction of her conversation to lighten it up some. "Just as well, I guess, since men don't tolerate emotional outpourings too well. I guess you've noticed that with Brownie too. Unless it's nighttime and the bedroom door is closed and you under the covers together, you know. Then they'll be all in your ear, 'Here, baby, you just cry, cry all over me, I'ma make it all all right.' Shoot, they'll even pick out their body parts for you to cry on. All for you, mind you. You watching your tears rain down all over his manhood making it sprout straight up, but it's all for you. Girl. What you talking?"

Now Louise was laughing out loud, laughter filling up in her head, thankfully replacing the deep-down stirrings she'd just felt. She gave in to the laughter so completely that she didn't even hear the babies crying at first, high-pitched cries, as if they'd both been slapped. And when she did hear and shook herself back to the porch, to her screaming child, she saw Shay alone on the blanket on the porch floor, arms stretching up and out as she hollered and bounced herself trying to lift herself to get to Neet. Neet hysterical too in Alberta's arms, twisting and hitting at Alberta, trying to free herself from Alberta's hold, trying to get back down on the blanketed porch floor to Shay.

Louise jumped up and scooped up her child to soothe her even as she tried to be heard over the wails to ask Alberta, What? What happened? Why did she interrupt the babies' play?

Alberta was already moving toward her door. "I'm sorry, Louise. That's so sad about your mother. It really is."

Louise could hear the ice in her voice as Alberta excused herself then, said she'd left something on the stove.

Alberta rushed into her house telling Neet it was okay; Don't cry, it's okay, Alberta said as Neet's cries filled the inside of the house. She shushed Neet and bounced her up and down and went to the fridge for something cold and sweet to pacify her. "Mnh," she said into the kitchen air as she spooned up tapioca pudding and fed it to Neet, kissed Neet on the forehead as the cold sweet of the tapioca quieted her some. "Waking up to a dead mother should have been my greatest life trauma." She snuggled Neet even closer to her because she was getting chills and she needed her baby's body warmth right then. She pulled a kitchen chair out from the table and sat. Neet, satisfied now from the tapioca, spread herself against her mother's bosom as if she knew already how to keep Alberta warm.

SHAY PASTED HERSELF at the window, her excitement building as she watched the back door of the cab edge open. Alberta got out first, Shay knew it was her as soon as her foot inched through the cab door, the telling piece of drab taffeta material that almost met her shoe. When Alberta was all the way out of the cab, she stood there with her hand out waiting for the cabdriver to give her change, and at first Shay's stomach started pushing up into her throat because it didn't seem as if anybody else was in the cab. Until the cabdriver, a wrinkled-looking man, walked around to the back passenger side and opened the door.

"Ooh, Neet, Neet," Shay said to herself and to the wide-open Venetian blinds at the living-room window, "if you only knew how much I've missed you." She bounced in front of the window as she watched the figure emerge from the back of the cab. She could no longer keep her excitement coiled in her muscles and now she was like a Slinky toy just loose and all over the place. Now she was at the front door and now she had the door open and now she was calling out to Neet. "Neet, Neet, welcome home," she said, trying not to sound too jovial out of respect for the circumstances, but jovial nonetheless just to know that Neet was really living and breathing. Had had the thought many times over the past week that Neet had died, that they'd kept it from her until they could figure out a soft way to tell her. Now her stomach did inch up into her throat because she was looking at Neet, seeing her. "My God, Neet," she whispered, "what's going on with you, my God."

It wasn't Neet's apparent frailness that Shay could see in the suddenly angled cheekbones that used to be much more subtle, nor was it the way her complexion seemed washed out to a shade that was more blanched than its usual coloring, which was a Crayola yellow with a hint of red. It wasn't even the long, shapeless dress that matched in style the one Alberta wore, nor was it the hat, a black felt number with netting that reached down to her eyebrows, the kind Alberta often wore to church and that would have Neet proclaiming to Shay that no matter what, she'd go to church, she'd dress like her mother insisted, unless she could find a way not to, she'd appear to be holy whenever she absolutely had to, she'd toe the line just to keep the peace, but no way, absolutely no way was she wearing that stupid little hat. And yet, disturbing as the hat was now, propped on Neet's head, that wasn't the worst of what Shay saw as she stood on the porch, barefoot, with her arms folded up across her chest. The worst of it was the way Neet carried herself. Back straighter than Shay had ever seen it especially when she was forced to wear her holy clothes. Shay knew that Neet so hated to be seen like that and yet the way she held herself right now, it was as if she was proud of her holy deportment. She walked with a stiffness, as if her insides would not be contained if she allowed herself to take a step without having first given it careful consideration. But mostly it was Neet's eyes that made Shay, standing at the edge of her porch, stifle a scream, because as Neet got closer and closer as she approached her steps, she looked over at Shay's house, right there into Shay's face, must have known how anxious Shay would be for her to get home, and there were Neet's eyes, soft brown like always but also hauntingly blank, like Shay had never seen them, like Alberta's eyes, my God, they were Alberta's eyes.

She tried to tell herself that she was wrong as Neet reached her porch and didn't even acknowledge that she was standing there, tried to convince herself that this was all a part of Neet's holy sham. But she knew Neet too well. There should have been a sign reassuring Shay that Neet had just taken her sham to a new level. Traumatized though Neet was, Shay should have seen a glimmer, a milder version of the play behind Neet's eyes that Shay could always pick up when Neet walked alongside her mother and she'd look at Shay as they passed and would allow the slightest twinkle to traipse across her eyes, which let Shay know that they were still on for the town-hall dance, or the movie, or the skating party, the arcade, the basketball game; that as soon as she could circumvent the dictates of this revival, or prayer meeting, or funeral, or special-call service, she'd be back. Have her change of clothes and her Kool filter tips ready because she'd be back. Shay would feel a coating of warm relief spread over her because of that suppressed fear that one day Neet might really catch fire for her mother's crazy religion. It appeared now that that very thing had happened, that this sanctified demeanor had not been forced on Neet. Now, this was who Neet truly was. And like Neet's botched abortion, Shay claimed responsibility for this too; it was her fault, hers. There it was, the guilt had broken through the dam of her father's good reasoning and was now soaking her up from the inside. It was no use, in Shay's mind. If Neet had really converted, she had carved out a joyless hell of a life for herself. Joyless. And Shay was drowning in guilt over this too.

LOUISE WAS CONFUSED by Shay's new reluctance to go next door. "What is it? Is it the cake?" she asked her.

"No, Mommy, the cake is perfect," Shay sighed more than said.

"And the bouquet you put together, now that's really perfect," Louise said, feigning cheeriness because really she felt so helpless and fought back her own tears as she watched Shay descending into herself again.

"Maybe tomorrow, Mommy. The cake will keep, won't it? Maybe we'll go over there tomorrow."

Louise didn't press the matter, thinking it was better not to force Shay. Shay had to be ready emotionally, Louise told herself, the whole time wishing that Joe was home because Shay really needed him right now to help her work through this. Where the hell was he anyhow, as late as it was getting. Off work since four this afternoon.

Joe got home around nine that Saturday. "At the barber's," he said to what looked like an accusation getting ready to pounce from Louise's mouth, the way her mouth was set right then, but it could just be all those missing teeth, he told himself. "We had such a good rap session going about how things might have turned out had Martin and Malcolm come together. Very provocative talk we had going, Louise." He said this with such sincerity that it didn't even feel like a lie.

The barbershop part was true enough, he had in fact gone. Though he'd spent the bulk of the time in the lavishly furnished apartment upstairs that Tim kept above the shop. Nathina was always on her husband to rent out the apartment. Tim told her he was trying to rent it out but first he'd have to get rid of the rats up there. She'd ask him why no one else on the block had rats, mice maybe, but not rats. He said that the site where the shop sat must have been a rat breeding ground years ago. Told her there were rats in the shop too, they just didn't come out when people were around. Offered to take her down there in the middle of the night if she didn't believe him. She didn't totally believe him, but she believed him enough not to test his story.

There were of course no rats, not the four-legged kind anyhow, because Tim used the apartment for the pleasure takings of his married customers. People from as far away as Southwest and North Philly tipped him heavily for the price of a haircut and a few hours upstairs. Prevented them from having to lie to their wives or girl-friends when they returned home and said they'd been at the barber's. The Cecil Street men rarely took advantage of this amenity other than using it for bachelor parties or smokers. Too close to home to be using if they were running around. "Like shitting where you eat, huh?" Tim would muse when he'd offered it in the past and they'd declined.

But Joe had been up in Tim's apartment earlier. Not with Valadean though. He'd been with Valadean the afternoon before at the Red Moon Hotel. Though he'd told himself that he wasn't going to see her again, it just wasn't prudent with her living across the street, he'd seen her again every other day since the tragedy with Neet last week. Valadean was such a welcome, willing distrac-tion to the heavy mood on the block, the sadness that thickened the closer and closer he got to his house. Could hardly get through his door because of the way the sadness seemed to coalesce there. He could laugh with Valadean and not feel guilty for laughing since she wasn't emotionally tied to the block. Yesterday they'd tickled each other under the arms and chins and wherever else they were ticklish until they were both hysterical. So freeing to laugh out loud, with abandon like that. Then they'd mixed pleasures in ways he hadn't done since he was a much younger man. He decided then that he would see Valadean again and again, as often as he wanted to, as often as he could without getting caught. Felt a defiance brewing in him. The defiance egged him on to ask Tim about his rat problem, the code the men used when referring to the apartment over the shop. Joe then pulled his horn from the back of the closet in the living room, where he'd slid it two weeks before. Spent this Saturday from the time he'd gotten off from work until now with his horn. He'd put it together and taken it apart; he'd cleaned it; shined it; sat it on the heart-shaped velvet couch and stared at it. He didn't put it to his lips though, not yet. Afraid of what would happen once he put it to his lips and transformed breath into sound again. Afraid of how he would feel, afraid of what he'd do after that.

"Yeah, baby," he said to Louise, feeling truly sincere as he said it, "I spent all afternoon until tonight down at Tim's."

"And how about Daddy's Girl?" He didn't miss a beat as he turned his sincerity on Shay where she sat so listlessly staring out of the window. "Did you have a nice visit with Neet, how she doing anyhow?"

When Shay said that they hadn't gone, that she had changed her mind, figured it was better to give Neet a little time at home first, Joe looked at Louise, asked Louise with his face what was going on with Shay. Louise hunched her shoulders, indicating that she couldn't figure it out either. Joe took over then. He insisted to Shay that he himself hadn't been able to even begin to move on and really get plain with what had happened to his friend until he'd stood over his buddy's hospital bed and watched the blankness in his eyes. "He didn't even recognize me, Shaylala, and at the same time it was as if he was looking right through me, right to my soul. I still get chills when I think about it. Mnh." He stopped talking then and both Shay and Louise fell silent, out of respect for the pain he was obviously remembering and, from the look on his face, feeling all over again. He shook himself back, then looked at Shay. "What do you say, Daddy's Girl, you ready?"

"But what if she doesn't want to see me? What if she's mad?" Shay whined.

"So she won't want to see you. So she'll be mad. Better that you go over there and Neet tell you to go f yourself than avoid that reaction by not going. You can't control how you're received, but you do need to go." He took her by the hand. "Come on, get yourself together," he said. "We going over there right now."

Louise hurriedly wrapped the cake in Saran Wrap, grateful that she was off the hook about setting foot in Alberta's house. She'd fretted herself over the possibility of a confrontation with Alberta, didn't know how she'd handle one either; it certainly wouldn't help Neet's condition to be forced to be privy to a bunch of hollering and cursing between two grown women. Not that Alberta would probably curse, but Louise knew that she surely would if the woman came off at her wrong, or especially Shay, she better not say shit to Shay, Louise had been thinking, and dreading since she'd promised Shay she'd go over there with her to welcome Neet back home. But now a confrontation was much less likely man to woman, as it would be now with Joe going instead of her.

She pushed the bouquet in Joe's hands and when Shay whispered that she'd made it for Neet, Joe said, "Well, why don't we give these to the mother? Nothing disarms an angry woman like a pretty vase filled with flowers."

"Well, why the hell you come home empty-handed, then, Negro?" Louise said to his back as she flicked on the porch light and watched Joe and Shay walk across the porch and then climb over the banister to go next door.

Chapter 11

LBERTA WAS IN Neet's room when the doorbell rang. She was putting her hand to Neet's forehead, checking for a fever the way she'd done every hour since Neet had come home. She listened to Neet's breaths come in long whispers and was relieved that Neet seemed to be in a settled stage of sleep. It was easy for Alberta to look at Neet now under the soft lamplight coming from the bedside table, Neet's eyes closed now, so at least it didn't hurt Alberta the way it did sometimes when she'd look at Neet and see her own mother's eyes looking back at her. Deucie's eyes. That terrified her, the way she'd been raised on the stories about her mother, Pat's stories. Whenever the dining room got too quiet at Pat's speakeasy bar and Pat needed a good story to get things lively, to keep her clientele drinking and buying, she'd start in on Deucie. She'd say that Deucie was half wolf, half human and had tried to bite Alberta's head off when she was born because she didn't like her scent. "Look at her forehead if you don't believe me," she'd say. "They committed her ass after she tried to bite the child's head off." Pat's stories would grow more and more outrageous, until she was saying that Deucie had claws instead of nails and had been spotted running naked on all fours through Black Road, in Fairmount Park. Alberta's chest would cave in on itself when she'd hear those stories.

Now she jumped at the sound of the doorbell. She knew who it was. Who else would lay on the doorbell at nine o'clock at night knowing that Neet had just been discharged from the hospital and was probably asleep. Such insensitivity they had. Shay and her mother, the whole block filled with people just like them. She'd hear Louise at night when she was entertaining women from the block in her kitchen. The way they'd talk about her at night from that bright yellow kitchen unaware that Alberta was out there on her steps hidden by the night, or that Louise's kitchen window was open, or that their voices carried so well on a summer breeze. The names she'd been called by them. Mean, just mean, fanatical, spiteful, hateful, pseudosanctified, mean, just mean. And then the way they tore down her church with their venomous words. She tried not to let it penetrate, tried to keep her skin tough. But she was still mostly a sensitive woman; no matter the dark, thick clothes she wore, their insults managed to wrangle on through anyhow and slice away at her overly delicate skin. She started to ignore their ringing of her doorbell right now, but decided they wouldn't leave without some sort of a response from her even if it was just to open the door so she could slam it in their faces.

SHAY AND JOE stiffened when they saw Alberta's door inch open and her face appear in the crack of the opening. Shay's breath caught in her throat so that a gaglike sound came out instead of hello. Joe wasn't much better, he was breathing hard and when he said, "Good evening, Alberta," it sounded more like a gasp.

"I guess you here to see Neet," she said as she inched the door to all the way open. She didn't know what made her open the door all the way like that, had planned to tell them that Neet wasn't up for visitors. Period. Maybe it was the sight of the bouquet the father held—she hadn't expected to see the father, had expected to see Louise—or maybe it was the timidity that was so unusual in Shay's eyes. Whatever it was, it propelled her to open the door all the way and invite them to step inside.

Shay and Joe almost tripped over each other and were lodged together in the doorway for some uncomfortable seconds as they hesitated and then started into the vestibule at the same time, and then stopped at the same time to let the other go through, both so surprised to be invited in so easily like that.

"Uh, yes, we did come to see about Neet, but we also came to see about you," Joe said, his breathing more under control as he half pushed Shay to go first and then followed her into the vestibule and handed Alberta the bouquet.

"I haven't suffered like my daughter has suffered, like so many should suffer but for whatever reasons are spared, but I do thank you just the same, for the flowers," Alberta said as she looked up at Joe and their eyes met in the small, dark vestibule that had taken on the odd mix of the heavy, sweet aroma of the flowers and the buttery chocolate scent wafting from the cake and Joe concentrated on the smells to take the edge off the coldness in Alberta's eyes, plus something about the way her face looked in the dark vestibule was disturbing. Alberta turned then and went into the living room and Joe nudged Shay to follow.

The lights were dimmed and the room was sparsely fur-nished, a normal living room. If Joe believed the rumors kept going by people like Johnetta, he guessed he should have expected candles and oils, or some kind of altar he'd have to bow before. But his point of view was confirmed and this was a normal enough living room with a couch and a coffee table and two chairs catty-corner at the window. Neutral walls with a smattering of framed pictures of Neet at various ages. No other pictures though. None of Alberta, no other family members, not even a picture of a white Jesus with wavy blond hair and piercing blue eyes looking down from the center of a puffy cloud. Not even a Bible on the coffee table, he noticed now. He shifted his weight from foot to foot and tried to settle himself down as Shay handed the cake to Alberta.

"This will only end up in the trash, I assure you. She's not eating a thing. Not a thing," Alberta said as she took the cake without looking at Shay, looked only at the cake as she shook her head back and forth. "Poor child is hardly even opening her mouth to talk. Most she's doing, which I'm very glad about, is praying. Been praying nonstop since this happened. If good always follows bad, then at least the fact that she's praying much more is the good coming from this whole torture."

"Well, um, Miss Alberta," Shay said, grasping for a clear, strong voice. "I guess we could take it back home if it's just going in the trash."

"We'll do no such thing," Joe interrupted.

"But Mommy worked on that cake all afternoon. I hate to see it end up in the trash." Shay directed her words to her father.

"And she did it for Neet and—and," he said, clearing his throat again. "She did it for Neet's mother too. She'll have a fit if that cake comes back into that house. We brought the cake here for Neet and her mother. Now come on, Shay, we can give the gift but we can't be responsible for how it's received. The cake's staying. Okay, Shay?"

His voice went stern, down a full octave when he said Shay's name, and she nodded and lowered her head, irritated with her father now, wondering whose side was he on anyhow.

Alberta walked into the dining room that was completely dark and set the cake on the table with a thump. "Have a seat," she said, her back to them. "Neet's been sleeping soundly all evening and I have no reason to suspect that that's changed, it is past nine after all. But so it can't be said that I'm acting funny with y'all and denying Neet the pleasure of your company after all she's been through, I'll go check. She's not supposed to take the steps though, so if she is awake and up to a short visit, have to be short, late as it is, I'll ask you to come upstairs."

She went through the dining room and Shay remembered then that this house had back stairs off the kitchen. The only house on the block that did, as far as they knew. Shay used to tell Neet how lucky she was when they were really young, back when Alberta used to allow Neet to invite company in before the brainwashing of her church took over and made her segregate herself from every-one on the block. Neet and Shay would race up and down the back stairs and play tricks on Alberta and have her running in circles trying to find them. And then later, when Neet would sneak out of the house late at night to go to some party with Shay, she'd joke as soon as she was safely outside, "Praise the Lord for that back staircase."

J OE WAS HAVING reminiscences of his own about this house as he took a seat on the couch and remembered it as the couch he'd helped Brownie unload from the top of his white Chevy wagon and lug in here. He motioned for Shay to come sit as he tried to make up for his sharp tone and whispered the story out to her. "Neet was a little thing, a charmer she was, just like you always been a charmer to your old dad. And her mother was more the quiet type and this was even before she got involved with that church, and Neet's father, Brownie, boy, I sure liked old Brownie, anyhow, this particular day Brownie needed somebody to help him get the couch in from off the top of his car. And I was available, said hell yeah I'd help him, what are neighbors for. And we had no sooner untied the couch from the top of the Chevy and both of us had a good hold of each end, we were young and strapping, if I do say so myself, when Alberta runs out on the porch, hollering, 'The baby, Brownie, I can't find the baby,' talking 'bout Neet of course. And Brownie stopped and dropped his end of the couch right where we were, in the middle of the street, and it went down so hard the leg broke from it, and he didn't even seem to mind the broken leg, he just said, 'What you mean, you can't find the baby?' and she said, 'What I mean is what I said, I just missed her, but now that I think about it, it's been about an hour.' 'An hour?' Brownie started shouting, and I told him to calm down, I'd have everybody out within five minutes scouring the place till we found her. Then I noticed that the blanket covering the couch had a lump in it 'bout the size of what Neet should be and I said, 'Yo, Brown, look, man,' and he snatched the blanket off and there Neet was, laughing like a hyena. Seems like she had hid in the back of the Chevy when he went over to M. Gross and Son to pick up the couch and somehow had managed to lay low and then found the opportunity to climb under the blanket and he was never the wiser. I said, 'Damn, man, I think your wife lied to you, I think this is really Houdini's child.' "

Shay let out a small laugh in spite of herself, just imagining Neet hiding under that blanket. That had always been one of her skills. The ability to hide, to sneak in and out of places.

"So we let her stay on the couch and swung it back and forth and gave her a ride on into the house and everybody was laughing, by then half the block had crowded in front of the house once they'd heard Alberta's frantic calls. Even Alberta seemed to be enjoying the moment 'cause she always had that serious streak to her even back then before the church fiasco came along and split up her and Brownie. We had a throw-down party that Saturday afternoon. I ran home and got my drill set and helped Brownie get the leg back on, though as I'm sitting here I swear to God this couch feels a little lopsided, would have been right there——"

"Please don't swear in my mother's house." The voice formed itself from the darkness of the dining room and startled Shay and Joe and they both jumped and Joe even stood.

"Neet? Is that you, sweetheart?" he said as he started walking toward the darkness. "How are you feeling, we would have come upstairs, your mother said you're not supposed to be tackling the stairs."

"What more can happen to me?" she said, and Shay felt the skin on her face burn, as if Neet had just smacked the words across Shay's face like a whip.

Joe was not deterred. He rushed to soften Neet. "I was just telling Shay about this couch and, uh, forgive me for swearing, I meant no disrespect, Lord knows—mnh. Sorry again. Neet? You gonna come on in the light so Shay and I can say a proper greeting, take a look at you. That's all Shay's been talking about, how glad she is that you're finally home."

Shay could feel the pulse in her temple throb as she kept her eyes fixed on the darkness surrounding the voice, waiting for Neet's frame to perforate the space under the dining-room archway. She could just make out her lips, the spot where her forehead jutted, the line of her nose. Guessed that she must be draped in black still because that's all she could see, the highlights of Neet. Wanted to see her eyes though. Wanted it confirmed that she had lost Neet for real.

Joe was still talking, telling Neet that Miss Louise had made her a cake. Asked if she planned to sample it soon because he could stand a taste of it himself knowing what a boss baker his wife was. "And you know your buddy Shay is not one to pass on sweets either," he said, laughing, forcibly, because Neet wasn't respond- ing, just breathing to fill the irregular spaces Joe left when he paused to think of another topic. This he did at least three more times. Moved from the cake, to the unseasonably warm weather, to the rerun of the block party planned for two weeks from then.

Shay wanted to tell him to be quiet, that he was sounding more and more foolish, that Neet was gone as far as she was concerned, might as well have died up there at BB's, Shay wanted to say to her father, but more, she wanted to say it to Neet. Because now she was angry with Neet for leaving her. Damn, Neet, she wanted to say, I was your motherfucking girl, why'd you die on me like this? If she'd had a bottle of cheap, fruity wine, she would have turned it upside down in the middle of the living room. This one's for my girl, she would have said. Instead she just sighed, said, "Come on, Daddy, we should go. Miss Alberta did say she might not be up for company. We should go."

Even Joe had to concede. "Neet, sweetheart," he said, "we'll keep you in our thoughts and our prayers." He turned and walked back into the remarkably normal-looking living room and Shay met him at the door. They stood in the close vestibule as Joe fumbled with the lock and Shay wanted to tell him to hurry up, she just needed to be out of there, because she needed to cry right now and she didn't want to leave her tears all over Alberta's vestibule floor. Then Joe forgot about the lock as the cracked sobs started pushing up from Shay's throat and he held on to her instead. They stood in Alberta's vestibule and Shay was racking against him and he soothed her with It's okay, Daddy's Girl, it's okay. That's all he could manage to get out because the magnitude of what Neet had been through, the death of any dreams that might include having children, and he was thinking, What if that was Shay? He held on to her and rubbed her back and swallowed hard so that he wouldn't stand there and start crying too.

Chapter 12

EET HAD BEEN home for almost two weeks and she still wouldn't talk to Shay, wouldn't talk to anybody except her mother and the people at her church. She was praying and studying her Bible and trying to prepare for the special session where the elders of the church would exonerate her of her sins. She asked them to call her Bonita because although she thought Little Freddie had given her back her name, since the abortion when she'd say her name out loud, Bonita, she'd feel chafed on the inside all over again, as if she was forced to sit on Mr. G's lap and he was saying her name. She told herself that she could tolerate the sound of her name from the Reverend Mister and the elders, though really it hurt still to hear her name even from them. Told herself that's because her insides were still raw from what she'd been through. Raw and scarred. So she studied her Bible, she prayed, she got in and out of cabs to go to church, and she slept. That was her life these days.

———

SHAY WAS TRYING to come back to normal. Returned to her summer job so that she was at least occupied during the day. Spent most evenings downtown with her mother's sister, Maggie, who'd treat Shay to nightly sips of Manischewitz Concord grape wine. Wished at times like this that she had a boyfriend. She'd go home and fall asleep trying not to notice that her father was staying out later and later these days. Made every effort to be nice to Louise though the tendency to disagree about the smallest things was still there and she'd forget herself and snap at her mother and then want to recall it because of the hurt look that came up in her mother's eyes.

JOE WAS STAYING out more and more. Pulling down a lot of overtime. Needed to, he reasoned, because of the added expense of Louise's dental work. Parceled out every minute beyond that he reasonably could between the Red Moon Hotel and Tim's furnished pad. Whistled every night coming in to deflect the complex of emotions that might likely show on his face. Spared Louise his kisses because her mouth was always swollen, or sore, or both. Sagging. He'd make general small talk with Louise about something he'd seen from his booth—he'd had to strong-arm an old geezer, he'd said the other night, to keep him from pissing on the tracks in clear view of a rush-hour crowd; he'd tell her about the progress being made for the next block party, less than a week away. And Louise would repeat all over again that another block party this soon was overkill.

WHEN LOUISE WASN'T at work, or at the dentist's, or in the bathroom soaking her mouth, she was in the backyard looking for the cat. Louise was worried about the cat. Though she should be the last one to worry about the cat since she'd never wanted him in the first place. Louise had had a cat when she was younger that had gotten out of their apartment somehow and was never seen by her again. This was around the time when her mother was sick and Louise had been devastated because she would talk to the cat about how much she wanted her mother to be healthy again. He would seem to understand, purr and lick her under her chin. But he ran away three days before her mother died, and some weeks later Maggie told her that cats can't stay in a house where someone's dying; they'll do everything they can to get away from death. She should have known, Maggie said, that after the cat left it was only a matter of days for their mother. So Louise had a resentment toward cats, having been abandoned by one when she needed him most. She insisted that the gray-and-white thing Joe and Shay dragged home couldn't live in the house because of what his claws would do to her floors. Insisted that if he was to be a house cat, then he'd have to be declawed. Both Shay and Joe were adamant that the cat shouldn't be declawed, said if he ever had to defend himself outside the house he wouldn't be able to. So they put together a little wooden cat house in the yard for him, and that seemed to satisfy them all. But now Louise was worried about the cat's erratic appetite, had been monitoring his food intake obsessively because she preferred worrying about the cat to worrying over Joe, or

Neet, or Shay. She'd rush home from work and go straight to the yard still in her nurse's uniform to check his bowl. For a couple of weeks, he was eating twice his usual, now he was down to half as much. When she cleaned out his bowl just now, she saw what she thought to be blood-tinged streaks of vomit. She was calling for him now. Wanted to look at him and see if he needed to go to the vet. "Cat, Cat," she trilled—they'd been no more inventive with his name than that. "Come here, baby, where are you, baby." She heard motion on the other side of the yard and walked toward the fence that separated her yard from Alberta's. "That you, Cat?" she said. She gasped and jumped then because she was staring in Alberta's face.

"Alberta," she said, hit suddenly, softened suddenly, with all that Alberta had been through. "Alberta," she went on, "I want you to know, if you need me, I mean, I'm just so, so sorry. Anything, Alberta, please ask, if you need anything." But now she was talking to Alberta's back as Alberta turned and walked away from her, up the steps and in through her back door. Louise didn't know which she felt to the greatest magnitude right now, anger or sadness. She fed the anger. Better to feel that than sad, she thought. Anger was easier for her to shake off. She looked up at her own back door flying open, Johnetta pushing herself out onto the back step. She hated the way Johnetta just took it upon herself to walk on in her house without ringing first. "Yeah, Johnetta?" she said, not even trying to disguise her irritation.

"Girl, come on in here," Johnetta said, "I just got some news."

J OE SAW JOHNETTA heave-hoing up his steps as soon as he turned onto Cecil. He'd come straight home today. He hadn't been straight home in a couple of weeks between spending time with Valadean and staring at his horn as it sat in the middle of the heart-shaped velvet couch in Tim's furnished apartment. The horn tried to seduce him as if it too were a beautiful woman. Except that he knew what to do with a beautiful woman, every follicle of his being acted out that script; he could tell himself he was being original, invent-ing moves not yet performed as Valadean writhed and moaned under him, but few things had changed as little since the beginning of time as the moves of a man with a woman. The horn though was different. There was no script for the horn, not as simple as jam-ming his hardness until it softened. The horn demanded originality, choice. Joe was afraid of what form that expression of choice would take, so he just stared at the horn after disassembling it, putting it back together again while the room expanded and an ocean opened up on the floor between the couch where the horn was and the arm-chair where he sat.

Now he wished he was up there in the apartment instead of on his way home, on time for a change, watching newsy-ass Johnetta head into his house. The block felt suddenly narrow. The shade that was usually so delightful on a summer afternoon hung now like a dark shape in the sky, waiting for interpretation. He sighed out his irritation and thought about turning back around. Then he saw Neet walking from her house toward a waiting cab. Her footsteps were slow and precise, old. Only seventeen, he thought, walking like she's seventy. This hurt Joe as much as the whole tragedy, that Neet's footsteps would appear so old in the man-looking shoes like her mother wore, long, bag-shaped dress, cap perched on her head. He wanted with everything in him to snatch that hat from her head, could have because he was right up on her now. He opened the cab door instead. "Neet, how you doing, sweetheart," he said as she slid into the back of the cab.

"Mr. Joe," she responded, just the way her mother always did. No hello, how are you, no good fucking day. Just said his name, Mr. Joe.

He watched the cab drive off. He turned then and started up his steps and listened to Johnetta's voice booming through his screen door. "But wait, you ain't heard the rest," she was saying. Joe stood on his porch unable to walk in through his screen door as Johnetta's words came in bursts through the door and she described some blue-black man with a scar from his mouth to his ear who was just around at Sonny's looking for a woman who'd disappeared a few weeks ago, last seen in a red, black, and green tie-dyed T-shirt. "Said she was headed for this block of Cecil looking for her daughter's house and ain't been heard from since. He don't know the daughter's name, but I 'clare to God it's got something to do with Alberta," Johnetta said.

Joe had heard enough. He couldn't open his door on his living room and be caught in the teeth of one of Johnetta's never-ending Alberta stories right now. He lifted his leg over the banister, onto Alberta's porch, quickly, before he talked himself out of it. He'd been preoccupied lately with how the block had always been a cushion for whoever was going through something, yet they'd pulled themselves out of the path of Alberta's fall when the tragedy with Neet happened. There'd been no streams of people coming and going with platters of food so she wouldn't have to cook, or offers to do her shopping this week, or mop down her porch, or just come over and sit and listen to her sigh if she didn't want to talk. Whether or not she accepted the overtures, the overtures should have been hers to refuse. Didn't know what he could do, but doing nothing seemed worst of all. So he listened to Johnetta's nonstop sentences pour through his screen as he rang Alberta's bell.

He focused on the manila-colored window shade and then Alberta's face as she cracked the door and said, "Joe?"

His throat went suddenly dry and he had to clear it several times. "Afternoon, Alberta, just stopped to see how Neet's making out, and you too of course. I just saw her leave and, I don't know, I thought, you know, I'd just stop and say hello."

Alberta stepped back and opened the door just enough for Joe to ease in. "Please don't let any flies follow you in, please," she said.

Joe turned around and looked over his head in an exaggerated way. "What you trying to say, Alberta, that I'm like that little ole dirty boy in the comic strip who always got a circle of flies over his head?" He laughed then, forgetting himself, forgetting whose black-and-white-tiled vestibule he'd just entered that smelled of Spic and Span. He remembered though as soon as his laugh was done and he was left looking in Alberta's eyes. She looked as though she'd been crying. He looked away, wishing he hadn't noticed that.

"You said it, not me," she said as she continued to look at him.

"Excuse me? Said what?"

"That you was like the little ole dirty boy in the comics with flies always circling your head."

She turned then and went through the vestibule door and into the living room and Joe followed her, convinced that he'd seen the murky outline of a smile trying to nudge at the corner of her mouth. He knew that was impossible though; he hadn't seen anything that even approached a smile coming from Alberta in the twelve or so years since she'd gotten caught up in that cultlike church and Brownie left. He'd been wondering about him since he'd told Shay the story of Brownie and the couch. Wondered if Brownie knew about this trauma Neet was going through. Brownie could certainly be one hell of an ally in all of this, maybe break through to Neet father-to-daughter. Maybe he could even track Brownie down, surely it couldn't hurt; he couldn't imagine that anything could bring Neet's disposition lower than it already was. He thought this as he followed Alberta through the tiny vestibule and into the living room. The blinds at the window were opened to halfway and he resisted the impulse to squint from the unexpected burst of slanted light. The room was neat, orderly, and Joe recognized Louise's good vase on the coffee table; the carnations Shay had arranged so artfully in the vase were gone though the baby's breath still made a nice adornment.

"Since you're here I can return the plate the German chocolate cake came in on," Alberta said as she thought about offering him a seat, then stopped herself from extending her arm toward the couch. "And the vase."

"Sure, sure thing, no problem, but first, uh, if it's okay, I wanted to ask you something. Uh, about Brownie, you ever hear from him?" He shifted his feet and looked behind him at the couch, and then resigned himself to standing.

"Brownie?" A mild surprise hung from her face as she stood in the sun and it illuminated all that was dowdy about her, the hairnet covering her head like a cage, the loose gray dress that buttoned all the way to her throat, the clunky lace-up shoes like his grandmother used to wear. He concentrated on the shoes though he wanted to look at her mouth, its poutiness, the sight of her mouth reminding him that though she tried like hell to disguise it, she was in fact a good-looking woman.

"Yeah," he said, "I was just thinking I'd like to try and catch up with Brownie. You know, old-times' sake and all."

"Well, I know nothing about old times' sake, but I do know you're not seeing Brownie anytime soon."

"Well, I know he was boxing over in Europe but I'd heard he was back in the States, what'd he do, leave the area?"

"Try left this earth," she said.

"No, Lord, no, you not telling me Brownie's dead."

"I'm telling you just that. Brownie passed about five years ago. Old devil of a wife had his remains cremated so fast that my poor child didn't even have a chance to say a proper Christian good-bye to her father." She pressed her eyelids tightly and tilted her narrow chin toward the ceiling as if she was praying.

"Well, don't look so shocked," she said when her eyes were back to Joe. "We all going that route sooner rather than later."

He mumbled out how sorry he was to hear about Brownie, could he do anything, for Neet, or he cleared his throat, for her.

"It's not like it just happened, not like we need chicken and potato salad for a fifty-person repast."

"Well, I'm just hearing about it, so it is like it just happened for me."

Alberta was struck then by how naturally Joe was taking up space in her living room. She couldn't remember the last time a visitor who wasn't part of her church had. This was wrong, she knew, giving him this much of an audience, worldly nonbeliever that he

180 • Diane McKinney-Whetstone

was. Even though she left him standing, she had still let him in, was still talking to him in ways that she rarely talked to people from the outside. Next thing she'd be having to confess to letting this man in her house the way Neet was on the way to the church to confess right now. How hard it had been the day before to leave Neet in the lower sanctuary, the dozen and a half disciplinarian Saints gathered to hear her put into words what she had done so that they could condemn and then forgive her. It had to be that way, the Reverend Mister had said as he'd gently led Alberta upstairs, away from the circle that had formed around Neet, chanting. The Reverend Mister had taken Alberta's face in his hands and with great tenderness and skill had kissed one cheek, then the other, then spoke directly in her eyes as he pointed out that Neet had to confess to the intention of the act, that she had intended to commit murder, that that's what separated God's law from man's, on the one hand, and the nature of man from the nature of beast, on the other, the level of intention. He'd whispered to Alberta then and said, "My dear sister Alberta, there are other sins as well, not just her murder of the baby in her womb, your daughter surrounded that act with a whole web of sins: the lying to you, the actual sin of coupling with a man outside of marriage. Other sins too, my dear sister Alberta," he'd said.

"They won't, you know, hit her, they won't hurt her, will they, Reverend Mister? She's still weak from her surgery," she had said and cried even as she'd said it. He'd dabbed at her tears with his thumbs and promised that Neet's condemnation would be only as severe as it needed to be, but it would be better for Neet, and for her, if she went on home, and perhaps she should send Neet to her sessions from here on and not actually come with her. When he talked into Alberta's eyes like that, with that haunting whisper to his voice and her face so gently molded between his hands, it was as if her will was a shimmering strand of a thread and his voice was the perfect touch of air to have her swaying in the direction he wanted her to go. But even though Alberta had acquiesced, allowed Neet to stay there yesterday, to go without her today, she felt uneasy, a gnawing in her stomach, as if she'd chosen wrong. Now she was picturing Neet the way she'd been when she'd left her at the church yesterday. So poised, sitting in the center of that circle, trying so hard to be righteous. Alberta went soft when she thought of Neet sitting like that.

Joe was going on and on about Brownie, man, what a good guy that Brownie had been, Joe was saying, always so personable, always so helpful, always had a good, hearty laugh for you. Alberta interrupted him because she was about to cry, over Brownie, over Neet, needed to cry, but she couldn't cry with Joe standing in the middle of her living room. "Listen, Joe," she said, "I have some things that need my immediate attention, you know, that you interrupted me from when you rang the bell . . ."

"Oh, uh, sorry, Alberta, if this is a bad time."

"It is, really and truly it is. I'm just going to get your plate and then you really do need to be on your way." She talked with such a flourish that she didn't even realize that she had already started to cry until Joe's face told her that she had, such concern, such sympathy covering his face and she couldn't tolerate him looking at her like that so she turned in a huff and rushed into the kitchen to get the plate.

Joe followed her into the kitchen and when she grabbed the plate from the old-style chrome-rimmed Formica table and turned and saw him standing there as if he was ready to hug her or otherwise lapse into some showy expression of condolence, she was outraged. "Are you some kind of fool?" she said, and her voice screeched from a combination of the sobs caught in her throat and from her voice going so suddenly loud like that.

"I, uh, I'm sorry, Alberta, but you just started crying from out of nowhere and I just wanted to make sure, I mean, you seemed—"

"Seemed, nothing! You got some bold nerve following me through my house. You don't have to go home, but you gotta get the—you gotta get on out of here," she said, censoring the expression that Pat used so often to the drunks who'd want to linger at her speakeasy bar past closing. Y'all ain't got to go home, but you gotta get the fuck outta here, Pat would say. Alberta hadn't heard those words in years and they just flew out of her mouth before she could even think about what she was saying.

"Whew, where you learn to talk like that?" Joe asked, eyeing Alberta now as if she were suddenly a stranger, though he had to admit that she was a stranger, really, how well did he even know her, really?

She pushed the plate toward him even as she looked down at the worn marks on her tiled kitchen floor. "Here, could you just take your wife's plate and go please?" Her eyes were stinging from a fresh crop of tears needing to fall and she sniffed and swallowed hard and then looked up at him. "Please, could you just go please," she said again.

Joe took the plate and his feet went to cement and he just stood there. He felt the need to do something, say something. Frail-looking woman just breaks out in tears right in front of a man he has to do something, whether she's a cold-skinned Holy Roller who takes a man down with a look or not, the right thing was to do something, at least help settle her down before he left, at least help her to stop crying. She pushed past him though, like a cold snap of air, and he had no choice then but to go on back into the front room. She was standing at the vestibule door wiping her face with the sleeve of her dark-colored dress when he got there. He touched her elbow and she yanked it away and opened the vestibule door with such force that the door hit her right on her forehead. "Holy shit, Alberta, are you okay?" he said as he grabbed her arm for real this time to pull her back away from the door, as if the door had wheels or feet and was coming in for another attack. He tried to look at her forehead, to make sure that she hadn't busted it wide open, hard as the door had hit, but she was covering it with her hand and telling him that she was fine, Just go, get, just go, she yelled at him now.

"I just want to help you," he said. "Why won't you let people help you?"

"If you want to help me, take your hand off of my arm and get out of my house." She had stopped crying now and the ice was back, at least in her voice. Not in her eyes though, Joe noticed just before he turned and walked on through the vestibule and out of the door. There was something else hanging in her eyes dead center and Joe tried to shake it as he walked across his porch.

Alberta rubbed her forehead as she watched Joe stomp across the porch to climb over the banister; her forehead was hot and beginning to throb, though she didn't know which burned more, the spot on her head where the door had hit, or the one on her arm where Joe's hand had just been. She went to the kitchen for ice. Shouldn't have been surprised that Joe's touch was still like fire, pulsing with life the way it used to all those years ago.

A LBERTA WAS ALWAYS cold back then. She'd been severely neglected as an infant raised in the speakeasy/ brothel by Jeffery's stepmother, Pat. The neglect had left her always feeling cold as a result, though Pat had never planned to have to accommodate a newborn given the nature of the business that she ran from her house. When Jeffery called every day from prison telling Pat that Deucie had given birth to a baby girl, that Deucie's mother decided she couldn't take the child, and could Pat claim the child since she was the legal stepgrandmother, Pat had told Jeffery, "No!" and slammed the phone in his ear. Every day for a week she slammed the phone in his ear. But one time when he called he added that Pat could get a relief check as long as the child was in her care, so she was persuaded then. Plus, Jeffery said that he'd be out the following month and he'd take over with the baby after that, and they probably wouldn't keep Deucie locked up in the crazy house much longer than ninety days, he'd promised. So Pat signed to have the baby released to her care on a Monday in case they needed to inspect where she would live. She did no business on Mondays and the house became a normal one. Mondays she cleaned all morning to get rid of the six nights of filth that had accumulated there. Then she'd sleep all the way through until Tuesday afternoon.

So Alberta went to live with Pat on a Monday. What was supposed to be a short stay took on a permanence because Jeffery couldn't manage to stay out of jail. He was in fact released the next month as he'd said he would be. He was anxious to do right by his baby girl, have a hand in her raising. But on his way to retrieve his child he saw the most beautiful stuffed teddy bear in the window of Lit Brothers department store. Thought he should present such a gift to his baby girl. He walked up the street to the PSFS bank and handed the teller a note, was surrounded by police before the teller even started filling a bag with dollar bills. Pat had screamed at him when he'd made his one call from the Round House to tell her he'd been rearrested. "You stupid motherfucker," she'd shouted at him. "Robbing a bank is a federal offense. Why didn't you just steal the gotdamned stuffed toy?"

So Alberta was trapped with Pat in a never-ending series of Mondays where Alberta would suffer gross neglect. Not that Pat didn't neglect her the other six days. But the other six days Alberta had the sad, honest drunks who sat at Pat's makeshift speakeasy bar. They'd pass Alberta from hand to hand and smile and coo. They'd rub her gums down with whiskey-soaked napkins when she was teething because they knew the importance of dulling pain; let her sip the juice from their bowls of collards when she was colicky because some nights that's about all they could keep down too. They'd tell her the stories of their lives because at least she listened without condemnation. They demanded that Pat change the child's diapers with regularity because they'd shitted and pissed on themselves recently enough and knew what torture it was to remain for too long in your own waste. They'd lift Alberta close to their chests and let her head find the warm spaces in the crooks of their necks because they felt like throwaway babies too. But too bad for Alberta that the drunks weren't there to care for her on Mondays, because on Mondays Alberta would cry for hours while Pat slept. She'd cry for food, she'd cry to be changed, to be held, looked at, talked to. But mostly she'd cry because she was cold on the inside, no matter how insulated the footed pajamas she wore, on the inside she was always cold. So that even when she got older she became accustomed to layering her clothes because she chilled easily. And though she was a pretty girl, soft brown eyes, nice lines to her cheekbones, subtle cleft to her chin, she was so pale and thin, and with all those clothes heaped on her all the time, she developed the affect of a homely child.

Pat put Alberta to work almost as soon as she was old enough to walk. She taught Alberta how to run the towels through the wringer washer, and then she slung a low line in the backyard that the child could reach so that she could hang them. She even taught her how to light a cigarette from the gas stove. And once Alberta started first grade—she'd skipped kindergarten because Pat said that the child's preference was to be at home with her—Pat made up for all that help she wasn't getting during the week by teaching Alberta how to take orders at Pat's Sunday dining-room speakeasy bar.

By the time Alberta was ten, she excelled at slinging shot-size glasses and wineglasses and brandy globes and beer mugs. She knew weights and measures like fingerfuls and nips. Don't ask her to fry an egg, but step back and watch her uncork a bottle of bubbly in record time. At least Pat would show her off that way. Would whisper to whoever was new at her bar, "They say she's Jefferey's. Her mother's a schizoid, she don't bond with people, more like a wild animal than a person. So I took Alberta in to live with me when she was seven days old, had to, mother might have eaten her alive, as it was, tried to bite her head off. Never verified that she's really Jeffery's, but my girl can sure tend a bar."

Alberta would sink a little deeper inside herself when she'd hear this. Sunday after Sunday she'd hear this. Instead of being at somebody's church like other girls her age, she'd be tending bar and listening to how her mother was no better than a wild coyote, or Doberman pinscher, or yellow-eyed panther, or whatever species Pat had decided would describe Deucie that day. And Alberta didn't even have any real friends, only the Sunday drunks who came to Pat's, but no friends at school, nor in the neighborhood. Anyhow, she'd push away anyone who tried to make friends, knowing the attempts would be severed once their mothers found out where she lived. Happened that way with Wilma, who lived on Catherine Street when Alberta was eight. She'd ventured home with Wilma after school one day, liking Wilma's strength, how Wilma stood up to other kids when they called her Sambo because of how dark she was. Wilma's apartment was warm and smelled of bacon and coffee beans. Alberta had gotten comfortable on the oversize couch as she waited for Wilma to change out of her school clothes. Then Wilma's mother came into the room. She looked like the perfect mother to Alberta in her flowered duster, brown-paper-bag curlers twisted in her bang, pretty brown face that seemed shaped for laughter. She was laughing, but when she looked at Alberta, her laugh hung unfinished in the room. She asked Alberta who was she, where did she live. Alberta answered in a whispered voice, the mark on her forehead burning the way Wilma's mother stared at it. The mother yelled for Wilma then. "Come in here and tell me what you done brought home with you today," she said. Wilma skipped into the living room wearing one scuffed play shoe with a run-down heel and one good black oxford.

"That's Alberta, Ma," she said, putting the other for-playing-in shoe to her mouth so she could unknot the shoelace with her teeth. "She's my friend. She don't even call me black Sambo."

"She's no friend of yours," the mother said, pulling the shoe from Wilma, trying to unknot the laces with her fingers and then using her teeth to get the knot out. "She live over in that whorehouse your uncle can't stay from 'round. She the one whose mother tried to bite her head off. Look at her forehead." She turned to Alberta then. "I'm sorry, honey, but you got to go on back round Mole Street. I don't need no extra mess. Got mess enough going on without letting you come 'round bringing your hard luck."

"She not hard luck, Ma."

"She is too. Live with a bunch of women taking down somebody else's man. Plus, her own mother marked her. Wilma, some things not explainable yet. Get me a knife so I can cut this knot out of your shoelaces. And stop kicking your shoes off without untying them first."

"But, Ma, she's nice—"

"What I say, girl? No more messes 'round here."

Alberta hadn't even waited to hear if Wilma would continue defending her. She'd slid down from the softness of the couch and on out of the living room. She didn't even turn around to tell Wilma good-bye, Wilma's mother threatening to hit Wilma with the shoe if she kept giving her word for word. Alberta went on back to Pat's cured of trying to be friends with anyone from school.

When Alberta was much older, sixteen, she did become friends with Brownie, the slick-dressing semiprofessional boxer. He would come into Pat's suited down, pointed edge of a cotton handkerchief peeking from his jacket pocket, big straw hat under his arm if it was summer, felt number if the weather outside was cold. He'd try to make conversation with Alberta, tell her what the text was for the service that Sunday, the hymn, ask her if she knew such and such a song, and Alberta, who didn't do much talking with the clientele anyhow, would mostly stare. Brownie was taken in by her stare, could see she was a cute girl once he got beyond the homely trappings, the layers of clothes that never even matched, the rag always tied over her hair. He would feel for Alberta as the tempo in the dining room picked up at her expense. He was affected by the way her cheeks would fill with air as if that's where she was holding the hurt. And in the midst of the uproarious laughter that would take over the dining-room bar when Pat got going good, Brownie would lean over and whisper in Alberta's ear something about Pat that had just occurred to him. "Like her hair, why she always got to have the worst-looking dos?" he'd ask Alberta. "I mean, look at her hair right now, pieces of it pressed, pieces of it tight, none of it smoothed down, puts you in mind of a bird's nest, doesn't it? Except it's not quite as organized as a bird's nest. You noticed any light-colored flakes on her shoulders, probably not dandruff, probably little flecks of eggshells. Probably a whole family of starlings living up there." And when it looked like a smile was trying to push up from Alberta's mouth that was otherwise set, almost pursed in cement, it was so unmovable, Brownie would keep it going. "Tweet, tweet, tweet," he'd say. Alberta couldn't hold her mouth closed and pursed like that and she'd allow a smile to break on through.

Brownie showed up at Pat's especially early one Sunday and told Pat he'd come to take her little barmaid of a granddaughter to church. Of course Pat protested. Hell no, Alberta had to help out at the bar. But Brownie told Pat to just get someone else for the day, and Pat insisted that couldn't nobody take Alberta's place behind that bar. So Brownie reached into his pocket, asked Pat how much was Alberta worth for the day. He started peeling off dollar bills and even fives as Pat salivated and said Keep going, you getting there, I'll tell you when to stop. He told Pat then to go find Alberta something decent to put on and at first Alberta didn't know which she enjoyed more, watching Pat hop around and fuss over her to get her ready for church, or the feel of the inside of Brownie's brand-new 1953 Chrysler.

But it was the church that she really loved about that day. She was so enthralled by everything once they left the morning humidity and stepped inside the church, and her self-consciousness about being as old as she was, sixteen, and never having been inside a church dissipated into the fan-swept air. The music, the preaching, the praying, the testifying, the beauty and the melody of all those words put together in combinations like she'd never considered, got inside her body and she cried and she laughed and was made dizzy from the words swirling around inside her. She became like a young child the way she was struck by the minutest of things, the white gloves the deacons wore when they passed out the Communion wine, the pleated sleeves of the choir's gold and navy robes, the paper fans attached to wooden Popsicle sticks, the felt-lined collection plates, the decorum, the sense of order, even when they lost control and started dancing and shaking convulsively, it had its own rhythm. She felt such a mighty clicking together, such a falling into place that first Sunday, that she begged Brownie to take her back, please, week after week she begged him to take her back to church.

Brownie was so tickled to do it. He was older than Alberta and felt protective, and so he reached into his pants pocket Sunday morning after Sunday morning and paid Pat for giving Alberta the day off, and never asked anything of Alberta in return; just the way her face settled down, as if she was allowing all of that hurt to finally seep from the inside of her jaws, was enough pay for him.

But one Sunday evening after a couple of months of Alberta's forays into Christian life, as she washed out the sinkful of shot glasses and Pat dried them, checking for especially stubborn red lipstick marks, Pat told Alberta that it was time for her to start carrying a little more of the weight around there.

Alberta just stood there with her arms immersed to her elbows in sudsy water, the kitchen walls recently painted the color of bile closing in on her. She knew what went on in those bedrooms on the second and third floors, and even sometimes during the card games downstairs. Knew it was only a matter of time before she'd have to paste the look of fake desire on her face the way she'd seen the other whores do, especially Penny, who would sit at the bar and talk to Alberta early evenings while she waited for her work to show. One minute Penny would be frowning, complaining about so-and-so who'd just walked in, how he grunts like a pig and sweats brown shit all over her from that cheap dye in his hair, the next minute Penny would be smiling at that same man, making her eyes go half closed, purring breathlessly about how she'd been waiting on him, what took him so long to get to her. Alberta would take it in as if she was being bred for that fake look of desire the same way she'd been bred to tend the bar.

Alberta's breaths went shallow then as she stood at the kitchen sink and she thought she might faint or vomit. She forced herself to look at Pat instead. Pat had thin lips that stretched from one end of her face to the other. Frog mouth, Brownie would whisper to Alberta when he was trying to make her laugh. "Ribbit," he'd say, and Alberta would indeed allow a smile to tug at her mouth. She concentrated on the movement of Pat's mouth now, hoping that in reading her lips she might find that her ears were mistaken, that Pat wasn't in fact asking her with that wide frog mouth of hers to start turning tricks. Though she'd seen it coming for weeks now. The first time Pat had helped her dress for church she'd told Alberta that she had a cute money-making ass. Then suddenly Pat was giving her bright red lipsticks to wear, nail polishes, cheap perfumes.

Alberta pretended that she didn't know what Pat was asking of her. "Huh?" she asked, raising her eyebrows and trying to force a dumb blankness to take over her face.

"Come on, Alberta," Pat said. "You can't be that damned stupid. You must see how the men look at you even though you got the look of Orphan Annie the way you piles clothes on."

Alberta knew that was true. She'd been hit on often enough by some of the men who'd take up seats at Pat's dining-room bar. Knew the difference between that kind of baseness and the genuine affection that Brownie seemed to have for her.

"Now you seventeen, Alberta," Pat went on. "And to my way of thinking, seventeen is grown, I was sure as hell a woman at seventeen. If truth be told, several of my best men clientele done asked about you, and quite frankly I can swear to you that this'll be the easiest money in the world a woman can make 'cause once they good and drunk, you don't even have to do nothing, just let them mount you. And believe me, nine times out of ten they gonna pass out before they can even get on top of you good, and trust me, they sure not in any condition to do no moving. And when they come to, you know, you give them a look like they the best you ever had, call 'em big daddy. Let 'em walk out with their dignity. All you got to really worry about is not getting caught and I can give you stuff to prevent a pregnancy. Easy money, Alberta, trust me."

"What if I don't want to?" Alberta asked.

Pat put down the shot glass and the dish towel and told Alberta to look at her. "As your father's stepmother I feel it my duty to explain to you right here and now that ninety percent of life, at least any colored person's life, is filled with doing what they don't want to do. You don't want to get up in the morning, you get up anyhow, you don't wanna brush your teeth, you brush 'em, don't feel like messing with your hair, you do it anyhow, sure as hell don't feel like waiting on no bus to get to no job being bossed around by white people all day, what you do? You wait on that bus, you get bossed around. You don't feel like cooking when you get in, or no man pulling on you when you finally take your tired black ass to bed. What you do? You stand over that stove and cook, feed that worthless-ass man till he's belching or farting or both, and then you still open yourself up once y'all under the covers. That's what you do. That's life, Alberta. I didn't draw it up that way, I'm just following the blueprint set before me. Now, you can leave here whenever you ready, you can take your cute yellow ass on out there and measure the ninety percent out there of what you don't want to do against the opportunity I'm offering you. Everybody don't get this opportunity."

Alberta didn't say anything. She turned back toward the sink and searched the water for more shot glasses to wash. The water was warm and felt good as it covered her hands in sudsy ripples. She tried to concentrate on what her hands were feeling, as if she needed some part of her not to be repulsed by what Pat had just said so that she could think about her options. What were her options? Father in jail, mother in the crazy house, outcast at school because of where she lived. No friends other than Brownie and a couple of the old-head drunks who'd cared for her when she was an infant and who hadn't yet succumbed to liver disease.

"I will allow you to keep all your tips, since you damned near blood," Pat said, her voice sounding farther and farther away to Alberta though she was talking practically in her ear. "And I will send only the best of them to you. That I will do. Plus, I'll give you the third-floor room."

"I don't want Brownie to know," Alberta said into the sink. "I think he likes me?"

Pat started laughing then. "Likes you, huh?" she said. "Don't worry 'bout Brownie. He won't be visiting you in that way anyhow. Can't. Had it shot off years ago in a street fight that turned dirty. Why you think he only comes around on Sundays? You ever seen him here on a Saturday night when the place is sizzling? Won't either. Guess he don't want to be reminded of what he can no longer do. Don't worry 'bout Brownie knowing. I'll conjure up some kind of story so he won't come looking for you no more."

Alberta was crying now, she was crying as much for Brownie as for herself. She would miss Brownie, miss how proud he used to be escorting her to church; she'd miss church too, but she couldn't be a prostitute Saturday night and take up space on a church pew Sunday morning. She wasn't letting any sound out, but her shoulders were moving up and down. Pat put her arm around Alberta's shoulders and told her that she could put together a nice little nest egg for when she was ready to go out on her own. "I promise you you'll be able to leave here in high style when the time comes 'cause your tip money gonna add up fast. You ain't ugly and horsey looking like these other bitches I got working here. Now what you wanna be called, can't let 'em call you by your real name. Let's call you C, take the end of your mother's name. You like that?"

Alberta just shook her head and went back to her dishes. And Pat said she needed to check the stock to see what she had to buy from the State store this week, could Alberta finish drying too. Alberta shook her head again yes. She actually preferred to work alone, preferred having a lot to do. Gave her life its structure when she had a lot to do, especially if it was some rote, repetitive thing, like washing these shot glasses, and drying them, putting them away, slinging the dish towels on the line, pouring vodka or Tokay wine, glass after glass. Sweeping up the crumbs from the beer nuts, mopping down the bar. Solitary things. So she started crying harder now that her chores were about to start being tangled up with another person. Now that she was about to have to start turning tricks.

Pat was still talking, telling Alberta that if it made her feel better, nobody even had to know it was her up there. "We'll give your room a no-lights rule. How you like that? Though I don't know any colored man that's gonna walk into a dark room. Let me think about it. We'll work it out. Plus, like I said, you have my word that I'll only be sending you the best up there. The gentlemen."

JOE WAS ALBERTA'S first. Horn-blowing, happy-go-lucky, intense and gentle and sad, Joe was her first. Still had his horn in his hand when he walked in the room, the room softly lit at first, Alberta's back to the door the way Pat had told her to do. Pat told Alberta just to leave the lights on long enough for them to get in the room and see what they were getting. She could let the room go black before she turned around so she'd never have to show her face. Alberta whispered out, "No lights, okay," as she turned the lamp switch and the room went dark.

Joe told Alberta that he didn't need lights, all he needed to know was that she had a pretty mouth. "You got a pretty mouth, baby?" he asked as he blew out a couple of notes on his horn and then laughed. "Oh you serious too, huh," he said to her silence, which hung in the air. He propped his horn in the chair and started undressing, talking the whole while. This was the first time he'd done Philly, he said. Liked it here, people here appreciated good sounds. He was from Pittsburgh, he said, no more though. Lost everything that ever mattered to him in Pittsburgh, buried his father, his only sister, and his mother there, he said, sitting on the side of the bed now. Saw his best friend beat down to a cripple-mute. "Five years since I left. Never going back to Pittsburgh," he said. "You got any places like that you buried? Huh? Come on, baby, talk to me now, can't see much of your face, least let me hear your voice."

Alberta was sitting up in the bed. She had on an emerald green robe given to her by Pat. The robe was silky and thin though she was used to flannel in bed, sometimes slept in a flannel gown over a thinner cotton duster because of her tendency to get chills. She was naked under this flimsy robe and the skin on her arms and back and legs was tightening into fine bumps. Joe was all the way in the bed now, the outline of his darkness moving in on her, still talking. "Tell me something, baby, come on, tell me something happy so I'll feel better about my lot in this life, or even something sad so I'll know I'm not the only one been through some tough shit." He was feeling her mouth with his fingers as he talked. Tracing the outline of her lips. "Damn, you got a beautiful mouth," he said. His breath was right in her face and she inhaled the mist that his voice left in the air. He was kissing her now, pushing against her lips, pulling her to him, all the way to him. His body was so thick and hot as it covered her and moved all over her. But it was too late. She yielded to her always cold self and there was nothing she could do to stop the chills. She shook convulsively and then she cried too. She cried and shook and shook and cried and Joe held her so tightly as he tried to keep his own nature at bay, his heat. He asked her what was wrong, damn, what was wrong, he was only joking when he asked her for a sad story, he said. Damn, damn, damn. And he couldn't hold on to his nature either as he exploded into her sadness and felt the explosion all the way to his marrow. Had never felt himself explode with such intensity before.

He was quiet afterward. He breathed hard and held Alberta while she cried. Though he hadn't cried since he was nine, he understood how necessary it was every now and then to create your own river to cross. He patted her back and declined the urge to ask her what was wrong. Life was wrong, just that simple. She was young and soft and colored, a whore. So wrong. He wrapped her up in the covers and rubbed her back until her chills went away. Until there was a one knock at the door signaling that his time was up, and he yelled at the door to just tally him up for the night. He was staying for the night.

Alberta sighed then. Felt her chest open up and she could

breathe again. Joe was getting up from the bed, going toward the chair, and at first she thought he was getting dressed to go. She wanted him to go, she wanted him to stay. She didn't want him to touch her ever again even as she did want him, wanted to feel him move all over her again. Was afraid of that feeling, the conflict, the duality of her that she couldn't understand. She watched the naked dark outline of him lift his horn from the chair. He put his horn to his lips and started to blow. Blew out "'Round Midnight," blew it softly at first. Then louder, until the sounds of his horn filled the room, and he might as well have been all over her again with what the sound was doing to her, the way it moved through her and settled inside and nestled there, sound embedded.

Joe would have continued playing except that there were knocks coming from the floor below and even cursing in the hall telling him to shut up with the gotdamn horn, take it to the Apollo or the Show Boat but get it the hell outta there. He started laughing then. His eyes had adjusted to the darkness and he could see Alberta just a little. At least her lips that were painted bright red and so pouty and perfectly formed. So he put his horn down and let the sight of her mouth draw him back again.

ALBERTA LOOKED FORWARD to Joe. With the other men she tried to grow a second self. A hardened, impenetrable self. Tried to go blank with the others, hollow and unfillable. Rote. She'd say "hut, two-three-four" in her mind as if she were a soldier on her way to die and the concentration in counting off each step kept her from focusing on the battle that would end when she'd meet the enemy face-to-face and take a bayonet to the stomach. Felt plunged into that way every time one of the others exploded inside her. But she was who she really was with Joe. She was shy and insecure and wanting to be held. She chilled easily. She was sad and lonely. She'd cry with Joe and he'd play his horn and comfort her. She really moved with Joe. Really moved, really felt.

They went on like that for two years. Joe walked into that dimly lit room once or twice a month, as often as he could get to Philly from wherever he was on the road, Alberta turning the lights off before he could really see her face. When there was talking it was mostly Joe. Alberta whispered rather than talked. Joe was loud though. His voice filled the room and Alberta cuddled up to the sound of it as he'd tell her about the clubs he'd played, who he'd played with, what songs, what the people in the audience had shouted. He mixed in stories about his growing up in Pittsburgh, described for her the size of the bullet hole that had gone through his father's head. Then he'd switch to something light, something funny that he could laugh about, he'd have Alberta laughing too. One night he told Alberta how some woman got saved during his solo at a club in Norfolk. "She started shouting and doing a holy dance right up on the little circle of a stage. People were laughing at first, then they were cussing and yelling at her that she wasn't in no damn church, get the hell off the stage." Joe laughed as he told the story. Then he found Alberta's mouth through the darkness and traced it with his fingers and whispered that he wanted to save her. Would that be possible? "Me and my music, baby, could we stand a chance with you?"

Alberta often laughed on the nights with Joe. But when he said that, she more than laughed. She giggled like a love-struck adolescent. Felt a giddiness that started in her toes, that started all the way to the day she was born; born not to a crazy mother who'd sunk her teeth in the middle of her forehead and marred her for life; born instead to the type of people she'd hear the drunks talk about: a mother who taught school and a father who was a doctor who kept his practice in a poor neighborhood and treated most of the people for free so that the people loved her and her parents and gushed when she walked down the street. The giddiness spread through her as she stared at the three unlit bulbs protruding from the ceiling and Joe nibbled at her ear, felt the giddiness in her chest and she was seventeen, but not like she'd been seventeen standing at the kitchen sink with Pat telling her she had to be a whore; she was seventeen sitting on the back porch of her parents' summer home in places that she heard about as she tended bar, places like Ocean City. She'd just left church and her hands were still in her white lacy gloves as she sat on the two-seated wooden swing next to the fine boy from the Sunday school class. His hands were dark and strong and warm like Joe's hands as he peeled her gloves and put her small hand to his lips and kissed her hand, then asked, "Can I stand a chance with you?" The giddiness was filling her up, all the way to her head, as Joe moved from nibbling her ears down to her neck. Usually by the time he started working his mouth the way he was now Alberta would be moaning, not giggling, but she was giggling now, uncontrollably. Her body was a spasm of the girlish sounds denied her throughout her life. Joe was grooving on the sounds, she could tell by the way he was moving, laughing now himself, asking her, What? Was she suddenly ticklish, had he hit her funny bone, tell him so he'd have the secret to know what to do to make her giggle like that. But right then the door burst open and frog-mouthed Pat was shouting that Joe's buddy had been stabbed in the ass, get him out of here right now or they would never be let back in Pat's Place again. Alberta had held Joe then, she'd never held him before to try to make him stay. "Let him die," she whispered in Joe's ear. "Don't leave me, please."

Joe said that he would be back. Had he never not been back? he asked. He kissed her then softly, as if she was his bride and he was on his way back to work after the honeymoon. He got a gnawing in his stomach then. A burst of reason as he sat up in the bed. How could she be his bride, she'd probably been with more men than he had women; he'd been with a lot of women given the lifestyle of a musician on the road. This was wrong, her asking him to stay. She was breaking the rules, he was a john, that's all. Then he did something he'd never done before, out of respect for her he'd never done it, but something about her desperation when she asked him to stay made him do it. He clicked on the light. She gasped when he did that and her hands went to her face to cover it, her face severely made up with lipsticks and rouges and mascaras, shadows and pencils that perverted her eyes. Though he did see her eyes. They were soft-brown beautiful eyes. He drew in a hard breath, said shit. Then got up and had to leave because he knew when he'd looked at her eyes, the desperation and longing and sadness in her eyes, that he'd fallen in love. Said shit again about having to spend a Friday night in an emergency room with a colored man who'd taken a knife to the ass. They'd treat a white man with a splinter in his finger first. Said shit a third time because it would never be the same again with her. Her asking him to stay had changed it; him glimpsing her under the light had too. In the dark she was a dream, a bit of a goddess who wasn't completely real, who'd cry over the big things: the condition of humanity, the plight of the colored man, the untouchable,

inescapable sadness that came with being alive, which he under-
stood, which he thought she had too. But now she'd pinned down
her sadness and made it too specific, made it about her needing him.
So he said shit three times and left, promising her that he'd be back
before the sun was up good, knowing that he was lying, had no
plans to come back. Felt no guilt over it either. Felt hardened in that
instant, as if he'd grown a crusty shell where his skin had been.

Chapter 13

ECIL STREET WAS trying to come back to itself, trying to use the setup for the second block party as a mood-enhancing activity to get beyond the tragedy with Neet. Trying to get beyond the edginess pervading the block even before Neet had attempted the abortion. Trying to get back to the way they used to be when the air on the block was loose and freeing, not thick and tight and sad. It helped that one of the block's favorite sons had just come back from the war in Vietnam, by all appearances intact, ten fingers and toes, steady walk, still able to smile and laugh. Wallace. "Looks good" was the refrain jumping the banisters from end to end. "Old Wallace sure looks good." They said it with relief, since the year before, Bunny's son, who lived three houses from the corner, had returned nodding and scratching, addicted to potent jungle smack, and the Smiths' boy from Ithan Street had returned and taken to directing traffic at Sixtieth and Spruce, imaginary whistle and all. But Wallace's mental health seemed good, and he'd even grown an inch, standing at taller than six feet, with square shoulders and a strongly set chin and a mother-loving face with big, honest-looking eyes. Joe liked him. Had always paid special attention to him since Wallace's mother was a single parent and Joe knew the life of a boy without a father. He'd turned Wallace on to jazz years ago and Wallace was a connoisseur. He was especially proud that now Wallace was college bound. He gave Wallace an enthusiastic multi-positioned handshake and they touched shoulders in a hug. It was a Thursday night and a half dozen men had gathered in Pinochle Eddie's basement to firm up security for the block for the weekend party. Though Wallace wasn't twenty-one yet, just twenty, but he'd been included because of his size and good sense.

They sat around the table and drew cards for time slots. Joe drew Saturday evening between seven and nine. Then they filled Wallace in on the last party that had been for the most part crime free. There had been a lightweight skirmish between the Corner Boys and a rival singing group from Delancey Street; two girls had tried to scratch each other's faces over some no-count boy. A couple of loud-talking bad-mouthers had too much to drink and hollered out insults to no one in particular. Nothing serious though: no pick-pockets, no silver salt and pepper shakers slipped out through the unlocked screen doors, no pervert tried to lure the children from the block. Though there was talk of the puffy-haired wild woman who'd challenged the Corner Boys. The story had grown so from when Johnetta had first fanned it until now. Now the story was that she'd appeared butt naked on the corner and asked the Corner Boys which one was gonna have her first. Then she'd gone straight for them and started pulling at their crotches and they'd shooed her away and she'd disappeared into the crowd. Wallace laughed out loud. Said that story was definitely more rumor than fact because the Corner Boys he knew would never have let a female get away who was willing to pat them down. Then Tim said hell, he might not have let her get away either. Pinochle Eddie offered Wallace a Miller High Life bottled beer, saying as he did that though he wasn't of legal age he'd probably seen as much, done as much in the jungles of 'Nam as any of them had right here on the streets of Philadelphia. Joe handed Wallace a cigar and said, "This is just our way of saying welcome home, young blood, we glad you made it back intact."

They drank beer and smoked cigars and pipes and cigarettes and got a card game working. Talked politics and women between hands. Talked about the big blue-black man who had gone into Sonny's store looking for the puffy-haired woman who'd supposedly exposed herself to the Corner Boys. Tim said he'd heard the man was a Black Panther. Eddie said he'd heard he was a crook. Joe said so what, Agnew's a crook. They all slapped hands in agreement about that, and that Nixon was an asshole, and that Valadean had the prettiest ass to sashay up Cecil Street since their wives were that young. Though Pinochle Eddie maintained that his wife's ass never looked that good. Swore to God that he loved his wife with all his heart, but damn, he said, her titties been living on her stomach instead of her chest since the birth of their child fourteen years ago. They laughed as they talked, Eddie always turning the conversation back to Valadean and how much he'd love to get a taste of that honey.

Joe didn't flinch. Took an extra-large swallow of beer and gave himself an excuse to cough. He turned to Wallace then. Asked Wallace was it true what everyone said about Asian women. Wallace said he guessed it was about as true as what everyone said about black women. "I guess it's all good when you're into it, Mr. Joe," he said, sliding the deck of cards in Joe's direction so that he could cut.

Tim put his hand on Wallace's shoulder then. Said, "My young blood, I'm gonna tell you something I don't tell everyone." He went on to describe for Wallace the apartment he kept over his barbershop that his wife, Nathina, thought was not rentable because of rats. Told him that since he was still in his mother's house, if he ever needed a little love nest, "Me crib, your crib, my young brother."

Wallace laughed, embarrassed, and Joe cut the deck of cards and slammed them on the table. Then Pinochle Eddie, back to Valadean again, said that from what he could tell, Valadean was already some lucky brother's taste of honey because his wife said that Johnetta said that Valadean had gotten into the habit of disappearing for hours at a time and would return glowing but not talking. "According to Joyce, Johnetta said she gonna follow the girl one of these days."

"Slow as Johnetta walks," Joe said, picking up his cards as Wallace dealt them his way. "Joyce probably said that shit to keep your ass in line, Eddie, to make sure you not the privileged one tasting that honey. In fact, where the hell were you between two and five today, nigger?"

Rousing laughter then as they played the hand out, talking between moves. They talked about racism on the police force, on the Phillies, on the school board, on the election commission. Tim said that he had a call in to the ward leader requesting that he get to whoever he needed to get to so that any cops having a presence around the area during the block party would be brothers. Said he reminded the ward leader of his civil suit against the city from when he was stomped by the cops on Fifty-second Street. Said the young folks crowding on the block to have a good time would be waiting for some racist white pigs to start some shit.

"You right about that," Joe said. "These youngsters not about to join hands singing 'We Shall Overcome.' They're gonna be looking for rocks to throw. That's why we needed a black ward leader anyhow. You wouldn't have even had to explain that shit if the ward leader was a brother."

They agreed on that and then the conversation went back to women, back to Valadean as Eddie told Wallace he should put the moves on her. Joe's irritation broke through then. He asked Eddie was he trying to get off vicariously through Wallace. "Leave the boy alone, let him go after who he wants to go after."

"Damn man, calm down," Eddie said, throwing his losing hand down. "Someone would think you boning her."

"If I was, I'd be there right now, sure wouldn't be sitting here looking at your ugly ass," Joe said as he tallied the score and declared Wallace the winner.

"Probably not your type anyhow, huh, young blood?" Joe said.

Wallace laughed, embarrassed again. Agreed with Joe that Valadean wasn't his type. Said that he preferred city girls, liked girls better when they didn't expose everything with their dress. Liked something left to the imagination.

"That'll change, tell him, fellows," Tim said. Tim and Eddie leaned into Wallace then, telling him man things about how it used to be for them, how it changes over time. Joe got up to leave. Said he was taking his old ass home and their response was yeah, please take your old ass home.

He was thinking as he walked out of how it had changed for him over time. Ten years ago every man on the block would have known he was hitting it with Valadean. A badge of honor back then. He knew better now. Knew how men let things slip during pillow talk about which husbands weren't true blue, jealous possibly that it wasn't they themselves running around. Increased their own pleasures that way too because what wife would deny such an honest, faithful man as the one telling on his cheating friend.

He was outside now. The streetlights were on and the children's laughter rose up from the steps where they played. The adults' chatter from the porches blended over his head and reminded him of how much he liked the block on a summer evening. Except that now he thought he heard Valadean's name from each porch as he walked past. He knew it wasn't so, but just the fact that he imagined it made him go tight inside. He felt guilty in the first place that he was running around, and in the second place that he hadn't gone to Valadean's defense when Eddie and Tim had described her in such base terms. Angry with Valadean now that she dressed the way she did and provoked those kinds of comments. Worried now too that his time with Valadean was fraying at the ends, headed to raggedy, he knew, if Johnetta was making comments. Was going to have to think about ending it altogether with Valadean, he knew that for sure. He was at his house now. Shay was sitting on the steps with her head propped up between her fists. Joe sat next to her. "What's going on, Daddy's Girl?" he said.

Shay shook her head. "Nothing much."

"Block party's gonna be boss this weekend," he said as he leaned into her shoulder, pushing her playfully.

"Nobody says boss anymore, Dad."

"Well, okay then, groovy."

"Dad, please, that's so white people."

"All right, well, how 'bout peace and love, my sister."

Shay laughed. The first time she'd laughed since the tragedy with Neet. Joe got filled up inside listening to her laugh. "Or should I just raise my fist and shout, 'Power to the people'?" he said. Or 'Sock it to me,' or 'Here come the judge.'" Shay laughed harder now. Joe kept it going, not loud though. He didn't want to let himself get too loud for fear he might miss this simplest, greatest pleasure of the sound of his daughter's laugh.

Nathina's daughter, Bobbi, came across the street then. She asked Shay if she wanted to go around the corner to Sonny's Store and get a milk shake and play the pinball machine. She was three years younger than Shay, only fourteen, a lifetime separated them at that age, but Shay was touched by the gesture and she could feel Joe nudging her on. "Only if you quit it with the slang, Dad," Shay said as she got up to leave and in her leaving gave Joe no other option than to go in the house.

THE HOUSE WAS dark and quiet. Joe whistled as he walked through the living room, toward the kitchen where he guessed Louise would be cleaning up the dinner dishes. She wasn't. The kitchen had neither the look nor smell of having just been through a meal. He was about to go upstairs, maybe Louise had turned in early though it wasn't even nine. She walked in through the back door then. She was still in her nurse's uniform and her eyes were red and wet. "Louise?" he said, concern wrapping around his voice. "What's wrong?" he asked as he went to her.

She pushed past him and went to the sink and ran the water and spit. "What is it, baby, your mouth?" he said at her back now.

"I can't find him, I think he's dead," she said.

"Who? Who, Louise, look at me and tell me what you're talking about."

She turned around and something about the sight of her now reminded him all over again of the first time they'd met.

Louise was crying out loud now. Her mouth was puffy and Joe could see that she'd had more teeth pulled today, from closer to the front this time. It was difficult for him to look at her mouth, she looked so comic and sad, and he almost wanted to cry himself. He pulled her to him. Asked her again who was she talking about, who died.

"Cat," she said. "I've been up and down the length of every alley between here and Alden Street. I can't find him. He's not even coming home to eat. And the other day there was even blood and vomit in his bowl. I think he's dead. Either that or he ran away. And if he ran away, then someone's getting ready to die."

Joe held Louise close to his chest. He rubbed her back. He told her that he was sure that Cat was alive and well, just keeping a low profile the way cats sometimes do. "And that business about some-body dying just because a cat runs away is foolishness, Louise."

Louise gave in to the feel of Joe's arms wrapped around her. Her first instinct was to pull away from him as if his arms were no longer meant for holding her. But his arms were so warm and solid. She held on to him. She cried and dripped blood from her mouth onto his shirt. Maybe it was the death of them, Joe and Louise as a couple, that had sent the cat away. She couldn't stand the thought of the death of them any more than she could picture Joe really dead, in a coffin. But she worked in a hospital, felt death hovering around all day long. As much as the hospital discriminated, death did not. People left here, just that simple. Never mind that they left next of kin hollering after them not to leave. The way she felt like hollering right now, Joe, don't leave us, give us a chance to live, to breathe together a while longer. But she had never been the hollering-after type. Didn't even holler after her mother's eternal stare. Sure wasn't going to holler after a man. She pulled herself from the sturdiness of his arms though she wanted him to hold her like that forever. She said she was okay. He was right, the cat would be home. Her mouth was sore, she said, and the temporary partial plate the dentist had made didn't fit right so she was gonna have to walk around with teeth missing near the front until Monday. She went back to the sink and ran the water to sponge away the blood that had fallen on her uniform. She said then that she hadn't cooked dinner. Maybe he could go around to Sonny's and get a cheese steak if he was hungry, she said, adding that Shay had eaten at Maggie's and she herself wasn't up for solid food tonight and anyhow he'd been keeping such irregular hours these days, who knew when he'd decide to come home. She surely wasn't going to try to guess. Don't look for her to plan meals around his schedule these days, she said as she walked past him. She needed to get the uniform off and soak it in cold water before the stain set, she said, telling him there was blood on his shirt too, and if he wanted, she'd clean up his shirt. "Going to bed after that, because I'm tired. You know what I mean, Joe. I'm tired."

She gave him one of those looks that he felt as a chill up and down the length of his arms. She left the room then, left him standing in the middle of the kitchen with the bright yellow walls. The walls were blazing at him now, spotlighting the shame that he felt over what he was doing, wronging two women in fact when he thought about how he'd listened so passively to the way the men had talked about what they wanted to do with Valadean. He couldn't stand how bright these walls were, was thinking that when they repainted he'd suggest a more muted shade. He walked out of the kitchen, headed back outside to the porch to catch a smoke. The porch was dark and soft and he inhaled deeply and settled in to the night sounds of Cecil Street. That's when he saw Alberta.

Actually, he didn't see her first, costumed in her usual long and dark something. He felt her presence at first until the night pulled back to reveal the outline of her face.

"Alberta," he said as she walked up the steps on her side of the thin railing that separated the houses. "How you doing this evening, Alberta?"

"Joe," she said and then disappeared into her house so quickly it seemed as if she'd just changed form and become air and seeped in through the brick porch wall. Joe felt a tightening in his stomach. Something about the way her face looked in the half-black air, a familiarity about her face. He suddenly needed to hear some music. Thought about going down to Tim's apartment and putting his horn to his mouth and making his own tunes. But he felt too incapable of blowing his horn, afraid still. He crushed his cigarette out and went back into his house, went to his stereo console and riffled through his albums and found what he was looking for. "Round Midnight." He put it on and settled down on the couch. He felt like such a fallen man right now, pieces of himself scattered all over the place, scattered all the way back to twenty or more years ago.

He was thinking now of the night he'd asked Louise to marry him. They'd been seeing each other for about half a year though their time together was erratic because of Joe's touring schedule. Louise was living with her sister on Queen Street and this night Joe had two bouquets when he showed up, one for Maggie, just to get through the door, and the other one with the white orchid in the center for Louise. He was loaded down with other offerings for Maggie that night: a double-decker box of Whitman's chocolates, silk nylons, a slab of steaming-hot barbecued ribs that he'd just gotten from D's on South Street. Maggie scanned the dining-room table and said that if these gifts were leading up to him asking for her sister's hand, he should take them back on out because her sister wasn't ready for marriage, furthermore, the sauce from the ribs was leaking through the bag and onto her good lace tablecloth. Joe snatched up the bag and carried it into the kitchen saying as he did that actually he hadn't come to propose to Louise. "Maggie," he said, "I wants to marry *you*, baby."

That got them all laughing and Maggie told Louise that though in her heart she thought that Louise should see the world before she carved out her rut in it, at least Joe would make her laugh. "That's not the worst trait for a son of a bitch," she said as she followed the aroma of the barbecued ribs and left Louise and Joe standing at the dining-room table.

Joe fumbled for the ring under the blazing light of the chandelier. He was quiet for once. Not talking, not making a joke. His hands were sweaty, and he thought cold too when he took Louise's hand and her hand was so soft and warm. He slipped the ring on her finger, chipped diamonds around a gold band that had swallowed up two months' worth of work. Louise was looking down. Her mountain of thick black hair had fallen forward and he couldn't see her face. He tilted her chin up so that he could see it. Wished then that he'd left it lowered because it was easier to look at the crinkles in her hair than what her face was doing, her eyes. Dark eyes that stared right through him, not spilling over with tears of joy, or sparkling with delight. Just barraging him with a steady, unblinking gaze.

"You sure it's me you want, Joe? Me?" Louise asked, her voice as steady as her gaze.

"What? Sure? Baby. Sure? Ask me anything, Louise, but don't ask me if I'm sure." Joe had had to look away then. Couldn't hold on to her eyes. Thought that if he didn't look away right then, Louise would have seen that he was anything but sure. He'd gone searching out C earlier. Just to make sure. Went back to Pat's speakeasy/brothel where he had not been since the night he'd first met Louise half a year before. He'd never been to Pat's during the day. During the day the normal three-story corner house with a storefront basement entrance gave no indication of the flesh and whiskey devoured there at night. Children played hopscotch out in the street, farther down the block a man proudly hosed down his '48 Chrysler. Joe walked around to the side street and down the three short steps and knocked on the door with two quick knocks, a pause, and two more, the code to get in. His door knocks went unanswered. The storefront window was tightly draped. He cupped his hands and peered through the square of the window at the door. Could see the card tables arranged, which meant that at least games still went on there at night. Then he saw a figure walking across the room, headed for the door. She was light and thin and his breaths quickened that it might be C. He had to admit that he might not even recognize C under the light of day. Chuckled at the thought that he'd have to stand her under darkness to know for sure it was her. This one almost to the door looked like a ragamuffin though, in two or three layers of clothes, scarf tied around her head, unmistakable pout to her stomach indicating a baby on the way.

"Nothing till ten," she shouted through the door and then closed the blinds, tightly blocking Joe's view into the room.

"Well, wait, hold up, please," Joe shouted through the door. "I'm looking for C. She still around?"

Silence then. "Hello," Joe called again. "Please just tell me whether or not she's still around."

"Long gone—"

"You know where, I mean, she working still?"

"Gone, got her a man, she married now, long gone."

He hadn't expected such news. Had imagined himself walking into that third-floor bedroom just like always, his heaviness lifting at the sight of the curves of C's back under that green silky robe, then the thrill of her in the dark. He told himself he should be happy for C that she'd escaped that life, been rescued from that life and made respectable by a husband. But he didn't feel happy. Felt a rock turning over in his stomach that he recognized as molten, craggy regret.

He walked away from the house, up the street and into the store on the corner to buy a *Tribune*. Made small talk with the old cat behind the counter. Told him he used to be a regular at Pat's Place but he'd been away for some months. "Still good action?" Joe asked.

"Naw, daddy," the old cat said as he twirled a toothpick around in his mouth. "Some crazy babe married to Pat's jailbird stepson got freed from Byberry and stabbed Pat in the chest with an ice pick. Didn't kill her, but it shook her up so much that she went back to Chicago where she's from. Pat's hos split even before the red car got there. Here tell those hos took the jewelry from 'round Pat's neck while she was bleeding on her kitchen shed floor. Nothing much goes on there at night anymore. A little card game, a little overproof liquor poured by some sweet little homely chick, some stepgrand-child to Pat. Try South Street, you want some action, daddy."

Joe stayed in the store for about an hour talking to the old cat, thought he was the age his father would have been had he lived. He told the old guy that he was a musician, that he was thinking about getting married, had even been looking at houses, had his eye on a two-story row on Cecil Street in West Philly. "Tree-lined block feels like heaven when you walk through," Joe said.

The old guy laughed and asked Joe if he was sure. "You a musi-cian, daddy? Plus, you out here looking for the likes of Pat's Place? You sure you sure?"

Joe tried to convince himself that he was sure as he focused on the china closet in Maggie's dining room where silver-framed pictures were propped behind the gleaming glass door. Even went to the china closet and opened the door and fingered the picture of Louise as a young girl snuggled under her mother's arms. He allowed his eyes to soften as he looked at the picture. Said to the pic-ture because he still couldn't look at Louise just yet, "Mnh, you asking me, am I sure? Baby, ask me anything, but don't ever ask me if I'm sure that it's you I want."

"ROUND MIDNIGHT" was easing in and out of Joe's consciousness as he sat on his living-room couch. He was moving his fingers through the air as if they were closing and opening over his saxophone. He'd always gotten a rousing ovation when he played that song. Even from C. Though when he thought about it now, never from Louise.

Chapter 14

T WAS FRIDAY morning and Cecil Street was setting up for the block party that would start tonight, culminating in the fireworks late on Saturday. Deucie was curled up under the cellar stairs, an array of Joe's and Louise's and Shay's clothes from the boxes down here spread out in a thickened mass for her deathbed. She'd found something white in one of the boxes, looked like the sort of robe someone might wear when they were baptized, so she put it on. That's the least she could do for the people who lived here who'd likely suffer through the smell of her body rotting before they had the presence of mind to investigate their own cellar. But their cellar had been a nice home the past weeks. And it sure beat the mental hospital, or jail, as a place to draw her final breath.

She'd done a brief stint at Muncy after she'd tried to kill Pat. Though the court-appointed lawyer could have gotten her off with an insanity plea given her recurrent stays at mental health facilities,

Deucie had protested. Told the judge at the arraignment that the truth of it was that she'd had every intention of killing Pat. That had been her premeditated plan, to stab Pat through the heart with the ice pick for turning her daughter out. She wasn't a liar, she insisted to the judge. Her daddy always said that a liar is worse than a thief because if you'll lie, you'll steal. She was a mother more than prepared to commit murder to right a wrong done to her child. She'd swear to it on a whole stack of Bibles, not just the one they pushed under her hand. The judge accepted her guilty plea and held her over for sentencing. Gave her a paltry sentence of one year and another four on probation. Though in her mind the only difference between jail and the crazy house was that in one the staff wore blue, in the other white. This cellar had eliminated both places as the likely site of her death and she was grateful. So she'd say thank you to these people for their hospitality by dressing herself in the robe. Thought that she wouldn't be such a frightful spectacle when she was discovered. Thought that dressed in the holy-looking white number she might look more like a fallen angel than a dead witch.

There was hammering going on outside, the sound of metal poles falling and clanging, wood being sawed. She wondered if Joe and Louise and Shay were out there helping. She'd learned their names when they talked in loud voices in certain spots in the house and their voices fell over her head. Knew that Louise was the mother and Shay was the smart-mouthed daughter and Joe was the husband who was running around. Knew he was running around because of the times of night she'd hear his heavy footsteps on the porch. And then silence in the house. Knew that silence was filled with accusations swallowed, unvented guilt. She'd ask the Big Man to turn a special eye on them when she beheld him finally face-to-

face. Had to behold him soon. It had been days since she'd eaten
solid food. Drained all of her energy just to make it back to the
spigot and get the water running so she could drink. She no longer
even considered hoisting herself up onto the windowsill to go for
the cat's bowl. Though she did squat under the window from time
to time just to have a few strokes of sunlight before she went back
to her curl under the steps to wait on death. She'd watched Louise
from her squat as Louise surveyed the cat's bowl. Saw the worry
lines come up on Louise's forehead. Thought it sweet that Louise
was worried about her diminishing appetite. Thought that Louise
could pretend all she wanted that it was the cat she was worried
about. "You ain't no dummy, Louise," Deucie had muttered to her-
self as she looked at Louise in her starched nurse's uniform calling
for the cat. "You know it's me down here you feeding. Can't admit
it to yourself that you know, but you know."

The closer Deucie got to death, the more she understood.
Believed now that people always know more than what they're will-
ing to admit. Deny to their death that they know because then
they'll have to act. Deucie understood that kind of denial because it
was much easier to not act. Had her own denial working about who
was living right next door. Whose high-yellow legs she'd see on
those steps out back. Whose screams had gotten under her skin
when the sirens were right outside. Could admit it to herself now
that she could do nothing about it. Deucie had watched Louise in
the white soft-soled shoes and white stockings walk to the same
fence that the cat was always creeping under. Had heard Louise say
the name, Alberta. Just like that. Alberta was just that close. Deucie
had let go a small gasping sound. Went to the drain to vomit. Then
back to her deathbed because she was powerless to do anything

more. Certainly didn't have the power to listen to the frightened screams her presence would surely generate. Nor did she have the power to keep them from carting her back to a hospital, heroic efforts to keep her living past her time. So she'd pretended the woman next door was just some random next-door neighbor who didn't mix in much with other people. Not her Alberta, that sweet, sweet child who'd been terror stricken when she'd seen her all those years ago and yet had kept her screams inside. The softness, the purity of that gesture filled Deucie up all over again. She would have cried right now over that gesture but she seemed to be dripping blood from every place these days, her nose, her mouth. So she didn't want to cry and see blood in her tears.

Except that this sensation of Alberta being right next door was such a big feeling. It rumbled through her now like an earthquake getting ready to happen. Suddenly Deucie was hearing her father's favorite song. Before her father was stricken with high sugar, Deucie knew when he was coming and going because he was always singing about how he said he wasn't gonna tell nobody, but he just couldn't keep it to himself, what the Lord had done for him. Suddenly Deucie couldn't keep this feeling to herself. The largeness of the feeling wouldn't allow her to lie here and die knowing that Alberta was right next door. Knowing that only a cellar window and a modest-size backyard separated her from getting one last peep at her daughter's face. She sat straight up then, forgetting her weakness, the dizziness prompted by sudden moves, the unpredictable thunderbolts of pain that owned her head these days. She clapped her hands. "Ain't this just like life," she said. "Just when you ready to turn out the lights for good, you see you got one more river to cross." She raised her hands in an optimistic hallelujah way.

She would try to get next door once quiet and darkness had fallen. She'd sneak into the house and look at her daughter while she slept. That's all she wanted to do. Look at the child one last time and whisper thank you.

JOE AND LOUISE WERE in the kitchen having an antagonistic breakfast. Joe was irritable, his neck and back stiff from having fallen asleep on the couch the night before while listening to "'Round Midnight" over and over. Hadn't even wakened when Shay came in after sitting out on the steps until eleven with Bobbi. Louise panicked at first when she woke at dawn and Joe wasn't in the bed. Tiptoed down the hall and heard him snoring downstairs. She was relieved, then sad, now angry as they sat across from each other, both having taken this Friday off, Louise because of her mouth, plus she had baking to do for the block party; Joe needed to help get the booths and stages put together. But right now Louise was quizzing Joe about the plate that she'd sent next door with the German chocolate cake when Neet had come home from the hospital. She was asking Joe how the plate had gotten back in the cabinet.

Her tongue went to all the empty spaces in her mouth as she listened to Joe stammer out a response. Louise had only noticed the plate because she was going through her dishes, ferreting out the chipped ones to box up and put down in the cellar along with the clothes she'd bagged, waiting in the back of her closet for Joe to carry down. At first she'd gotten excited when she'd seen the plate because she thought that Neet and Shay were talking again. But she'd asked Shay as Shay left the house this morning for work.

Shay's dark eyes had lowered and she'd said that no, she'd had no contact with Neet.

"I still don't understand why you went over there in the first place," Louise said to Joe through barely parted lips. The soft scrambled eggs were sticking to her gums and she tried to fleck at her gums without opening her mouth.

"I went to try and find out about Brownie's whereabouts," Joe answered, trying to swallow his agitation with the eggs that he scooped up on a crust of toast.

Louise asked him what made him think about Brownie after all of these years.

"The couch, Louise. Didn't I tell you I even told Shay the story about Neet hiding in the couch?"

"Yeah, but to go from thinking about a couch to suddenly wanting to find Brownie?"

Joe tilted his coffee cup, drained it, taking his time so that he looked at the flower pattern at the bottom of the cup as opposed to looking at Louise, especially at her gums, which were purple and pink and prominent. "I said I thought maybe Brownie could help Neet get through this thing," he said, talking into the cup.

"And you don't know anybody else who might have known where Brownie was, all the people you know in this city—"

"Louise, come on, where we going with this?" He hit his cup against the saucer. "You don't have better breakfast conversation than this?"

Louise persisted though. "All I'm saying," she continued, the tiniest quiver to her voice, "is that the woman's made her point over the years that she wants nothing to do with any of us. I tried to talk to her the other day when I was in the yard looking for Cat and she turned her back on me like she was giving me her ass to kiss." She closed her mouth again, realized by Joe's expression that she was showing her gums. She watched as Joe cut a corner of butter for his toast; he left jelly and bread crumbs all around the stick of butter. She stopped herself from remarking about how he always did that, couldn't he just use the clean butter knife that was sitting on the dish and not the one he was eating with. "What did Brownie die from anyhow?" she asked instead.

"I don't know."

"You don't know? What you mean, you don't know?"

"What did I say, Louise, I don't know. I hadn't intended on going over there. Intended on coming home until I heard Johnetta in here talking loud and saying nothing."

"Wait a minute, that particular day Johnetta was saying something. According to her some big black man with a gun in his pants pocket and a scar from his mouth to his ear was around at Sonny's asking 'bout some woman who fit the description of the one who had the Corner Boys all riled up at the last block party. The man said she'd been missing for weeks. Said when he saw her last she had on a red, black, and green tie-dyed T-shirt—"

"Louise, I know the story—"

"Well, tell me this, then," she said, still trying to talk with her mouth closed, so her words were muffled, "how you go next door to find out where Brownie is and you find out he's dead and you don't know what killed him?"

"I forgot to ask, okay? I was just so shocked I forgot to ask. And then she pissed me off so much." He bit down on the toast, and crumb shavings that looked like sawdust came out of his mouth as he talked.

"Well, I'm trying to understand what pissed you off so much."

He wanted to say he was trying to understand it too. That he'd felt as if he'd been assaulted when he'd left there. "I was pissed because I didn't know that Brownie was dead," he said, trying to put some finality to his tone.

"Joe. The man's been dead for five years."

"Well, I didn't know the man was dead and I feel as if I should have known—"

"Well, wait a minute now, she didn't owe you an explanation about her ex-husband's life or death status."

"Well, I didn't see you jumping at the chance to go over there."

"You right about that. I'm not comfortable around the woman outside her house, I'm sure not gonna compound my discomfort by going inside her house if I don't have to."

"Well, they went through a trauma, Louise, shit, and you call yourself a Christian."

"What? She try to convert you?"

"All I'm saying is that Neet went through a terrible thing and if I can do something to help her pull through it I'm gonna at least try, if for no other reason than because of my own daughter who has been devastated by this whole thing as well, and on top of that, Neet doesn't have a father—"

"But you didn't know her father was dead when you went over there."

"So."

"So all I'm asking is what were you doing going over there?"

"You know what, I'm going into work today." He shoved back from the table, dragging his chair as he stood, knowing how Louise hated to have chairs dragged across her flawless floors. "Gonna see if I can pick up some hours. If I got to be getting shit, I might as well be getting paid."

"Well, good, I should make a dentist appointment, getting teeth pulled is more enjoyable than trying to have a conversation with you."

He felt bad when she said that, knew how tormented she was over all the dental work. "Look, Louise," he said. "If we don't have to talk about Alberta, I won't go to work—"

"If you got to put conditions on what we talk about, then go the fuck to work," she said.

She huffed out of the kitchen. She went upstairs, first to the bathroom to soak her mouth. She muffled sobs at the feel of the grains of salt separating from the warm water and attaching to her gums. She grabbed one of her good display towels, the dusty rose with the brown embroidered trim that matched the bedroom. She held the towel to her mouth and cried into it so no sound would escape. Either that or tell Joe that if their marriage had come down to him sleeping on the couch, then he might as well make it official and leave, parade whoever he was running around with out in the open. There, she'd allowed herself to think it. Had been feeling it since the night he was five hours late getting home, but now was the first time she'd allowed the feeling to form a concrete thought and stream through her conscious mind. She wanted to get hysterical and tear up the bathroom in a rage. She went into her bedroom instead. Added one more thing to the bags needing to go in the cellar, the green silky robe Joe had given her last month for her birthday. She made sure it was hanging over the top of the bag as she moved that bag to the front of the closet.

NEET AND SHAY STEPPED out on the side-by-side porches at exactly the same moment this Friday morning. Neet was on her way to church, Shay to work. At first they were like people who wake the morning after someone close has died and in those first seconds of consciousness don't remember the loss; they stretch and maybe even smile if the sun is pouring in through the window shears, until the reality falls and clicks into place like a cage locking and the loss takes over the room, blocking the daylight. Neet and Shay looked at each other at first as if they were about to go to the banister and kiss on the mouth the way they'd always done. But the reality of what had happened at BB's thickened the air between them, turning it muddy, and they both stared straight ahead as they walked down their steps, the activity in the street of the booths going up a welcome distraction.

Neet's cab sat at the corner, unable to drive through Cecil Street, and she walked slowly, aware that Shay was just steps behind. She wished she could run. She could feel Shay's energy blazing up and down her back, Shay's anger and hurt trying to burn through the black taffeta dress Neet wore. But Neet couldn't run, could barely walk, the way her insides felt, loosely packed, as if what was left of her insides would slip right on out onto the ground if she separated her legs more than the inches necessary to put one foot in front of the other. She counted her steps so that she could concentrate on something other than Shay's breath that she could almost feel at her neck. Shay getting ready to say something, Neet could tell.

Neet bracing herself so that Shay's words wouldn't penetrate, she couldn't let them penetrate, couldn't allow her efforts to live devoutly to be hampered by whatever Shay was about to say.

"It's gonna be hot today, you're gonna burn up in that long black dress and that ugly little hat," Shay said, almost in Neet's ear, she was that close.

"Hell's hot too. I'd rather burn for a day than for all eternity," Neet replied without turning around to look at Shay, just focused straight ahead at the cab at the corner, raising her finger to let the cabdriver know that she was his fare.

Like lightning striking, Shay was in front of Neet now, blocking her from moving forward. Neet stopped short because she didn't have the energy to push Shay out of her face. Shay's hair was pulled back in a bushy puff, a barrette adorning each side. She'd bought Shay the barrettes at Connie's on her employees' discount. Now Johnetta was turning the corner with her morning paper under her arm. Neet looked at the ground so that she wouldn't have to take in Johnetta's expression, which was filled with pity for Neet. "Excuse me, please, Shay," Neet said to the ground.

"Why are you acting like this, Neet?" Shay said, and Neet could tell how hard Shay was working to keep from crying. "This is not you, Neet. You know this is not who you are. Look me in my face and tell me that this is who you are."

Neet couldn't look at Shay because she wasn't even sure of who she was. She just knew that at least her mother's religion held out the promise of pulling her up from where she was now. This place inside her where she'd fallen that was beyond sadness; sadness at least provoked tears, salt and water and life. But she'd fallen to a place of suffocating dust and dryness. Splintered, like the feeling she'd gotten when she'd been handled by Mr. G, though worse because it surrounded her all the time now, not just when she was called Bonita, but every waking minute. So she couldn't look at Shay because Shay couldn't help her. Shay was no wiser than she was. If Shay had been even a little wiser, Neet was thinking now, she would have come to understand how much affection Neet had had for that dot that had spread out and grown inside her; she'd loved it really; its absence had carved out a hollow deeper than Neet imagined possible. So Neet couldn't look at Shay even as Neet recognized how unfair it was to try to make it Shay's fault. That in and of itself was a sin, she thought now. Her church would never understand it since they'd been filling Neet's head with the notion that it had been her association with demons like Shay that had caused her current state of damnation, but Neet recognized that trying to make it Shay's fault was the real sin.

Shay had her hands on Neet's arms now, shaking her. Yelling at her that she was a liar for pretending that this was who she was. "You were supposed to be my girl, Neet. My motherfucking girl," Shay cried. "You promised no matter what, we'd always be girls."

Neet could feel a quiet descend over the block as the workmen stopped assembling the party's machinery to see what was going on. Neet still focused on the ground, the pavement that was a conglomeration of smooth and rough-edged stones fused together in a slab, the cracks that she and Shay would try not to step on in their little-girl rhyming game. Shay was sobbing now, her sobs filling up inside Neet's head. Now Johnetta was peeling Shay's hands from Neet's arms. She was talking in a soothing voice. "Come on, baby, let her go," Johnetta said as she pulled Shay to her chest. "You can't rush her to come around any sooner than she's gonna come around.

Neet knows how much we all love her. Come on, Shay, don't you have you a summer job you got to get to this morning? Miss Johnetta gonna walk with you to the bus stop."

Johnetta touched Neet's arm as she led Shay away. Neet still didn't look up. Waited for them to turn the corner, the sounds of Shay's sobs hung back though, followed Neet even as she walked to where her cab waited.

Chapter 15

ALBERTA WAS SITTING on her back steps. The sounds of the party preparations out front filtered into her yard and she could even hear through the opened window the electric mixer going in Louise's kitchen. She didn't usually sit out here this early in the day. Usually sat out here in the evening around the time the Corner Boys sang. But she was reversing herself today. Had been reversing herself the past few days. Had gone on the third floor of Lit Brothers yesterday instead of the basement where she usually shopped. Bought a two-piece night set that came to the knee, pink and white with a wide pink satin ribbon instead of the one-color, to-the-floor flannel she usually bought for sleeping. Allowed herself a piece of jewelry hidden under her high-collar dress though self-adornment was against the dictates of her church. Had even reversed herself and told Neet that if she didn't feel up to it, she could take the day off from church though Neet had declined the gesture and left for church first thing this morning. Alberta had been reversing herself for several days, now that she thought about it, ever since she'd allowed Joe to take up space in her living room and bring up Brownie's name.

She heard a scratching sound coming from Louise's yard and she got up and walked to the Cyclone fence. She was barefoot and the dirt yard was cool and hard under her feet. She made a whispery sound, her attempt at whistling, thinking that maybe the cat was back. She hadn't seen the cat in several days now and she missed the way he'd come and rub against her legs evenings when she sat out here and tried to make peace for the wrong she'd done. She didn't see the cat though, and went back and took a seat on the steps thinking how she really needed the cat's soft purring now because she hadn't been able to get Brownie from her mind since Joe had mentioned him. Though thoughts of Brownie drifted into her mind often enough, it was usually something having to do with Neet as a little girl that made her smile inside: the way he'd let Neet dance on his feet, or swing Neet from his arm and have her squealing, or come in every other night with a special treat for Neet hidden in his hands, behind his back. But now she was thinking about how she'd run Brownie off after all he'd done for her. He'd made her respectable after all, married her though she was pregnant. He'd given the child who wasn't his a name and treated her better than if she'd been his. And yet Alberta had forced him out after she'd taken up with her church, told him that if he couldn't join in with her, he couldn't be with her. He'd told her he was a straight-up Baptist, no way could he go to the extreme measures they advocated with their dress and their having to sever ties with everyone not part of that church body, the denying themselves of the simple pleasures of life. Alberta had said that that's who she was now, and if he couldn't be that too, he had to go. And just like that, he'd left.

Though Alberta had not planned on things turning out that way. After Pat was stabbed and spent twenty-eight days in the hospital and then fled the area for Chicago, Alberta changed the tenor of Pat's Place from a whorehouse to a speakeasy. As much as Alberta hated Deucie for being crazy, for the shame she'd felt being born to a woman who'd bite her newborn's forehead, she'd often thought how she had Deucie to thank for half killing Pat. That ice pick to Pat's chest ended Alberta's nights of being shoved and rammed, handled over and over by greedy, insistent men.

Pat's other girls took what wasn't nailed down and left, though Alberta was the only one privy to the whereabouts of Pat's cash box, which included the deed to the house, paid for in full. She added to what cash had accumulated there in the box by selling liquor on Friday and Saturday nights to the regular faithful drunks. She brought in more than enough to keep the utilities paid and otherwise maintain her modest lifestyle, plus she rented out the rooms on the second floor and was able to significantly pad the cash box so that she could quit this life altogether once she'd discovered she was pregnant. Didn't know how she'd gotten caught, was careful with all the jellies and foams Pat had given her but figured Pat had probably watered those down like she did everything else. Didn't know who the father was though she had her hopes that it was Joe. She went into a depression during the early weeks. Cried and vomited and slept and waited for Joe to show up again, sinking deeper inside herself each day that he did not. Were it not for Pops, who owned the convenience store on the corner and who stepped in and tended the bar, she probably would have closed the speakeasy. She came back to herself a little at a time. Started pouring liquor again, listening to the details of the lives of the drunks again, noting as she did who was in town playing at the Showboat or the Bijou Cafe or some neighborhood bar. Summoned all of her energy one cold Saturday morning when the sky was gray and fat with the threat of snow. She went to Eighth and Market and put a baby crib on layaway and registered with a diaper service. She splurged then on a two-piece wool suit with a foxtail collar that hung along the shoulders like a cape. She stopped in a beauty parlor that did walk-ins and the cosmetologists fought over who would do her since her hair was soft and long and a beautiful brown shade with the slightest hint of red. When she went to visit Pops after getting her hair done, he'd let go with a long whistle. Ran and snapped a few Polaroids and inscribed one on the back and gave it to Alberta because he said he'd never known she could look so good. She asked him to tend the bar for her tonight because she was stepping out, he could take his usual cut. He said as good as she looked, he'd tend her bar for free.

She went home and took a long, hot bath and lotioned herself down with a sweet, thick cream, another splurge of the day. She unrolled black stockings up her legs and put on the suit that was tight through the hips though luckily the baby hadn't really started to show. She colored her lips in with red and dabbed the same under her cheekbones to blush them. Just a touch of glittering shadow for her lids, no whore's makeup tonight, tonight she was going out as a lady. She ordered a cab for nine and got to the club right as he was beginning his set. She took a seat in the back and tried not to cry as Joe played "Sentimental Mood."

The notes he blew went all through her, just like they had the first night they'd been together and he'd tried to comfort her when she'd cried and gone into chills. She was getting filled up and flushed as she listened to him play, the notes settling deeper inside her, filling places that she hadn't known were empty. Sound into fingers touching the bruised spots, so many bruises, so many men, the feel of them erased right now by what Joe was doing with his horn.

He closed his eyes as he played and she did too, imagined that they were together in the same dark place, the way they'd been, without the benefit of light so that their other senses predominated, making him more familiar to her than if she'd studied him in the light. Though she had studied the look of him too, peeped at him when he played cards at Pat's, watched him from her window when he left and the sight of him was caught in the headlights of a passing car. So she knew his look too in ways that he didn't know hers. Not yet, she thought, as he came to the end of his song and bowed and then beamed as he looked around the club and his eyes fell on her. He nodded at her, let a barely perceptible smile tease the corner of his dark lips. She lowered her eyes, acknowledging his, and when she looked up again his eyes had moved on. She realized then that he hadn't recognized her. She sipped her ginger ale as she felt other eyes on her now coming from the front of the club. A dark-eyed woman with thick, black hair staring at her; Alberta had felt the woman's severe eyes looking her up and down when she'd first walked in. She wondered now what the woman had seen on her face as she closed her eyes and listened to Joe play. Wondered if she'd seen the desire, the desperation for Joe. Alberta sat up straighter and adjusted her foxtail collar lower on her shoulders, she'd dusted her shoulders with powder to give them just a hint of glitter. The band was on a break and milling around over by the bar.

She pulled her stomach in and stood, though at that moment she felt the baby move. First time she'd felt the baby move. She sat back down so she could pat her stomach, thinking that maybe the waistband on the skirt was too tight, maybe she should undo it so the baby could stretch out some. That's when she saw the dark-haired woman with the witch's eyes walk toward Joe as he sipped a drink at the bar. He was surrounded by three or four admirers, but he excused himself to open a path for her as she walked toward him. Alberta felt as if she was watching a collision about to happen, wanted to holler out No! No! as Joe opened his arms for the woman and took her face in his hands and kissed her, a long kiss. Alberta felt the kiss as a jolt, as if she'd just put her wet fingers to fraying live wires. The jolt moved through her and she shook sitting there even as she felt the flutters the baby was stirring up.

The electric mixer in Louise's kitchen was going full blast now. Louise had always had the conveniences, the soft touches of life. Such a lady Louise was, Alberta was thinking now as she moved down to the bottom step so that she could push her bare feet into the hard, cool, dirt floor of her yard. Of course Joe would end up with a lady, not the likes of her, who he didn't even recognize sitting up. An ass-on-the-bed bitch was all she'd been to Joe. Better that he hadn't recognized her so she didn't have to be reminded of what she truly was.

She'd stumbled out of the club. It was snowing and the whitened streets shocked the night, purified it. Alberta undid the hook on the back of the skirt so the baby could breathe. She cried then. She cried and vomited and stumbled in the high heels she was so unaccustomed to walking in. She had the appearance of a drunk with all the vomiting and staggering, her skirt hanging crookedly below her coat. If it weren't for the baby, she thought, she would have taken the men up on their offers as she walked, the snow not stopping the serious clubgoers or men on the prowl. Would have found an alley and taken them one after the other, allowed them to moan inside her and deposit their droppings like so much bird shit. That's all she was, she thought, even as the baby kicked up a storm as if in disagreement, forcing Alberta to vomit, to spit it up, spit it out, get rid of that debased image of herself.

She made it all the way to Christian Street and then she did end up in an alley. The alley was warm and close, a covered breezeway, actually, that ran along the side of a beautiful brick building. A church. Brownie's church. The church where he'd so proudly escorted Alberta Sunday after Sunday when her innocence was intact. How taken care of she'd felt sitting next to Brownie, the hymns sung with a beat that made her chest expand and she could really breathe, she'd felt so alive when she'd gone to that church.

The sun was moving to almost directly over her back steps. She dug her toes deeper into the dirt that was softer below the surface, moist. The mixer in Louise's kitchen was silent now and she could smell the butter and sugar coming together in the oven over there. It was a miracle she hadn't lost toes to frostbite that night, sleeping, or passing out, in that alley, still not sure which. When she came to, the sun was rising and the air felt fresh and new. The aroma of yeast rolls baking came to her in waves and warmed her on the inside. She slipped into the church through the side door and tiptoed past the women cooking in the kitchen. She went into the bathroom and cleaned herself up, then stood by the front entrance until she saw him, suited down like a proper man just like she'd known he'd be. Brownie. The only man outside Pops who knew her for who she was—shy, soft Alberta—because he wasn't privy to how she'd once earned her keep. Her Brownie became her Brownie anyhow after she cried in his arms, told him a concocted story of having been jilted by a sailor who'd gotten her pregnant. She wanted a real life for the baby, she said. She wanted to close the bar before the baby was born, move to somewhere else, she wanted respectability, couldn't have that as a woman without being attached to a man.

"Awl, Brownie," she said out loud as she watched a worm emerge through the holes in the dirt her toes were making. He'd been a prince the way he'd acquiesced to her every desire. After she'd quizzed Pops the day she'd closed the blinds in Joe's face when he'd appeared from out of nowhere asking for C, and Pops told her what he could remember of their conversation, "something 'bout getting married and buying a house somewhere in West Philly, Cecil Street, or somewhere," Pops had said. Alberta told Brownie she wanted to move to West Philly, heard there were nice houses for sale on Cecil Street. Convinced Brownie that they could rent his house out—though he loved it downtown, insisted that he didn't want to move from downtown. But he yielded to Alberta on that. Shortly after Neet was born, Brownie told Alberta he'd found the perfect house on a tree-lined street. Cecil Street.

She'd never expected the house to be right next door to Joe and Louise. Almost told Brownie they should move back downtown, especially when she'd be caught on the porch with Louise and she'd remember how much she'd hated her that night when she'd watched Joe kiss her so tenderly. Joe, typical man, was completely oblivious to who she was, not an inkling about who she was. Except for one night when he played his horn on the porch, played "'Round Midnight" with all the passion he'd had when he'd played for Alberta in that third-floor room of Pat's Place, and his playing moved through her on the porch just as it had back then. When he walked back up his Cecil Street steps that night leaking sweat and looking like a little boy who'd just done some wonderful thing, she'd turned to him from her darkened porch and said, "Nice, Joe. That was real nice." She used her whispery C voice and she could tell he was trying to figure out how he knew that voice. When he looked at her in the dark, she thought he was close to knowing who she was. But then Louise called him in a sharp, biting voice. And Joe never played his horn again.

The sun was in Alberta's eyes now, telling her that it was past noon. She'd thought she'd take the bus to Jersey and make a few dollars picking strawberries today. Not that she actually needed the money since she still collected rent from Pat's house downtown, and she and Brownie had paid for this house with cash. But she did need the torture of that hard work, the sun burning her skin, the stooping and standing, needed to feel whipped, punished, at the end of the day, absolved. Needed her church for that reason too, the severity of it. Though she'd loved Brownie's church, loved the promises of salvation that poured from the pulpit, the purity of the energy that would fill up the place when the Spirit hit, the goodwill that flowed from arm to arm when they greeted her with hugs, the warmth in the "God bless" they said to her over and over again; though she loved it, could have wrapped herself up in the perfect affection the church showered on her, she didn't trust it. Trusted only what she knew: that if the truth of who she was came out, that church would do like Joe and refuse to recognize her. They'd pass her by and withhold their affection, give it to a less-stained, less-handled, more respectable version of a child of God.

But her church, the one she put Brownie down in favor of, understood her need to be punished. Even the Bible they studied used only verse that shouted out the unworthiness of mankind. She needed that. Needed to be reminded that she was unworthy, always would be. Needed to know that the best she could hope for was that the next life would be brighter; the only way to know that brightness was by denying herself in this life. Needed to deny herself. Needed to suffer. But she hadn't suffered picking strawberries today. Hadn't gone to church today either. Worried now about the fact that Neet had. Neet still weak from her surgery; her forehead had even been slightly warm this morning. She thought she might go to church in a bit and bring Neet home. Just because she needed a religion that bludgeoned her daily didn't mean that Neet did too. She shocked herself now giving life to such a thought. Another reversal, she thought, and she got a woozy feeling, as if she was on a train that had suddenly changed direction, moving backward now instead of forward.

She heard movement in the yard next door. Heard Louise out there calling for the cat, sounded as if she was crying as she called for the cat. She got up from her steps then and walked to the fence, told Louise that she truly hoped the cat turned up. "I love him too," she said to the shock in Louise's eyes. She didn't wait for Louise to answer, walked back up her steps and into her house wondering what else she would do today that would reverse the idea of who she was.

Chapter 16

VENING WAS FALLING over Cecil Street and the excitement was building. The block was determined to shed its sadness tonight. Already laughter mixed with pop-up noisemakers and the sounds of the live band warming up. Gas balloons floated to the sky like the smoke from the oversize barbecue grills. Even Louise, who thought the whole notion of two block parties in one summer overkill, baked two pound cakes and half a dozen sweet potato pies and was now readying her dining-room table for the assemblages that would likely filter in. Plus her sister was coming up from downtown for the night, and she liked to show off for Maggie, knew it made her feel good, that despite Maggie's own tendency toward baseness, she'd still managed to raise her baby sister up with class. So Louise arranged her better glasses in the center of the dining-room table. Planned which trays she'd use for the cheeses and Ritz crackers, and olives and fantail shrimp. She'd given Joe a list of last-minute things she needed, like pineapple to garnish the ham she'd just decided to stick in the oven.

Joe hadn't gone into work after all. He'd gone upstairs behind Louise and listened to her sob into the towel, then went in the bedroom after her and asked why she was getting rid of the good robe he'd just given her. She said it wasn't so much the robe, just what the robe represented. He begged her then to please keep the robe. Please give him a chance to prove how much he deserved for her to keep the robe. He grabbed her and held her and said that he wouldn't let go until she agreed to keep the robe, to keep what the robe represented. Louise had let herself go in his arms. She'd tried to remain stiff and unwavering but his arms were so warm and strong and desperate that she relented and let herself go soft in his arms, let him hug her as she held on.

IN THE AFTERNOON Joe met Valadean at the Red Moon Hotel. The sunlight looked frayed pushing in through the dirty windows and he cringed at the gray-spotted patterns on the gold-colored bedspread. Suddenly he didn't want to touch anything in here. Rather than sitting in the brocaded armchair that sagged in the center, he stood, leaned slightly against the chest of drawers. Valadean was perched on the edge of the bed. Such a contrast to this room, she was dressed in white from head to toe. So clean and fresh, like a commercial for Tide or a minty mouthwash, a clean-burning fuel that put a tiger in the tank. Felt himself stirring when he thought that. Though that's not why he was here, even as he mulled over the possibility of one for the road. Especially when she walked to where he was and started pulling on him, purring into his neck.

He kissed her then, a hungry, open-mouthed kiss as he started moving against her, telling her as he did that this had to be their swan song. His feelings for her were running too deep and he had to get out now while he still had the ability to be reasonable.

She pulled herself from him. It was an abrupt move that was almost painful to Joe the way he'd gotten himself worked up moving against her.

"What?" she said, and he was surprised that she could in fact end her words without drawing them out the way she did his name.

"Come on, baby, you knew the deal," he said. "You knew I had a wife—"

She reared back on her heels and he thought, Here we go with the hysterics. He'd forgotten the red-colored drama that went with ending a fling. He watched Valadean's hands come up from her sides and he thought she was about to start pulling at her hair. But these weren't hands moving through the dingy air. These were fists. His head snapped back after the first one landed on his mouth and he felt his lips go to pulp. Before he could react there was the other fist coming at him from the left, catching him again in the mouth. "Whoa," he said, putting his hands up to cover himself, tasting blood. "Come on now, what the fuck is your problem?" he said even as he felt his mouth throbbing, ballooning. Gotdamn, he thought, this country bitch just cold-cocked the shit out of me.

Valadean snatched her clutch bag up from the bed. She told Joe that Pinochle Eddie moved better than he ever did anyhow. She walked out of the room, slamming the door as she did, leaving him alone in here with the accumulation of lies told in the dark that now sparkled in the light of day, crawling up the walls in here and making his skin itch. He waited until he was sure she was gone, then went to the bar downstairs to get ice for his busted lip and straight scotch, no chaser, for the harder hit she'd delivered to his manhood.

H E S T O P P E D A T Tim's barbershop on the way home. Tim was cutting hair and raised his eyebrows at the sight of Joe's busted lip. Joe held up his hand to deflect questions. "It's a long story, man, what's doing with the rats?"

"Exterminator coming at ten tonight," Tim said over the buzz of the electric clippers.

"Solid," Joe said. "Just need to cool my mouth down."

He went up to the apartment and iced his lips and thought about how he'd explain the swollen mouth to Louise. Got into a tussle with some young boy, he'd say. It had gotten out of hand, and before he knew it, they were duking it out. He'd laugh it off, tell her she should see what he did to the young boy.

The sun was splashing around in here and he went to the window and closed the drapes. He sat down on the heart-shaped couch next to his horn and nursed his mouth with the ice and thought about how Valadean had looked coming at him with her fists. He figured it was better for her to take her shit out on him rather than running around getting Louise involved. He was grateful now that he'd gotten out of it with only a busted lip, actually two busted lips, but a small price to pay. Thought she must have put some kung fu moves on him, she came at him so fast. He laughed at the thought. He imagined her kicking and flying through the air, whipping his ass. He laughed harder, picturing now how easily she'd be able to take Pinochle Eddie down. She'd probably go for his eyes. Could see her landing her fists one-two, blackening both of Eddie's eyes. He tossed the melting cube of ice in the ashtray and laughed harder still. He was doubled over, he laughed so hard. Laughed so hard that at first he didn't realize he'd knocked his horn off the couch until he heard the brassy sound it made as it hit the glass-topped table and then the thud as it landed on the shag carpet.

He scooped up the horn as if it was a newborn he'd just dropped on its head. He cradled it, then inspected it, drawing his fingers along the curve, touching the instrument from top to bottom. Before he could stop himself, he moved the mouthpiece to his lips. He could feel the pressure of the metal against the inside of his mouth threatening to open his lip, which had started to scab over some. He pushed a small breath through. Just a note. The note was harsh and off-key but it was still a note. A breath transformed. He was shaking as he pushed out another note, his stomach was turning in on itself and he thought he might cry. He didn't cry. He was playing nothing and everything as he went up and down the scale. His chest opened up for him then. His fingers had grown stiffer over the years, his fingertips soft. But his fingers were moving just enough to direct his breaths. He was making music. Yeah. He blew harder as he stood up and walked around the room, danced around the room to the tunes of his own making. His mouth was bleeding now but he didn't stop. Didn't acknowledge the feel of metal against his raw, open skin. Acknowledged only the feeling in his chest, felt like he was flying, he felt so free. Felt strong, more than strong, felt as if Jesus was standing there snapping his fingers to the beat, smiling, pleased. Yeah.

He played for over an hour. Guessed they could hear him down in the shop, but still he played. He was both spent and revived when he sat down holding his horn close to his chest. He packed it away in the case then. He was taking his instrument home.

SHAY WAS AROUND the corner at the bus stop waiting for her aunt Maggie. She'd hoped that she'd see Neet so that she could overtly ignore her to make up for the way she'd groveled this morning, begging Neet to come back to herself, crying. Though she consoled herself whenever she thought about it during the day by noting that Neet had cried too. She hadn't cried out the way that Shay had, but she'd cried just as hard on the inside. Shay knew Neet well enough to be able to tell when she was crying. But during the day Shay could feel her depression lifting, going outward into an anger toward Neet that was at least active. At least she wasn't just sitting, sighing, crying to herself. The anger was at least energizing, so that if nothing else, it made her move her body. She'd even cleaned her room after she'd gotten in from work. Punched her pillows to fluff them, beat her dresser and her chest of drawers with the dust rag, banged the minutest specks of dust out of the corners the way she hit the floor with the broom, even moved her furniture around, threw it around really, she had so much energy from the outward expression of her anger. Hoped that Neet was up there in her own room while she did this, hoped the furniture bumping against the wall like that was irritating the shit out of her and keeping her from praying or sleeping or whatever she did up there all day. Shay had taken a warm bath after that, settled into her immaculate and rearranged room and started to read. She'd drifted off into a sleep that was so deep and restorative that she felt mildly transformed when she woke. Even her thinking seemed clearer, more upbeat, as she stood on the corner of Walnut and waited for the bus carrying her aunt.

The bus pulled up and Shay's aunt Maggie was the first one off. She was limping as she got off and huffing, "Oh Lord, oh my Lord."

Shay ran to the curb and grabbed her aunt's oversize vinyl tote bag and her cosmetics case that looked like a miniature suitcase. "Aunt Maggie! What happened? Why you limping?" Shay asked as she slipped her free arm under her aunt's arm and kissed her cheek.

"Oh Lord, Shay, that was so sweet of you to meet your old aunt here at the bus stop, oh Lord."

She turned then and looked around her, making sure the throngs of people who'd followed her off the bus had already dispersed. She straightened her back and her steps went quicker and steadier. "You believe that shit?" she said, tugging Shay's arm so that Shay would lean her head in some. She was short, a good six inches shorter than Shay and barely making it to five feet. "I had to pretend I was a cripple so those lazy, trifling, no-raised sons of bitches would get up and offer me a damned seat. I tell you, Shay, all the civility is leaving this world, the main ones shouting black power don't even have the power of good manners, and don't let me start on those motherfucking shaggy-haired hippies. Calling out peace to each other as they got off the bus. Shit, how they gonna sit there in peace and watch a half cripple struggling up the length of the bus looking for a seat? Shit. Peace. I bet none of their peace-saying asses rode a block past the university into the real West Philly. I bet you they ain't getting caught up here after dark. Peace, my ass."

Shay threw her head back and laughed out loud. "You a mess,

Aunt Maggie. But you scared the you-know-what out of me, I thought you were really hurt."

"Yeah, feelings hurt. The bus driver actually had to pull over and look through his rearview and say, How about somebody offering this lady a seat? And then the bad part about it, the man who got up for me was almost as old as me. Pretty mouth though," she said, stretching to try to talk into Shay's ear as they waited for traffic so they could cross the street, "mouth looked like a pussy, it was so pretty."

Shay laughed again. Suddenly she wasn't even missing Neet as much.

"Any change in your girlfriend's mood?" Maggie asked, and Shay just shook her head. "'Cause I got our little nightcap in the bottom of my bag," Maggie said, not missing a beat. "I bought us our Manischewitz Concord grape, and I got a shot glass with your name on it."

Shay saw her father coming toward them, dressed all in black, and nudged her aunt to stop talking about the wine and asked her father where was he headed.

"Your mother decided to slice up a ham to put on the table to add to everything else she's in there cooking up," Joe said, his hand cupped over his mouth. "So now she needs a can of pineapple for garnish. Maggie, how you tonight, sweetheart," he said as he leaned down to peck Maggie on the cheek.

"I'm doing, I'm doing, and you looking mighty good for a son of a bitch," she said.

"Well, as long as you doing and I'm a good-looking son of a bitch, I guess I can make it through the night."

He forgot and dropped his hand and Shay said, "Dad, eeh, what happened to your mouth?"

"Long story, baby girl," he said. "But you should see the other guy."

They could hear him still laughing as he rounded the corner and Maggie said a string of how-dos as they tunneled through Cecil Street, which had already accumulated a crowd.

T HE FIRST PEOPLE were beginning to stream into the living room at Joe and Louise's and Louise and Maggie were forced to stop talking about people who lived on the block as they finished setting the dining-room table that had grown to include not only the ham with a pineapple garnish, but Maggie's macaroni and cheese that she tinted orange with food coloring so that it tasted even more like butter and cheese.

Joe was still high from having blown into his horn earlier, plus Johnny Hartman was oozing from his stereo console and he thought right then that he had a damned good life. Beautiful wife—or certainly would be beautiful again once her new teeth were ready, nice house that his wife could afford to redecorate every so often, solid, close-knit block, stable job, daughter headed for college, jazz collection that wouldn't quit, and Acoustic Research speakers to boot. He felt a surge right then. He wasn't a religious man, except when Shay was baptized or getting an award or Louise was heading up a women's day, he never went to church, but right then he felt, what? He had to admit it, he felt blessed. He clapped his hands together. "Yeah!" he shouted. "Where's my wife? Louise, they're playing our song, dolling, so come on in here and melt into my ever-loving arms because I loves you, baby."

"Listen to Joe, he's such a mess," rippled throughout the living room and dining room. Even Louise said it in the kitchen. But Maggie untied the apron from around Louise's waist. Told her she better take her fine ass in there and dance with her husband before one of those other bitches in there did. "Go," she said as she pushed Louise out of the kitchen. "And shake your hips when you walk through."

Johnny Hartman was singing "You are too beautiful and I am a fool for beauty" as Louise and Joe swayed together. He cupped her hand in his and held it close to his cheek, and with his swollen mouth looked as if he was about to cry. Now Maggie wasn't even watching Joe and Louise as she leaned against the archway, her arms folded in a tight clasp across her chest. She was watching the perimeter instead. Looking for a woman whose eyes were tight with envy, whose smiling face was cracking around the edges. Because she'd had two husbands and two who had come close to being husbands, meaning they hadn't quite made it to the requisite seven years to be considered common law. And she knew that when a man started publicly proclaiming his love like that after all these years he was either drunk or trying to convince himself right along with everybody else.

Joe's heart was racing now. He held Louise as close as he could, praying that if he squeezed her hard enough and long enough his heartbeat would settle down. He proclaimed his love for Louise all in her ear, telling her how he loved her so much that it hurt, Jesus Christ, I love you, baby, he whispered, hoping his love for her would be enough because the high he'd felt playing his horn was boomeranging on him now, the way that any high would, leaving you lower than you would have been had you not been lifted up in the first place. He felt a sinking inside now. He held Louise closer still even as he felt himself being pried away.

T HE PARTY AT Louise and Joe's had grown to wall-to-wall and after that first slow dance with Louise, Joe forced himself to be happy as he cha-chaed and boogalooed and did every step from the twist to the funky Broadway. His face ached from laughing so hard and a warm tightness was starting to spread across his back and he half seriously wondered if he was having a heart attack. Still, he clapped and did the bop when he moved toward the door because suddenly he realized that the tightness across his back wasn't coming from inside him, it was in the house, the air inside his house had gotten so close, so claustrophobic. He stepped out onto the porch and inhaled deeply.

Joe took in the scene from his porch. Nearly two hundred people curved through his block right now; they looked sinewy and connected, like those mammoth caterpillars in African dances, dozens of feet moving under vibrantly colored cloth as they went back and forth across the street and in between concession stands and rides and makeshift circular stages. He enjoyed all of this collected motion and energy. The infectious laughter of the children spinning in circles on the cup-and-saucer ride made him throw his head back and laugh too. Yeah, Cecil Street needed this block party to get back to itself, he thought, something happened in the air when they all got together like this. He was thinking now how it had been a block-party night last month when he'd lifted his horn from the basement, took another block party to actually make him play. People like

Johnetta who noticed such things swore that a new crop of babies turned up every year nine months after the block party. She maintained that old couples broke up that weekend, new ones got together, churches were more filled than usual on the Sunday after because something in the air changed people, made them put down ways, or pick up ways, made them turn around and reverse course, pedal uphill if they'd been having it easy, or coast on down and rest if the road had been rough. Johnetta said—and Joe was inclined to agree, though he was generally not so inclined when it came to what Johnetta said—that it was their coming together for a good purpose that unleashed that spirit of change. The hashing out and in the hashing out getting involved in each other's lives at a new, deeper level; the touching and agreeing over the same plans, the excitement that built up from the pavements scrubbed extra clean for the event, the cooking and the hammering and the building up. Joe guessed that's really what it was, they rebuilt their community every summer around block-party time, rebuilt parts of themselves as they did so.

He leaned against the banister and allowed the air to deal with the droplets of sweat that had formed on his forehead. Picked out of the continuous stream of motion what appeared to be a pair of drunks staggering right for his steps. He was about to say something like sorry, private party until he realized that they weren't headed for his steps, they were headed next door and it was in fact Alberta and Neet.

Neet was leaned so completely on her mother that it was making it difficult for Alberta to walk straight and almost impossible for her to maneuver the steps. Joe hopped over the banister, took the eight steps in two skips, and lifted Neet and carried her onto the porch, the whole time asking, "Is she all right, she's shivering so, Alberta, is everything all right?"

"I'm okay," Neet said. "Really, Mr. Joe, I'm okay."

"How can everything be all right when the cab couldn't even get any closer than the corner thanks to all that foolishness in the middle of the street," Alberta said as she lifted her key from her purse. "Suppose there was a real emergency and a person needed an ambulance."

"Ambulances, cops, fire rescue got license to ride on through up the sidewalk. That party going on down there wouldn't hardly hamper real help getting through," Joe said as he held on to Neet despite her protests that she could stand up, really she could, she insisted.

Alberta had the door open and Joe carried Neet inside, on through the vestibule, and Alberta said that if it wasn't too much to ask, he might as well take her all the way upstairs. She ran ahead of them and had an outstretched blanket waiting for Neet. She covered her while she was still in Joe's arms and then he eased Neet down onto the bed. Alberta was fussing over her, feeling her forehead, going to the top of the closet to get another blanket, asking her what did she want, did she want soup, tea, really, she should have something cold for chills because that would jump-start her body's thermometer, and Joe stood there feeling awkward in this teenager's room, average-looking room, could have been Shay's room.

He cleared his throat and Neet said that she just wanted to sleep. That's all she wanted right now, to fall into a long, deep sleep. Her eyes were puffy and her nose was red and Joe could see that she'd been doing some heavy-duty crying, but at least her shivering seemed to have stopped. "Neet, sweetheart," he said, measuring his words because his previous attempts at talking to Neet had been such disasters. "Anything I can do, anything at all, Mr. Joe is right next door, you remember that, okay?"

She nodded weakly and as he turned to leave, she called behind him, "Could you tell Shay please that she was right about what she said this morning. Could you tell her please that she's still my girl," her voice cracked as she spoke. "Tell her I still love her, no matter what."

Joe had to swallow what felt like a choke hold coming up his own throat when Neet said that. "She feels the same way 'bout you, Neet. In fact, why don't I go get her, right now. She'd want more than anything to hear that."

Neet said that she was really tired, exhausted. She would talk to Shay tomorrow. Alberta told her to rest then. "I'll make you some tea and set it on your nightstand and every time you wake up, I want you to sip it. You need fluids, Neet." She felt Neet's forehead again and asked her if she was warm enough and Neet nodded, already half asleep.

Alberta turned to Joe. "I'll see you out," she said as she motioned Joe toward the door, and her voice sounded as small and as weak as Neet's. When Joe looked in her face, he could see that she had been crying too.

Alberta dropped her hand and stood there and showed her eyes, knew how they must look by Joe's expression, as if he were in here because someone had just died. She didn't even lower her eyes. What was the sense in trying to hide it? She had been crying. Cried over everything during that cab ride home after she'd followed her mind and gone to the church to bring Neet back. Ended almost in a fight with the Saints, who'd said that they were too close, on the verge really of expelling that devil that had such a hold on Neet. They said Alberta should go, let them have their way, let them break down Neet's resistance, Neet was too strong willed, they said. But Alberta wouldn't leave. She remembered her own confessional session years ago when she'd been hit and punched and slapped in an effort to drive the devil away. Beaten, beaten down as they chanted and prayed until they were satisfied that her will was no longer her own. Then the Reverend Mister, who'd otherwise not taken part, came into the candlelit room. He'd nursed Alberta's bruises and soothed her cries and held cool compresses to her head. He'd kissed one cheek, then the other, and owned her will after that. Even convinced her to put Brownie down. But she'd deserved it, she reasoned, after all, she'd been a whore in her life. She had the memory of countless nameless men to expunge. Neet was so much better than she'd ever been. Neet was honest and sweet and loved. She rose up against the Saints then. Told them no, no, she was taking her daughter home. Reverend Mister came in as they fought over Neet. Raised his finger and said to let Neet go. They held no one there against their will. And Alberta had run from the church, dragging Neet as she did, not turning around, afraid that if she looked at the Reverend Mister's beautiful face, she'd be under his power again.

So she'd cried over leaving the church like that, afraid of where her life would go without the confines of that church directing her path. She'd cried over what Neet had said to her on the cab ride home, how Neet had sobbed that she was a good girl, "I'm a good girl, Mommy," she'd said over and over. "I am, I am." It had never been her intention to be bad, to disappoint her, the only reason she'd lain with Little Freddie was because of how he'd given her back her name. She'd then told Alberta how she'd lost her name to Mr. G those Friday nights during revival when she was just eight. Alberta swallowed her horrified gasps. She'd held Neet then, she'd rocked her and shushed her as she felt her own heart tearing at what Neet told her.

"You are good, Neet," Alberta said. "It was my mistake, not yours, letting that monster, that devil, take you by the hand. That was my failing, Lord Jesus, not yours, never yours. You're so good. You're what's good in my life. The good in my life is you. Dear, dear Lord, sweet Jesus, what have I done to my child? It's gonna be all right. Mommy's gonna make it better. Let Mommy say your name. Bonita. Bonita. Bonita. My good, good child, Bonita. Mommy's sorry, Bonita. Bonita. So good you are, Bonita." Then Alberta couldn't talk anymore because she was crying too hard, even as Neet stopped crying and nestled against her mother's chest, sighing sweetly each time her mother said her name.

So Alberta didn't try to hide her face from Joe, the evidence of her tears. She'd cried over Neet's scarred womb, realizing now that the scars from the abortion were minimal compared with how she'd been scarred when she was just a little girl. She'd missed Brownie all over again as she cried. Then she'd cried over the sadness in her mother Deucie's eyes when she'd come into that third-floor bedroom at Pat's Place and Alberta had known immediately that it was Deucie by pictures she'd seen, plus they looked just alike. She'd put her spit-tinged fingers to Alberta's forehead all those years ago and told Alberta, "You mine, you 'member that too. You the only perfect thing I ever made. And you mine." She cried over the softness, the purity of her mother's touch, realizing for the first time that day that her mother wasn't a wild animal as Pat had maintained. Her mother was a person, a real woman with sad eyes blaming herself no doubt for her daughter's outcome, the way she faulted herself for Neet's. Felt a kinship with Deucie during that cab ride home. A closeness, and she even missed her too. Sorry now that she'd not tried to hunt her down. Alberta cried as if she was a baby all over again on a Monday at Pat's when Pat slept all day and there was no one to answer the baby Alberta's cries. She was tired of crying. Tired period. Guessed that's why she just stood there and let Joe look in her cried-out face, too tired to even try to hide it.

"Alberta, uh, forgive me please if I'm overstepping as I sometimes have the tendency to do, but if you feel like Neet may need to see a doctor later on, please let me know. I'll be happy to—you know, or Louise even, if I'm not around, we really care about what happens to Neet, we really do. And you, we care about you."

Alberta said thank you, said she thought Neet might be coming down with a flu. Prayed it was nothing more serious than that. They had moved out into the narrow hallway that was dark and close and Joe was struck by the sight of Alberta's face, the outline of it in the near darkness.

She started down the steps ahead of him, had to, otherwise she might have pulled him to her.

Joe could hear music as he followed Alberta down the stairs. The music was so clear, so unfiltered that at first he thought Alberta had a stereo going in her living room. He said so as they reached the bottom and stood in the living room.

Alberta felt suddenly better down here facing Joe under the lights. Felt her chest open up. "Now you ought to know better than that, you know I don't listen to that devil music," Alberta said, "unless you count the past sixteen or so years where I've had to listen to yours by default."

"Well, you been listening to some good music," Joe said as he smoothed his black T-shirt and his black pleated dress slacks. "Not all of it's devil music either, as you call it. I got some soul-stirring pieces over there, may not mention the Lord by name but some of my music lifts up His name just the same. What you talking, even the father of gospel music, Tom Dorsey, played the blues." He patted his T-shirt pocket to make sure his cigarettes hadn't fallen out. "I mean, I apologize for the volume—"

"And for the way that bass has my floors shaking," she said.

"Come on, Alberta, you exaggerating, my stereo don't hardly make your floors shake."

"Stand right there by the coffee table."

He did, then he smirked, acknowledging that the floor was in fact shaking. "But that's only 'cause they're over there dancing, you know, a little gathering in honor of the block party—"

She raised her finger, telling him to be quiet. "You hear that, now that's one of the few tunes coming from over there that I do like," she said.

He focused his ear toward the living-room wall, then slapped his leg excitedly. " ' 'Round Midnight.' That's a classic."

"I know what it is," Alberta said as if she'd just been insulted. "Didn't you used to play that on your saxophone? I mean, back when you used to play."

"Wow, you got quite a memory there, Miss Lady," Joe said as his eyes lit up. "That's been years and years."

"Well, I guess it was memorable, then," she said. " 'Cause it was sure nuff loud."

Joe smiled, let his smile take its time forming. "Talk about giving a brother a compliment and then snatching it right back," he said. Now he laughed. "It was sure nuff loud," he said, mocking Alberta. "I just knew you were about to say, 'Joe, you sure could do something mean on that saxophone.'" He looked behind him, at the couch. Wanted to sit. Felt relaxed in here with Alberta right now, the music from next door, the party sounds out in the street, felt removed from the night's happening but still a participant. Plus, there was something about the way Alberta looked standing here, eyes red and swollen but something about the eyes that he thought he needed to figure out. "You mind if I sit?" he asked, taking it upon himself, not waiting to be asked.

"Don't you have a party in your house you need to be at?"

"Party's gonna be spilling out into the street any minute now. That's where the real party is. Just a little impromptu gathering in my house."

Alberta told him to suit himself. Said she was making tea for Neet, he was welcome to a cup, or she could pour him a glass of tap water. Or bring an ice cube for him to hold to his mouth. "Somebody punch you in the mouth, Joe?" she said as she walked into the kitchen without waiting for his reply.

JOE STAYED OVER there for more than an hour. He wasn't even surprised by how easily conversation had flowed from both of them. He had been surprised by how much Alberta knew about worldly music though, especially when she pointed out that that was Joe Williams singing "My Foolish Heart." When he asked her how did she know so much, she told him she'd been raised in a

house that was more worldly than churched. He said he couldn't
even picture that. And she said she knew that he couldn't.

But if her musical knowledge surprised him, he was even more
amazed by how insightful she was when their conversation turned
to people on the block. He even tried to hide his embarrassment
when she mentioned that of all the nieces and cousins and what-
evers who had stayed with Johnetta over the years, that one there
now had the hottest nature she'd ever seen.

"Darn, what you do, Alberta, spend all of your time at your
living-room window casing the block? You might have Johnetta
beat."

"I just see and hear things when I walk through, that's all. Block
gets so quiet whenever I walk through that I can pick up the raw-
ness really of what's just been said, it just hangs over my head when
I walk through."

Joe wanted to apologize then for the way the people on Cecil
Street had ostracized her over the years. Almost formed his mouth
to say how sorry he was that she'd had to endure the rawness in
their words when she walked through. But the music stopped next
door. The party was already spilling out into the street and Joe said
that he should go.

Joe found Louise laughing with Maggie down at the corner
where the live band was doing its thing. A James Brown imper-
sonator had them hollering to "Say It Loud, I'm Black and I'm
Proud." Louise and Maggie were laughing with two men Joe
didn't know, but who Maggie obviously did. Louise's mouth was
wide open and Joe could see all the empty spaces in the back of
her mouth and even a couple missing from the sides. He kissed
Louise on the cheek and asked if she'd seen Shay. He was anxious

to tell Shay what Neet had said about loving her still. Wanted to tell Shay before he even told Louise. Louise said that Shay was out here somewhere with Nathina's Bobbi. He backed out of the crowd that had formed around the band. He winked at Louise and mouthed out that he would be back. He went to the corner and was disturbed to see mounted cops. White cops. Now he wanted to find Tim or Eddie to find out what was up with the mounted police.

J OE WALKED UP and down the length of the block. He finally found Eddie, who told him he'd been promised that the police presence would be discreet. Said it got worse around on Spruce Street where they were lined up in riot gear. He'd put in a call to that honky-ass ward leader, he said, who'd told him he was sure it had nothing to do with anything on the block. Joe felt his stomach tightening as he listened. Sometimes shrimp did that to him and he'd had a half dozen before Louise had even set them out on the dining-room table. Eddie asked him then who'd punched him in the kisser. "Fuck you, man," Joe said, forcing a laugh, and then walked to the other end of the block.

All of West Philly seemed crammed down here now in anticipation of the drill team and the climactic fireworks. He elbowed his way back to Louise and Maggie, joined now by Nathina and Joyce. They were bobbing to the rhythm of the excitement building. Joe felt as if the shrimp, or whatever he'd eaten, needed to come out, didn't know at this point from which end, but he knew for sure the food was on the way out. He told Louise he was going to take an Alka-Seltzer and he'd be back in a few. Maggie told him to take his time, nothing wrong with him that a good shit wouldn't take care of since he was so full of it. Even Louise laughed when she said that. He made a checkmark in the air and told Maggie he'd give her a point for that one, that one had been pretty good, he said as he walked toward his house, glad to see Shay sitting on the steps. He hadn't seen her since he'd seen Neet, so he hadn't been able to deliver the message from her. She looked so sad sitting there too. Sad and lonely. Broke his heart to see her sitting there like that. That's when he saw another figure beating him to the steps. His young blood, Wallace. Wallace was at his steps now, leaning in, handing Shay what looked like a cherry-water ice. Joe hung back and watched the scene playing out on the steps, Wallace smiling, bowing, then Shay blushing, moving over some to give him space to sit next to her on the steps. He crossed the street then, where the rides and concession stands would block their view of him. Figured Shay could use a new friend tonight.

He felt himself about to vomit and walked around to the alley. He did vomit then, right in the alley in the back of his house. He was embarrassed, hoped no one had seen him. He went into his yard and unrolled the hose to wash down the alley. Turned on the spigot right above the cellar window. Never even looked down to notice that the cellar window was open, Deucie crouching on the sill because she was too weak to jump down when Joe had come into the yard. He looked up instead, at Alberta's kitchen window. Her kitchen was dark and he imagined her face surrounded by darkness. He turned the water off and went back around the front.

Shay and Wallace had left the steps, he could see them headed to the same corner where the entire city seemed to be right now. He went into the house. The house was in disarray. He pushed corks back into wine bottles and recapped his blended scotch whiskeys and put the orange juice back into the fridge. He emptied the ice bucket of water and took the spoon out of the potato salad and even went through and picked up pieces of crackers and nuts that had fallen onto Louise's flawless floors. She must have been tasting big time to leave the dining room like this, he thought as he poured himself some ginger ale, then went into the living room and sat down. The lid to his stereo console was up and the power was still on and he went to turn it off, close the lid. He sat on the couch and rubbed his stomach. The quiet in here right now was disconcerting so he shuffled through his albums for something to listen to just until he could take the edge off whatever was going on with his stomach. He found it without even having to look. " 'Round Midnight." Alberta had remembered he used to play that. He put the album on, but before the needle could lift all the way he clicked the stereo off. He went to the closet instead. Pulled out his horn and played it. Stood right by the wall that separated his house from Alberta's and played " 'Round Midnight" with everything he had. Played through the upset stomach and the swollen mouth. His lip opened and started to bleed and still he played. He erased time as he played, played through the years as he allowed himself to see Alberta minus the hairnet or the holy cap, her hair out and loose; her pouty mouth covered in red lipstick; her holy dress exchanged for a green silky robe. That was her. C. Right next door. He played through the recognition. How he'd been seeing her most days, and then unseeing her, knew who she was but didn't allow the knowledge to sift through to his conscious mind. Felt her softness night after night over there on that darkened porch, her sadness, but covering himself so that what he felt didn't even penetrate beneath his skin. His mouth was expanding in excruciating circles of pain, he deserved this pain, he told himself as he continued to play. When he stopped he set his horn on the high-backed corner chair. He picked up a napkin from the stack fanned out on the coffee table and pressed it to his lips. He walked out onto the porch and closed the front door behind him.

He swung one leg, then the other over that banister separating his porch from Alberta's. Quick as a shadow of air. He situated himself inside the darkness of Alberta's porch. Despite the glitter and the blasts of light from the street below, the space of her porch that would have been illuminated if she'd been a cooperative neighbor and turned on the outside light was instead a welcome patch of blackness. How nicely his black T-shirt and black gabardine pleated dress slacks meshed with the blackness of her porch as he mashed her doorbell and held on as if he had every right to lay on it like that. He swallowed his breath as a half-drunk couple laughed themselves silly as they passed on the street below. They never even looked up in his direction and he focused himself again at Alberta's door and watched it now as it seemed to inch open in slow motion. "Alberta," he whispered when her face appeared from behind the door, and she stared up at him with those eyes. And he could see now that they were remarkable eyes, soft brown with a shyness about them. Knew now why he'd been so affected when she'd look at him and he interpreted her look as disdain. It hadn't been disdain. It was desire, affection, love? It was a reflection of his own muddle of feelings, his own love and desire and guilt and regret that had stared back at him and shook him so, no wonder he'd feel so wrangled after looking in her eyes.

"Alberta, can I come in? Please. Please, Alberta. Please let me in."

ALBERTA OPENED THE door all the way. Already knew that it would be Joe mashing her doorbell like that. Especially when she'd listened to him playing his horn. She'd felt herself going loose and weak-kneed when the first notes had filtered through the wall. By the time he'd played it through once, she'd gone up to her bathroom and run water in the tub. She stepped out of her holy clothes and left them in a pile in the middle of the bathroom floor and immersed herself in the steamy water and stretched out in the tub and lay there and enjoyed the heat of the water playing against her back and her thighs and her chest. She soaped down with slow strokes and concentrated on the feel of the slick hardness of the soap bar against her skin. When she got out of the tub, she stood on top of the mound that was her holy clothes. She allowed the thirsty clothes to sop up the water running off her nakedness. She rubbed herself down with mineral oil, then walked into her bedroom and looked at herself in the mirror with a detached eye. She lifted the hairnet from her head and ran her fingers through her hair that had curled up from the bathroom steam. She shook her hair out and then brushed it and allowed it to just fall around her face in tousled wisps. She smoothed her eyebrows down and coated her lips with petroleum jelly and pinched her cheeks to redden them some. She went to the drawer where she'd folded her new night set with the fat pink sash. She was usually so cold at night, even in the summer she slept in flannel, but it was warm in here now because she'd turned the heat on to protect Neet from a recurrence of chills. She decided on just the robe. Hurried it on and secured it with the ribbon tie. She went into the hallway and cocked her ear for Neet's room and heard her deep, rhythmic, sleeping breaths. She walked barefoot down the steps. The notes had stopped vibrating through the wall and the house was absolutely still save for the rotating fan on the table. Until the doorbell rang. Felt as if the ground underneath her house shifted when the doorbell rang. She held on to the walls as she went through the black-and-white-tiled vestibule. Had to hold on to the walls because she was dizzy from the sudden tilting happening in the vestibule. Except that the room was still, quiet, the blurring of the stark black-and-white tiles to a muted gray wasn't from the room spinning but from her perspective shifting, inverting itself. She balanced herself against one wall and reached for the doorknob, realizing as she did that she'd had it all wrong, her beliefs, her foundation, all that she'd based her actions on, her lifestyle upon. It had been inside out, wrong side in, seams showing, linings exposed. And she knew once she opened that door that things would never be the same again.

Chapter 17

IT WAS WARM in here since the windows were closed tight and the heat had been turned on. The small rotating fan on top of the end table made a buzzing sound as it rotated from Joe to Alberta as if it had a bet on who would make the first move. The cup-and-saucer ride spinning in front of this house cast, against the ceiling, intermittent spools of light that seemed to move to the whir and click of the fan blades. The table lamp was steady though, with a soft, yellow glow, and Alberta focused on that because she was feeling dizzy from all the circular motion and the warmth as she sat on the edge of the chair by the window and waited for Joe to say something.

But Joe wasn't saying anything, he was just standing by the vestibule door with his hand still on the knob, asking himself what he'd just done. What was he going to do now, because after his bold move of laying on Alberta's doorbell like he owned it, he really didn't have any other moves planned. He felt like wood right now, so unlike him to feel this self-conscious, and he was ready to claim what small piece of him that didn't look like a fool and head right back out the door.

"Joe." She said his name as a complete sentence when she saw him turn to leave. His name was the subject and the verb right then and her voice shook. But Joe still wasn't talking as he turned back around to face her, he was just standing there in the half glow of the table lamp, so she said her sentence again, phrased it as a question so that he wouldn't leave. "Joe?"

All he could muster up right then in response was a comment about her appearance. "You look very nice, Alberta, I mean, with your hair out and all, very nice," he said, and Alberta could see his eyes go larger from across the room.

"Take a seat," she said, and her voice didn't even feel like her own rising up through her throat. Joe did and wished at that moment that he'd left some music playing next door, something to fill the stretch of space between the chair by the window where Alberta sat and the couch where he did. She was even hard to look at, sitting there. Short robe that barely covered her knees, slender legs leading down to bare feet, hair out of that cage she usually locked it in, all fluffy now, lips shining, pouty lips, the only part of her he'd been able to see back then in that darkened room at Pat's was her lips. He remembered now how he'd trace them with his fingers, telling her what a beautiful mouth she had. He started to remind her that he used to do that, but he wasn't sure how she'd take to being reminded about that life. He himself hardly wanted to recall that life of hers that extended beyond him. And it had extended beyond him. Hated to think about all the men she'd probably had; base, drunken dogs most of them. Though she looked so far removed from that life sitting there now. So small, frail even. So inexperienced. She looked exposed right now, sitting there, and he felt as though he'd just opened her bathroom door by accident and caught her naked. So out of respect he tried not to look at her, even as he was drawn to look at her and ended up then looking at her pretty bare feet.

"I honestly don't know what to say, Alberta," he began in a dry, cracking voice. He reached into his T-shirt pocket and pulled out his smokes. "Guess I can't do this in here?" he asked.

"I don't own any ashtrays," she said as she shifted in the chair, and her thighs felt so soft rubbing against each other from the way she'd lavished on the mineral oil.

He let the pack of cigarettes fall on the coffee table and cleared his throat. "My apologies, Alberta. I mean, I swear to you I really can't explain it, you know, why I never realized, but then you never said, I mean, who would think, I mean, right next door. You knew? I mean, all this time, I mean years and years? Did you remember me? It's just that one minute I'm playing my horn and the next minute I'm seeing what I couldn't see, the past, what, seventeen years?"

"And?" she said, wanting him to go on while the oil was still slick along the surface of her skin before she reverted back to what she'd been for the past years, a hate-filled woman in a holy dress.

Joe was still grappling with his words, trying to make her understand how he felt, once he could understand it. Just knew that he was sitting in her half-dark house getting all worked up over the sight of her now with her hair out and her bare legs. He meant no disrespect, he was saying right now, when he hadn't come back like he'd promised the night that Cheeks was stabbed.

She was thinking, as he talked, that nor did she mean him any. That she knew he had a wife who he loved, knew it was wrong of her to entice him the way she was doing right now, but she wanted to turn her life around, she told herself now. Because she was like a car that was trying to come out of a skid and that had to veer in the other direction to right itself. And that's all she was doing right now, she told herself, she was just going to the other extreme for a minute while she got back on course. That's all.

"I mean you no disrespect either, Joe," she said as she stood and watched Joe walk toward her, watched his strong, dark hands lightly caress the pink satin ribbon that held her thin robe in place. "As God is my witness, I mean you no disrespect." She was half crying now as she said that she just needed to be held tonight, that's all. Because she'd been through a lot and she was tired and lonely and sad.

"Oh God, Alberta. Come 'ere. Let me hold you. Let me. Everything's gonna be okay in the long run," he whispered. "You right too, 'cause you do need some comforting. I always could comfort you too, couldn't I, Alberta. Damn." He ran his thumbs along the perimeter of her hairline, from her forehead to her cheekbones. "It's such a sin the way you kept all your prettiness all caged up like you were ashamed of it. Don't you believe the Lord wouldn't have made you so beautiful if he didn't want to show you off? Huh?" He smoothed his fingers through her hair. "You pretty as an angel, you know that." His swollen lips touched the skin on her forehead right where her mother had marked her. He pulled his lips from her forehead and let them slide down the bridge of her nose. "If I don't hear you say for me to stop," he whispered, "I'm just gonna assume that you don't want me to stop. Huh, Alberta, 'cause Lord knows I don't want to stop, and soon I won't be able to anyhow. Lord. Alberta. It's on you, now. Damn. I know you must miss the feel of a man's arms holding you closelike, tenderly. Don't you? Let me. Please, Alberta, let me." He had all of her in the circle of his arms. She was a small woman, slight shoulders, thin arms, her arms hung loosely at her sides. He wanted her to lift her arms, to hold him. Told himself that he wouldn't go any further if she didn't hold him too. She was too vulnerable right now, so as hard as it would be for him, if she didn't give him some kind of signal besides standing here with her passivity intact, he'd just peel himself away.

She lifted her arms and hung them around his neck. How natural it felt, as if she'd hung her arms around his neck every night for the past seventeen years. His mouth was at hers now as their breaths got all tangled up and they could no longer tell which heart was thumping in which chest, whose sobs were whose. He undid the pink satiny ribbon holding the robe together and pulled it through the loops and let it fall to the floor. He slid his hands under the robe and almost gasped at the feel of her skin that was giving off an oily steam. He thought he might explode right there against her in the middle of her living room and there was nothing he could do about it until he felt her pulling him, nudging him, and when he became aware of his surroundings, they were all the way through the house, at the basement door. He scooped her up and carried her down. And the darkness down there was so movable, so loud, that they didn't even hear the fireworks going off outside. And Alberta thought that it was like cotton down there with Joe. So loose. So free. Finally, free.

Chapter 18

EET SAT STRAIGHT up when she heard the boom boom boom of the fireworks outside. She was groggy, as if she'd had too much sleep, or too little, she wasn't sure which. She was sure that it was hot in here. She swung her legs over the side of the bed and listened for her mother. Her radiator hissed and she remembered her mother telling her that she was going to start up the heater so that Neet wouldn't have a recurrence of those god-awful chills. She sipped from the tea on her nightstand and tried to determine whether she was really awake or if this was an extended dream where you woke up and were still dreaming. Had she really cursed at them at the church earlier, she wondered as she started to unpeel the blankets from around her. By the time she pushed the third blanket away and propped herself up in the bed and fingered the blanket's satiny border, she knew that that fiasco at the church had been real enough.

She dabbed at her eyes with the border of her blanket as she felt a new crop of tears boiling up in her eyes, burning her eyes because she'd cried so much the past few days. Didn't think it was possible to cry so much. She remembered now how she'd shaken uncontrollably in the cab when she'd told her mother about Mr. G. Her mother had taken her sweater off and wrapped it around Neet and asked the driver to turn on the heat please because her baby had caught a chill. Then she'd listened to Neet as she held her like she was a baby. She'd rocked her all the way home and said her name, Bonita, Bonita, she'd whispered all the way home. The sound of her name oozing through her mother's lips was like a balm to Neet, smoothing over the places where she'd been damaged, stripped raw, softening the roughness, erasing the pain, healing; healing all the way from deep inside back to the surface of her skin. It had felt to Neet as if her mother's singular voice had been joined by a choir of angels telling Neet that she was good. She was. Except that the real beauty of it had been that it was just her mother's voice, nothing like it in the world, she'd thought then, such a simple, precious thing, your own mother's voice soothing you as you cry. Neet had been so filled up in that instant, so grateful that she hadn't given up on her mother, she still filled up at the thought. So she cried and blew her nose and felt as if a wicked spell that had been cast over her had been broken.

She finished the tea that had been patient on her nightstand. Now she wanted to talk to Shay, was burning to talk to Shay. She stuffed a pair of jeans over her pajamas and threw a sweater over her shoulders and slid her penny loafers onto her bare feet. She stopped in the bathroom and was perplexed by the sight of her mother's clothes in the middle of the bathroom floor. Her mother wasn't in her bedroom and Neet started down the stairs and heard the back door closing as she did. Guessed that her mother had gone to sit out in the yard. She would go sit with her, she thought, once she found Shay. She was halfway through the living room, headed for the front door, when she saw a pack of cigarettes on the coffee table. She picked it up and turned the pack around in her hands. She remembered then that Mr. Joe had helped her mother get her into the house when they'd gotten back from church and Neet was so exhausted that she could barely walk. She told herself she'd thank him by returning his smokes. She put the cigarettes in the lapel pocket of her pajama top and was about to head for the vestibule door when she saw it. A pink satiny ribbon curved along the living-room floor. This she picked up too and fingered and now she reversed her steps and headed for the back door instead of the front, now she wanted to find her mother and ask her about this most unlikely find on the living-room floor, a pink satiny ribbon that looked like a sash.

She walked through the darkness of the dining room into the yellow-lit kitchen and on through to the back. The back door was unlocked and the black wrought-iron gate was ajar but Alberta wasn't out here. Alberta often came out here and sat on the back steps at night, but she never used the yard and the alley as an entrance or exit the way that Neet did when she was trying to sneak in and out. She jumped at a sound in Shay's yard, a scratching and a weak cry. She looked in the direction of the Cyclone fence that separated the yards and saw a patch of white against the ground and told herself to get a grip, it could only be the cat. She walked on through the gate and out into the alley. A shallow column of chilly air moved through the alley and she folded the ribbon accordion style and put it in the pocket with Joe's cigarettes and pushed her arms through the sweater sleeves and pulled the sweater close around her. Remnants of barbecue smoke drifted in and out of view and Neet had to push back stems of ivy that dangled from the Cyclone fence and protruded into the narrow walkway. She was thinking about that pink ribbon that felt like lead in her pajama pocket.

The block party had thinned out considerably when Neet turned onto Cecil Street, at least this end of the block had. Storms of people were crowded at the other end though, and Neet could see the last of the fireworks draining through the sky. Neet tried to see down there to locate Shay. She was so out of breath from that short trek through the alley and her heart was beating so fast and so loudly that she could feel it in her ears. She realized she could never make it down to the other end with her stamina so diminished from this flu or whatever she had and the exhaustion from the near fight at the church. She inched her way up the street, trying to make it back home. She got to her house and collapsed on the steps. She tried to take slow, deep breaths and then jumped and turned sharply when she heard someone coming down the steps on Shay's side. It was only Joe. She lifted her hand in a weak wave. "You scared me, Mr. Joe," she said.

"I'm sorry, sweetheart, and what you doing out here anyhow? Thought you were out for the count earlier."

"I was, but then I woke up and I was looking for, well, first I was looking for Shay, then my mother. It's been a long night, Mr. Joe, I feel like I'm dreaming. Maybe I'm sleep deprived. Were the fireworks good?"

"I, uh, I didn't see them. My stomach's been messed up, I was, uh, just in the house trying to recuperate."

"Well here, Mr. Joe, I almost forgot, you left these when you helped me out earlier. Thanks, by the way."

She reached into the lapel pocket of her pajamas and pulled out the pack of cigarettes and the pink satiny ribbon came out too. The spotlights around the cup-and-saucer ride were turned on full blast and illuminated Neet's hand right then as she extended it to Joe. He looked from her hand to her face and back and made no move toward her hand.

"Well, aren't these yours?" she asked, and then she looked down at her hand and saw the ribbon and was about to say, well, of course the ribbon's not yours, Mr. Joe. But then she couldn't say it because of his expression caught in the revolving bright lights, his face so drained of color suddenly, so pulled back in that instant until it seemed as though she was seeing him through a fun-house mirror and his head was set a yard back from the rest of his body. It was all beginning to click into place: the ribbon, the clothes on the bathroom floor, the thump of the back door closing, the gate left open, him missing the fireworks over some excuse of a stomachache, his expression right now, even his voice that was so dry and strained sounding.

"The cigarettes are mine," he said. "Thank you, Neet. Mnh."

Neet didn't say anything else as he took the pack of cigarettes from her hand. She watched him light a cigarette and take a deep drag and stare off into the lights surrounding the ride. Then he walked down off the steps. She just sat there and held on to the ribbon as its satiny pinkness shocked the night. She wanted to cry again. She was crying, thinking that perhaps her mother had used Mr. Joe the way she'd used Little Freddie, as an attempt to reclaim her goodness. Sobbed at the irony, that her mother's church had never been able to do that, convince her that she was good. Cried now wondering what about her mother's life had been so damaged that she needed that church in the first place. Alberta would never talk about her upbringing, her parents, other than to say that they had both disappeared when she was born. So Neet cried over her mother's past, or rather the absence of it, the fact that it was so horrible that she'd felt the need to try to erase it. Even Neet understood that that was impossible. She pulled the sweater tighter around her shoulders and felt herself going into chills again. Thought she should go back in the house and get under the covers. But she was crying too hard to even pull herself up to standing. Crying so hard that at first she didn't even feel the hands rubbing against the sweater, going up and down her arms, warming her. Didn't even have to look up when she did. Knew these hands, always there for her when she needed them most, since they were babies and they'd reach their hands out to be picked up over the banister so they could be together. Shay's hands these were. Shay, her girl. Her girl, Shay.

Chapter 19

HE FIREWORKS HAD ended. Though the thunder-claps of color generally closed out the block party, the music was flowing again at this end of the block. The mounted police had retreated from their stance on Spruce Street, though they'd left calling cards in the form of horse shit. Murmurs of complaints rippled through the crowd about the white racist pigs trying to crash their party. The James Brown impersonator had taken to the stage again in a glowing orange-sequined pantsuit and high-heeled boots. Somebody yelled, "Hey, where's your cape?" This brought laughter and applause from the crowd. The band leader called back, "Attheend, my man, canwe give thedrummer some, huh!" running his words together so that only every third or fourth one was intelligible. The audience loved it, laughing hysterically. Joe laughed in spite of himself as he moved into the crowd, relieved to see that the cops were leaving. He scanned the crowd for Louise. Saw Valadean and Johnetta,

Johnetta whispering something in Valadean's ear. Valadean put her hand to her mouth as she laughed, and Joe could see that her knuckles were wrapped with gauze. He looked away quickly, his mouth throbbing all over again at the memory of Valadean's fists punching his mouth to a bloody pulp. He spotted Louise then with Maggie, up on Nathina's porch. He wouldn't allow thoughts right now of what he'd just done with Alberta. What he'd just done with Alberta was too complex and he knew he'd grapple with it until his dying day. Joe headed in Louise's direction, weaving through the bodies dancing out here now. Clara grabbed his arm, and before he knew it he was caught in a dance, unable to get through the tight press of bodies. When the song was over and space opened up, he went directly for Nathina's porch. But when he got there, Louise was gone. It felt to Joe as if he was looking at a snapshot where Louise's image had been carefully, meticulously cut away, leaving just the outline of her against the backdrop of Cecil Street.

LOUISE HAD BEEN talking to the man Luther, who had returned to Cecil Street again looking for Deucie. Luther told Louise that he was very attached to Deucie because she reminded him of his mother. "She's prone to headaches," he said, his voice cracking even as he halfway shouted to be heard over the drums and the crowd's enthusiasm for the James Brown impersonator. "Plus, her liver's gone." Louise stood so close to Luther under the archway of Nathina's porch that she could see the sweat glistening on his mustache. She was mesmerized by the scar across his face that hadn't been properly stitched. She was captivated too by the outline of the gun in his waistband, shadowing against his T-shirt.

He was a bad man with his gun and scar and his black, black skin, his heat that Louise could feel moving inside her as they talked. She asked him what hospital should be held responsible for the botched repair job to his face. She was a nurse, she explained, she noticed people's work, that's why she was asking. He said he'd stitched it himself. He told her that if she had some time, he could tell her how he'd gotten his face slit in the first place. Most women couldn't handle the description of how it had happened, he said, but being a nurse and all, he was sure that she could handle it.

Oh, she could definitely handle it, she laughed, as she thought then how easy it would be, given the right set of circumstances, to leave this block of Cecil Street and go home with this Luther, wrap herself around his badness, lose control. She rarely had such thoughts and was getting worked up over this one, squeezing her thighs together, looking right into his eyes that were hard and kind.

"You a pretty lady," he said. "Married?"

She felt her cheeks going hot and flush as she hunched her shoulders, as if to say she didn't know. He raised his eyebrows and started moving his shoulders and his arms and his hips and before she knew it they were dancing on Nathina's porch to the tune of the James Brown impersonator singing out, "I got the feeling, now." Louise snapped her fingers and shimmied around and around as Luther moved into her back and she could feel the butt of his gun brush against her. She raised her arms and hollered, "All right now." She pulled her hair straight up and let it fall back disheveled and wild. Luther had his hand on her waist and she slowed herself so that they were moving in perfect sync. His large hands were callused, she could tell as he pressed them against her lightweight dotted-swiss shirt. She imagined how tender his touch would be as he compensated for his rough skin. By the time the song was over and they laughed together, out of breath, Louise was considering inviting him inside Nathina's house. Who was there to stop her? Maggie certainly wouldn't; Nathina would probably wink her eye. She reached in and touched Luther's scar that was the texture of steak gristle. Thought she would pee on herself when she did, and told him that she could definitely handle the story of his scar. But right then she caught a glimpse of Joe far off in her peripheral vision; she hated that she always knew exactly where Joe was in a crowd, even now when she was allowing a desire for another man to build inside her, she was focusing in on Joe.

Now she had to go to the bathroom, urgently. She asked Luther if he would excuse her for just a minute. She ran into Nathina's house. Barely made it upstairs to the bathroom without wetting herself. Realized then how long she'd been holding in her need to go. Had been holding her water since before she'd even left her house to come down here. Left her house in uncharacteristic disarray because once the house had emptied and the music had stopped, she was frightened by sounds coming up from her basement. For several weeks had been hearing sounds, coming up from the basement but was afraid to go down there until Joe fixed the light switch, afraid there might be rats down there the way that Nathina said there were rats in the apartment above her husband's shop. It dawned on her now that Tim was lying, there were no rats above the shop. Realized now that there were no rats in her basement either. Her head cleared as she peed. Felt the desire for Luther dissipating with the pee. Now she thought about the woman Luther had come here to find.

She washed her hands as she said the name out loud, Deucie. She dried her hands on Nathina's satin-edged hand towel. Then she washed and dried her hands again. Then one more time. Always washed her hands three times when she went to care for the dying. She moved through Nathina's house then, to the back of the house, and left through the back door. Walked quickly through the alley, ducking out of the way of the protruding ivy, taking in the honey-suckle as she turned at the Cyclone fence of her backyard and then to the window that led to her cellar.

The window was open. Louise stooped and pushed her head in and peered through the darkness. Was immediately struck by the smell as she climbed through the window and down into the cellar and followed the odor to the front of the basement, under the steps. Her eyes adjusted to the darkness, her nose to the smell that rose up from the mattress of clothes spread out on the floor. Louise knew the smell of death. Not the smell of death that was antiseptic and cleaned up, neutralized, which she worked around all day long in the hospital. She knew the smell of death when it came into a home where people lived trying to deny its approach. It rose off the skin like a fog in the morning if you were willing to look it in the face, know that this was death and that it was mostly a blessing. She hadn't been able to look at it straight on. She'd cover her face as if she was watching a horror movie, separating her fingers only once in a while to peek through. Though her sister Maggie had tried to prepare her, in her own way. She'd take both Louise's hands in her own and say, Louise, what are we going to do when we have to tell Mother good-bye? Louise would cover her ears then. She was just a little girl, only ten. She couldn't even fathom such a thing.

H ER MOTHER HAD called for her that morning. She had gasped out Louise's name over and over. She was struggling to breathe, Louise could tell by the choking sounds she made, the way she was clutching at her throat as Louise walked into her room that morning. Louise didn't know what to do when she saw her mother flailing about like that. She ran back into her own room and threw herself on the bed and covered her head with the pillow. She stayed like that with the pillow shielding her from those awful gasping sounds for almost an hour. When she unfolded herself from the bed, the house was silent, so still. She went to make her mother's tea then. The tea brewing always calmed her down as she'd sit and watch the leaves turn the water to a greenish brown. The tea seemed to be taking a long time this morning and she kept boiling more water to rush it. Then she went into her mother's room, anxious to see her mother smile the way she always did when Louise brought her morning tea. Mama loves her little helper so, she'd gush.

But no smile greeted Louise this time. Just her mother's eyes, wide open and still. And the stench of death. She thought now as she reversed herself and started walking again through the dark cellar, toward the back window, that it had been the smell that had shocked her and made her hands shake and the teacup rattle around on the saucer, tilting completely, streaming the hot liquid right down her mother's chest, causing her to worry from then on if her mother had felt the tea scald her as she sat propped up against the headboard, already dead.

Louise followed this stench now to the back of the cellar, this stench a mixture of urine and bile, dried blood, sour skin. She was at the window now, the wooden pony under the wide-open window. She hopped up and pushed herself up and out again into the backyard. Light from the alley lamp drizzled down and she could see drops of blood in the yard, like bread crumbs, leading to Alberta's yard. She went into Alberta's yard and up the back steps and knocked. When she didn't get an answer, she pushed through the door and went on in. She alternated between calling for Alberta or Neet as she walked through the kitchen and into the dining room and living room, following the droplets of blood and the occasional spots of watery shit. She caught a whiff of Brut aftershave in the living room, recognized it as such because that's what Joe wore. She called louder as she walked up the stairs, thought she even smelled Joe in the close hallway, shook off the thought because she was at the bedroom door that she guessed must be Alberta's room. She saw a white-robed figure in the center of the bed. Her hands were opening and closing and she was making clucking sounds. Louise could see even from where she was the jaundice that had yellowed her eyes, her skin.

"Deucie?" Louise said as she walked all the way into the room, recognized the robe as her mother's robe that had been packed away so many years ago.

"Alberta?" Deucie replied.

"I'm sorry, no, I'm not Alberta, I'm Louise. I live next door. You must be Alberta's mother, right? Deucie. A man named Luther's been looking for you, Deucie."

"Chile, I know," Deucie said, her voice high like a whistle, slow, as if she was translating her words from a different language as she spoke, and had to first think about the pronunciation. She paused. "But I'm dying," she said, finally.

"I know you are, baby," Louise said. "You want to go to the hospital?"

"Lord, no. Please, no!"

"All right, all right. I can understand that. But I'ma stay here with you till Alberta gets back. I don't know where she is, Neet either. Might have gone to church. I'ma help you though. You don't mind, do you? If I stay right here and help you, maybe soften it for you some?"

Deucie shrugged her shoulders. "You done enough," she said. "Feeding me."

Louise lifted Deucie's hand and held it, taking her pulse as she did. "So you been in my cellar for, what was it? A month?"

"That place sure brought my appetite on."

"You hurting?"

"Not so bad." She motioned then to the spot just above her stomach.

"Cirrhosis?" Louise asked.

Alberta nodded.

Louise put her hand to Deucie's forehead. Then she rubbed her hand down the side of her face, stopping at the gash just below her cheekbone. "You were a fighter, huh?"

"Chile, I kicked some ass in my day," Deucie said.

Louise smiled as she tried to imagine Deucie with clear eyes, a plumpness to her sagging cheeks, her soft gray hair combed out. She told Deucie that a nice sponge bath would help right now.

Deucie had fallen off to sleep by the time Louise was back in the room. She set a pot filled with water on the floor next to the bed and dampened a washcloth and proceeded to wipe the dried mucus from the corners of Deucie's eyes, then moved on to clear away the blood caked under her nose. She gently pulled the robe down from around her shoulders, the bones in her shoulders protruding. By the time she had sponged down her arms, wiping between her fingers, flexing and bending her fingers in a tender massage, Deucie was awake, staring at her, her face softer now after having been cleaned up.

Louise smiled at Deucie. "You and Alberta favor one another," she said. "Y'all both pretty."

"Shit, you crazy," Deucie said, the whistle still in her voice, though her voice had more energy to it now. "Nothing pretty 'bout me."

"You wrong. I bet you had many a man weak in the knees in your day."

"Had 'em doing it on their knees," she said. And Louise could tell that she was trying to laugh though the laugh caught in her throat and she grimaced instead. So Louise squeezed her hand until her face relaxed.

"All right now with your little fresh self," Louise said. "I need to change this water and then turn you over and do your back. Can I trust you to behave while I go get some more water?" She thought Deucie winked as she quickly backed out of the room, flooded suddenly with an intensity of feeling for Deucie.

She sat the pot in the tub and ran the water, then went down the hall to Neet's room looking for a picture of Alberta to show to Deucie. Had already searched Alberta's walls and dresser and seen pictures of Neet at various stages, but none of Alberta. In Neet's room, she opened a heart-shaped photo album with picture after picture of Neet and Shay, Neet and Little Freddie, even Neet and Brownie, but none of Alberta. She noticed Neet's Bible then. There in the inside flap was a yellowed Polaroid of a breathtakingly beautiful woman. Louise gasped because she'd seen this woman before in that foxtail-collared suit that hung off the shoulder. Years ago. She'd not forgotten. How could she ever forget the look on the woman's face that night sitting alone at a table in the back of the club. Louise had wanted to slap that look of heat, of desire, that had come over the woman's face as Joe played his horn. It was that look, that face that convinced Louise that night that Joe would have to put his horn down. Realized that night that she couldn't, wouldn't compete with every pretty woman in a club affected by Joe's playing, allowing their passions to accumulate as he played, showing so shamelessly on their faces what he was doing to them as he played, enticing him, pulling on him with their looks of base desire, calling him away from her. Night after night. That couldn't be her life, she'd decided that night as she'd watched that woman with her shoulders sparkling in the fox-collared suit jacket. No way. He'd have to cut the strap that hung that sax around his neck. Relegate his playing to a hobby instead of a vocation. Pick up the habits of a nine-to-five-type man. The picture shook in her hands as she told herself that no way could this be Alberta, not dowdy, stiff Alberta. She turned the picture over, her eyesight blurring as she took in the words on the back, "Alberta, you are one fine lady. Your Always Friend, Pops."

She swallowed hard as she left Neet's room, trying to submerge the dense compress of emotions expanding and edging up her throat. She wondered if Joe knew Alberta back then, wondered if

Alberta had just been an adoring fan, or someone attached to Joe's emotions.

By the time she was back in the room where Deucie was, Louise wanted to ball the photo up in her hands, but the sight of Deucie softened her. She showed Deucie the picture. "I bet you were prettier even than Alberta in your day," she said as Deucie grabbed for the picture and stared at it, a thin stream of water running from her eyes.

They were both quiet as Louise finished cleaning up Deucie, Deucie watching her intently as she tried to help Louise out by rolling in the direction Louise nudged her. Louise dressed Deucie in a lightweight cotton nightgown from Neet's drawer. Told Deucie it was her granddaughter's. Told her what a lovable child Neet was, smart, honor-roll student, so pleasant to be around, so giving, bright, bright future waiting. She felt a surge of emotion coating her words as she talked about Neet. Telling Deucie now that Neet had been through a trauma recently. Said that she faulted herself partially. Had she only allowed herself to know consciously what she knew deep inside, she could have helped Neet before things got too far gone, taken her to a safe, clean place. "I just pray to God she doesn't suffer permanent damage as a result. She doesn't deserve that." Louise was no longer looking at Deucie, she was looking at Alberta's dresser, the hairnet on the dresser, bothered by the sight of the hairnet, but then she felt Deucie's hand wrap around her wrist, pulling Louise's attention back to her. "She'll heal," Deucie said. "Already has."

Louise felt a great relief opening up in her chest even as she dabbed at the trickles of blood draining from Deucie's nose. Figured that she could trust what Deucie had just said, that Neet would heal. Deucie was too close to death not to know such things.

"Wonder if me and Joe will heal," she said, more to herself than to Deucie.

"Chile, nothing better than loving what you ain't got to own," Deucie replied, eyes closed now, already half asleep.

Louise couldn't tell if Deucie was rambling or if her words meant something. She didn't try to keep her awake and talking to find out. She propped herself up in the bed and listened to Deucie breathe. The room was still and the outside sounds floated up here, the block-party sounds that Louise had been oblivious to once she'd washed her hands in Nathina's bathroom. She focused in now on the scatters of voices, remnants of music, laughter. "Thank you, Jesus," she shouted at the realization that Neet would heal. "Thank you, Lord." She hadn't intended to shout like that, didn't want to pull Deucie from her sleep. Deucie was smiling in her sleep, as if she understood why Louise had just shouted. Louise bent over and kissed Deucie's forehead that smelled now of Ivory soap.

She leaned back against the headboard. Her thoughts bounced around the way they always did when she was about to fall asleep. Thoughts running the gamut from the hairnet on the dresser to the way she'd swung her hips when she danced with Luther, to Neet, to Alberta in that picture. She picked the picture up from the bed where it had fallen from Deucie's hands and propped it up on the nightstand. After all of her cajoling, her sweet persuasion, her turning her dark eyes on and off, teasing one minute, threatening the next, after all of that—the one in the picture had ended up right next door. She had the thought as she drifted off to sleep that maybe Alberta and Joe had run off together. That had been the problem with Joe, or when she thought about it, the problem with her—she'd always been waiting for him to leave her. Always focused on what he was doing. How many of her own years had she lost trying to keep Joe, trying to own Joe.

IT WAS ALMOST dawn and Joe was a wreck not knowing where Louise was. He'd been unable to go to bed, had half slept in the chair by the bedroom window, waking with a start every fifteen minutes, calling for Louise, walking through the house all over again. Nobody else had seemed to be worried about Louise as the block party had finally begun to fizzle out and even the most die-hard dancers had taken to a step, a porch, and finally inside a house. Joe had gone up and down the block and around the corner. Went to Nathina's and Joyce's and Clara's, Johnetta's, BB's. Each time he came back to his own house praying for Louise to be here but was met with her absence, her absence shuttling his emotions from concern to the near hysteria he was feeling now. Shay and Neet were each curled up in a chair in the living room, having reunited on the porch with a crying then a laughing fest, joined by Maggie later. Maggie, snoring openmouthed now on the couch, a half-empty bottle of Manischewitz Concord grape on the floor next to her bag; wine-stained shot glasses next to the chairs where Neet and Shay slept. Joe would ordinarily have been amused by such a scene, but now the scene made Louise's absence all the more stark. He picked up the phone to call the police, then put it down, strangled by the thought that Louise might have left him. He walked through the house one more time just to make sure she hadn't come in. His horn was sitting in the high-backed corner chair where he'd left it after he'd played last night. Played last night really for Alberta. "What have I done?" he said out loud as he picked up the horn and put the strap around himself, and walked out onto the porch. "Damn, what I have done. Awl man, what have I done?"

Daylight was organizing itself over Cecil Street in layers of royal blue and red and orange and pink. Joe stood on his porch and put his horn to his mouth. He played tenuously at first, trying not to cry as he realized that he'd never done this before. Played for Louise. He'd played for his dead father and sister and mother, played for the Pittsburgh he'd left years ago, played for Alberta, played for the many nameless women who'd sit front and center during his shows, played for Cecil Street and the surrounding blocks that could likely hear him when he played. But he'd never played for Louise. He did now. Begged as he played that she'd come back. Swore his love as he played. Asked her forgiveness as he played. Didn't know he had the song in him that he now played. A song of his own creation. It was wide and beautiful and just for Louise. Right now he played for Louise.

Louise was coming to from the surprisingly deep sleep she'd fallen into propped up in the bed next to Deucie. Deucie was still asleep, still alive, though Louise could hear the phlegm attached to her breathing now, the death rattle. She tiptoed to the hallway and cocked her ear. The house was still. No Alberta yet. Wondered where Alberta could be. She started for downstairs to get salt so she could rinse out her mouth. Then stopped because she thought she heard a horn playing. A saxophone. Couldn't be. But there it was. Had to be Joe. Was he crazy? Out on the porch this time of morning playing his horn. She ran back into the bedroom certain that the sound of the horn would rouse Deucie. It did, and now Louise was already planning how she was going to bang that fucking horn like it was a tin can. Deucie sat straight up then. Her shoulders were squared and her head was high. Louise thought she should be too weak to hold herself erect like that. She was pulling at her neck as if she was trying to speak. Louise put her ear in close so she could hear what Deucie was trying to say. "What is it, sweetheart?" Louise asked.

"Alberta? That you, Alberta?" The whistle was gone from her voice, not enough air for a whistle now.

Louise nodded, her eyes misting over as Deucie took in her face.

"You—really made—you softened it—" she said, breaking between her words to try to breathe. "And—and Gab—? Gabriel's horn?"

Louise nodded again as she lightly rubbed Deucie's hands. "Yeah, sweetheart, that's Gabriel's horn," she said.

"Blow for me, baby," Deucie said. "Yeah, Gabriel, yeah."

Louise felt a breeze then that seemed to start at the bottom of the nightgown that Deucie wore. She watched the breeze gently ripple up the gown and then onto Deucie's face, tilting her chin like a lover seeking a kiss, opening her eyes all the way, moving through her hair like the swipe of a wide-tooth comb. And just like that, Deucie was gone. Louise drew her hands over Deucie's eyes to close them. She rubbed Deucie's hand even as the warmth was leaving the top of her skin. She rubbed her hand and cried. Cried finally. Finally, cried. She listened to Joe play as she cried. Allowed Joe's playing to move inside her. She'd never allowed herself to really listen to him before. Such a nice backdrop his playing was now to this room crowded with the angels guiding Deucie home.

She cried now over how beautiful it was, his playing, Deucie's passing. How big. Thought now that she could forgive almost anything from a man who knew to blow his horn at the exact moment when it had the power to soften death. She cried now like she'd been meant to cry over the years since her own mother had died, but never could. Now she could.

She sat with Deucie and cried until Deucie's skin started to cool, until the angels left the room, as Maggie would say, until she heard Joe calling for her. His voice fading in and out as he walked up and down Cecil Street calling her name. Louise dialed for the medical examiner and then went home.

JOE'S PLAYING MUST have wakened the block, Louise thought, because it was more like five in the evening and not the morning out here. Chatter jumped over the banisters from end to end about how last night's had been the best block party ever. Assemblages gathered in the street now to bag the trash and hose down under the rides with water and bleach. Louise stepped over the banister and onto her porch and into the living room to the sight of three beautiful sleeping lumps. Maggie on the couch, and Shay and Neet each in a chair. Louise just stood there and took in the scene, wondering how they'd slept through Joe's horn playing just now. As if on cue, Shay sprang suddenly awake. She almost knocked Louise over the way she ran for her and jumped on her and hugged her and asked her where had she been. "God, Mom, Dad was going crazy, and me and Aunt Maggie and Bonita were even getting worried."

Louise buried her chin in the softness of Shay's 'fro and told her it was such a long story. They should wake up Neet, she whispered. She'd been next door caring for Neet's grandmother who'd just died. Maybe Neet knew where Alberta was. Did Neet say last night where her mother might be?

Shay shook her head, stunned. "Neet's grandmother died?" Then she started to cry.

Joe blasted through the front door like a gunshot then, calling out Louise's name. He dropped his saxophone from around his neck when he saw Shay standing there crying. "Louise, don't, please don't," he said, thinking that Louise had just told Shay that she was leaving. He pulled her into the barricade he made with his arms, held her there as he begged her to stay. "Please, Louise, stay. Please. Stay."

Louise didn't say anything. She let Joe hold her. Remnants of his Brut aftershave still clung to the space under his neck. And something else. The smell of leather and brass and mint. The way he'd always smell after he'd just done a show and she would breathe in his essence, trying to pick up another woman's scent. Trying to figure out why he looked so drained in a satisfied way, as if he'd just prayed and seen God. Only knew of one thing that made a man look that way. She gobbled up the smell now, understood it now. Just his breaths, that's all. His breaths transformed in the notes he played, changing him. This time, changing her too.

Chapter 20

LBERTA LEFT CECIL STREET that block-party night. The decent thing to do, she reasoned, considering how she'd used Joe to break her out of her skid, veer her off into the opposite direction so that she could ultimately right herself. Could not, would not continue to live next door to Joe after the way they'd exploded the air in her basement. So she left Cecil Street when the party was at its height. She went back downtown to the house where she was raised, Pat's Place. She sat on the front steps and took in the scent of the hydrangeas blooming in the garden. She thought about what she would do now without the dictates of her church directing her path. She sat on the steps and thought and cried and prayed and dreamed. When the first signs of daylight began to sift overhead, she let herself into the house and tiptoed past the second floor where the renters lived. Up to the third floor, which had been unoccupied for years and years. She'd been the last one to live up here. She pushed open the door on the empty room. The air in the room was musty and close. She lifted the window high and waved her hands to hurry in the fresh air, to make the air in here breathable. This would be her bedroom again. She'd give the renters notice and let Neet have the second floor. Enough rooms down there for Neet's sleepover company to stay. She thought she might turn the basement into an apartment, rent it out and bring in enough to keep the real estate taxes paid. But who knew, down the road she might want that space for a playroom for the children Neet would one day have.

A breeze rode in through the open window. It carried the scent of the hydrangeas blooming in the garden out front as it rippled through the room, mixing in now, she noticed, with a smell like soap, Ivory, she thought. Alberta tilted her head to the ceiling and allowed the soap-scented breeze to move on through her. It felt like new life coming, this breeze, like possibilities. She spread her arms out and arched her back and hung there on the breeze as it wrapped her up and held her.

THOUGH ALBERTA LEFT Cecil Street that night, this time Cecil Street didn't leave her. They streamed in and out of the house downtown where she was living now to console her, to bring her food, to help her clean, to help her move. They understood her tearful reluctance to come back to Cecil Street given the circumstances of her mother's death, her mother dying in her bed like that. Johnetta said Neet could stay with her until Alberta's renters moved, though of course Shay's house was the most logical. So Neet ended up splitting her time between Shay's and her mother's third floor. As much as she loved Shay, Neet needed to be with Alberta when nighttime fell. Johnetta organized a grand repast to follow Deucie's funeral service. Nathina had secured their Baptist church for the occasion and a steady stream of mourners stood in line to get a glimpse of the woman who'd lived in Joe and Louise's cellar for a month just so she could get close to her daughter before she died.

C ECIL STREET RETURNED to the way it used to be after they buried Deucie. Though different too. The tree-lined block was still a pleasure to walk through as the little girls jumped double Dutch to the beat. Tim never could get rid of those rats, and Clara still opened extra early on Saturdays to fry and clip and color and curl some hair. There was still a good card game to be had at Pinochle Eddie's. The Corner Boys were still a trifling lot except when they graced the block with their evening songs and everybody paused, connected for the moments while the a cappella melodies held. The youngsters were still growing their 'fros and talking of revolution and power to the people and to be young gifted and black. And Louise's dentures were finally ready, her smile taking over a room again.

But it was different now too because Joe was blowing his horn. He'd stand out on his porch in the mellow warmth of a summer night after the Corner Boys were done. He'd transform his breaths and reconcile his past in the notes he played. The music was so pleasing to the ear. And to the heart. Where it all went anyhow, he thought, once you brought it on home.

Insights,
Interviews
& More . . .

About the author

About the book

Read on

Diane McKinney-Whetstone

Bill Cardoni

Meet
Diane McKinney-Whetstone

DIANE MCKINNEY-WHETSTONE is the author of the nationally acclaimed bestselling novel *Tumbling*. She also wrote *Tempest Rising*, published in 1998, and *Blues Dancing*, published in 1999.

A native Philadelphian, Diane's father served two terms as a Pennsylvania state senator in the 1970s. Diane grew up in a close-knit family with five sisters and one brother, attended public schools and graduated from the University of Pennsylvania in 1975 with a bachelor's degree in English. She has been a contributor to *Philadelphia* magazine. Her work has appeared in *Essence* and the *Sunday Philadelphia Inquirer* magazine, and the anthology *The Bluelight Corner: Black Women Writing on Passion, Sex, and Romantic Love*.

She teaches fiction writing at her alma mater, the University of Pennsylvania. She lives in Philadelphia with her husband, Greg. They are the parents of twentysomething twins, a son and a daughter. ∾

How I Came to Write
Leaving Cecil Street
"The Promise of Place"

WHEN I BEGIN A NOVEL I know very little of the story: the characters are merely sensations, the plot not even a sigh. What I do know, however, in sometimes startling detail, is the world—the place—of the story. I'll sometimes write pages and pages evoking the smells and colors and eccentricities of the place. What is its emotional content? Does the air whistle or bounce as it moves on through the place, or does it sag? I'll get inside the place through the writing and live there for sometimes weeks before the characters emerge. While writing *Leaving Cecil Street* . . . I was on that block. I could hear the smack of the double Dutch rope and Joe's saxophone. I could smell the dinner aromas through the cracked kitchen windows and the hair sizzling in the hot combs. Before I was aware of the characters' identities, the core of who they were to become was already inextricably fused with the block. For me character grows from place. . . . The two develop a symbiotic relationship so that the more I know of the world I'm creating, the more sharply drawn the characters become. And as the characters begin to breathe and live in the world, as they evolve, the place reacts in kind. *Leaving Cecil Street* took five years to write, partly because, in early drafts of the novel, I was attempting to discover the story through characters alone. I was setting the characters in a contemporary venue—a middle-aged woman remembering a summer of her teen years on a close-knit Philadelphia block—yet I couldn't feel her ▶

> ❝ While writing *Leaving Cecil Street* . . . I could smell the dinner aromas through the cracked kitchen windows and the hair sizzling in the hot combs. ❞

How I Came to Write *Leaving Cecil Street*
(*continued*)

contemporary world, her place. She lived in a
big suburban house on a private road that I
could describe well enough, but it had no
atmosphere, no emotional leaning. As a result,
the character never really came to life for me.
Significant portions of the story, however,
were extended flashbacks to her teen years
on Cecil Street. It was not just her story then,
it was a community's story. The block
was the world, and then I was thoroughly
engaged with the material. The story came
to life with energy and color and sound.
After several years and drafts of trying to
get the contemporary parts to at least come
close to the engagement I felt on that block,
I realized I had to let go of the middle-aged
woman and push the entire story on Cecil
Street circa 1969. I yielded to the promise
of place.

Diane McKinney-Whetstone
Philadelphia, PA
September 2004

> 66 The block
> was the world,
> and then I was
> thoroughly
> engaged with the
> material. The
> story came to
> life with energy
> and color and
> sound. 99

4

Q&A with **Diane McKinney-Whetstone**

Your debut, Tumbling, *was received with extremely high praise, earning rave reviews as well as a comparison to the work of Toni Morrison. Did you find it hard to live up to these expectations as a writer and did you feel pressure while writing your second novel,* Tempest Rising?

Yes, I felt tremendous pressure. *Tempest Rising* was a difficult book to write because *Tumbling* had been so well received. With *Tumbling* I had no deadline, no conception of an audience waiting for the book, no thought of sales and marketing and tours, no fears of being a one-book wonder. And though my editor insisted over and over that it was her job to consider the marketing aspects, that my only obligation was the story, I still had to work very hard to distance myself from those considerations so that I could reclaim the magic that was always with me during the writing of the first novel. I felt a tremendous sense of accomplishment when I completed the second novel.

> " I still had to work very hard to distance myself from those considerations so that I could reclaim the magic that was always with me during the writing of the first novel. "

A backroom abortion plays a central role in Leaving Cecil Street. *Why did you choose to write about abortion?*

I actually did not plan to write about abortion. I generally begin my novels with a place, ▶

> As the block came more in focus I was able to peek in between the Venetian blinds and see the secrets living inside the houses.

an atmosphere, the shadowed frames of one or two characters. The story follows from that. The story of *Leaving Cecil Street* began with the flashback to the block, the rhythms and clatter, the shade trees, the cherry ice, the corner boys singing a capella as the sun set. As the block came more in focus I was able to peek in between the Venetian blinds and see the secrets living inside the houses. When I first realized that Neet, one of the main characters, a teenager with a bright future, was pregnant, I was not sure how it would play out. Would she terminate the pregnancy or not? Run away? Get married? But once I started writing that abortion scene—man, that scene just rumbled out of me and caught me by surprise. I was out of breath after I wrote it as if I'd run a marathon. It was as if everything I knew about writing had come together on the page before me. My best writing happens like that and I wish I knew exactly what to do to hurry it along, or make it happen more often. So, though I didn't plan to write about a backroom abortion, I went with it because it works in the context of that block. Women of my generation perhaps know people who've had what we called backroom abortions. Perhaps younger women who take their right to choose for granted might get a glimpse of how it could be if they suddenly no longer had a choice—which could happen. But the abortion theme came out of the story, the story unplanned, emerging and catching me by surprise as I went along.

What message do you hope readers will take with them after reading Leaving Cecil Street?

Well, certainly I hope that people take with them the beauty, the closeness, of this block. . . . So much is made of the negative aspects of African American communities— the crime, the drugs, the poverty—and I am not suggesting that those conditions do not exist, particularly when communities do not benefit from basic services because those services are deployed to more well-heeled sections of a city, but all over the country there have been African American communities that thrive, that are desirable places to live.

I hope that people also take something from the story about the nature and degrees of right and wrong. That what may appear to be the worst thing a person could do, could actually be less so when one considers the intentions behind the act.

Are any of the characters in Leaving Cecil Street *based on people whom you know or have known?*

Not really. I knew people who got pregnant young, but in my day you got married or were sent to live with relatives down south. There were always a group of boys singing love songs on some corner steps, always one person on the block whom everybody else gossiped about, always some child who had to go to church *all* the time. So in terms of broad characteristics, yes, I borrow liberally from what was. The characters ▶

> ❝ I hope that people take with them the beauty, the closeness, of this block . . . all over the country there have been African American communities that thrive, that are desirable places to live. ❞

themselves, though, get so filtered through my imagination, changed so from their original rendering, that had they started off as a real person, they'd probably be unrecognizable by the end.

Leaving Cecil Street *was five years in the making. What was the writing process like for this novel? What are your rules for writing? What are your inspirations?*

September 11 happened during the writing of this novel and, for a time, everything I wrote felt so small, so trivial, until I was able again to connect with what is important in my work: the universality of human connectedness, of suffering or joy, the nature of compassion, betrayal, redemption. I had many starts and stops with this novel, many revisions.

My only rule for writing is that I begin early. I have access to imaginative powers at five in the morning that I just can't tap into at noon. This doesn't mean that I don't work later in the day, just that I do a different type of writing, more logical and sequential.

I'm sometimes inspired by music, jazzy ballads are nice, a good horn sound. Other times it's by being up close with people I don't know. I lived out of the city for a while and spent a lot of time in the car. After I moved back to Philly I realized that I missed the way the city forces you into spaces with strangers, on busses and trains, for example,

66 My only rule for writing is that I begin early. I have access to imaginative powers at five in the morning that I just can't tap into at noon. 99

when you can watch people for the length of the ride, see what happens to their face when they laugh or frown, notice the pattern of their wrinkles. I walk a lot more now and hear snatches of conversations; the rhythms and inflections of human speech are fascinating. You miss that in a car.

All four of your novels are set between the 1940s and 1970s. What is your affinity with these eras?

I wish I knew. This novel started off actually set in contemporary times with extended flashbacks to Cecil Street. Except that the block and the era were much more exciting to me than the frame at the beginning and end set in the present. My editor agreed. I think that when writing about the past I'm forced to use my imagination more, not to settle for chronicling how things are today but to see it first as a blur, and then through sharpening the image allow a story to unfold. I'm working on my next novel that also seems to be set in the present . . . we'll see.

I imagine that it is a tough balancing act being a writer, mother, wife, and teacher. What are the biggest challenges you face or have faced?

Time, time, time. When I'm in the intensive phase of writing, when the deeper meanings of the story are beginning to emerge and the characters have taken on lives of their own, I'm almost always in that world, or at least want to be. This was a particular challenge ▶

> " I walk a lot more now and hear snatches of conversations; the rhythms and inflections of human speech are fascinating. "

❝ When I'm really into the deepest phases of the writing … life gets messy because the story takes me over. I've accepted the reality of that, perhaps even the necessity. ❞

Q&A with Diane McKinney-Whetstone
(continued)

when my children were younger. I have to confess that much of our quality time was spent with me reading portions of the novel to them *and* soliciting their input.

I find it difficult to get a lot of writing done while I'm teaching, so I just teach one semester a year. But when I'm really into the deepest phases of the writing, I don't answer the phone or e-mail; I rely on my husband to relay important information. Life gets messy because the story takes me over. I've accepted the reality of that, perhaps even the necessity.

How do your own life experiences influence your novels?

My life experiences influence my worldview, and it is that view that falls onto the page naturally, without any effort on my part.

What made you start writing?

Writing was always something I knew I did well. I was raised to believe that everybody had a special talent. I don't sing or dance or draw or paint. It was writing, or why was I born? Yet I was years and years coming to fiction writing. I was approaching a big birthday and doing the life-evaluating thing people do as they enter a new decade. I'd always told myself that at some point

I would write fiction but I kept putting it off because I simply did not have the time. I realized that if I didn't at least attempt it, at that point, I never would, and that it would be a regret that would eat at me from then on. Once I became conscious of the urgency, it actually took more effort to continue deferring the writing. I started by waking up a couple of hours early each morning. That became my magic time. It still is. ～

> 66 I realized that if I didn't at least attempt it, at that point, I never would, and that it would be a regret that would eat at me from then on. 99

Enter the World of
Diane McKinney-Whetstone's
Philadelphia

Blues Dancing

McKinney-Whetstone's strength is apparent in all her work.... Her novels have a page-turning quality, long the most overlooked skill in novel writing. *Blues Dancing* is McKinney-Whetstone's most writerly novel to date.

—*Philadelphia Weekly*

Blues Dancing fuses past and present, character and place with a transfixing lyricism that shimmers in its detail. A richly spun story of love, passion, betrayal, and redemption, *Blues Dancing* grapples with the meaning of faith, forgiveness, and familial bonds in a narrative that moves seamlessly between the Philadelphia of contemporary times and the city in the early 1970s. Verdi, the pampered daughter of a Southern preacher, comes to Philadelphia in the 1970s to enroll at the University and is immediately drawn to Johnson, a University student as well, though a city boy, poor and militant. Their differences seal their hearts to each other until Johnson teaches her the one thing that will change her life forever—how to love heroin. Enter Rowe, the conservative professor who rescues Verdi from her ugly addiction even as he falls in love with her himself, leaving his sophisticated wife for this very confused Southern girl. As the novel opens, Verdi and Rowe have been living a comfortable existence for the past twenty years—she is the newly appointed principal at a school for special learners, but she feels her world teeter off balance when she unpins a note from the blouse of her most precious student, the daughter of a cousin whom she is close to, and learns that Johnson is back in town. Once Verdi and Johnson lay eyes on each other they know that the years have not dulled their passions and they skid uncontrollably toward the desires of their youth.

Tumbling

"Even the air is palpable in *Tumbling* ....
The story moves forth on the power of Ms. McKinney-Whetstone's characters. Ms. McKinney-Whetstone captures the formidable struggle to protect both a community and a family."
—*New York Times Book Review*

Set in south Philadelphia during the 1940s and 1950s, *Tumbling* combines the mood of an urban community with the vitality of its inhabitants to tell a story in which sorrow and joy come in equal measure. At the heart of the story are Herbie and Noon, who care deeply for each other but have been unable to ▶

66 Even the air is palpable in *Tumbling* ....
99

TOUCHSTONE
A Division of Simon & Schuster
A VIACOM COMPANY
ISBN 0-684-83724-2

consummate their marriage because of a vicious sexual attack in Noon's past. While Noon finds comfort and solace in her church, club-hopping Herbie finds friendship and sexual gratification with a jazz singer named Ethel. Herbie and Noon are then blessed with daughters when, on two separate occasions, the children are left on their doorstep. On the advice of the community, they take the children into their home, where the girls become inseparable, as if blood sisters. But when a devastating city proposal threatens to put a road through the area, the community must pull together to avoid being pulled apart.

Tempest Rising

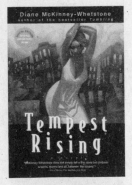

"McKinney-Whetstone solidifies her position as a writer of well-crafted, serious popular fiction.... McKinney-Whetstone is masterful at rendering the spaces between people, giving to the air that separates them a taste, a texture, a soul."

—*Philadelphia Inquirer*

Tempest Rising, set in west Philadelphia in the early 1960s, tells the story of three sisters, Bliss, Victoria, and Shern. They are budding adolescents raised in a world of financial privilege among the black upper-class, but their lives quickly unravel as their father's lucrative catering business collapses. He disappears and is presumed dead, and their mother suffers an apparent breakdown.

The girls are wrenched from their mother, and as the novel opens they are living in foster care in a working-class neighborhood in the home of Mae, a politically connected card shark, who is filled with syrupy sweetness for the foster girls but is abusive to her own child, Ramona, a twenty-something stunning beauty. As Ramona struggles with Mae's abuse and her own hatred for the foster children, she also tries to keep at bay a powerful attraction she has for her boyfriend's father. ∾

66 It's been said that Diane McKinney-Whetstone writes 'like Toni Morrison.' That's not true. McKinney-Whetstone writes like herself. She creates a unique, believable black middle-class world where there are no villains—just individuals trying their very best to get through life while inflicting minimum pain on each other, or themselves. . . . The thing about these characters is, they show up for life. They don't leave. These people are flawed, human, engaging in the best sense. Outside of the troubles, it must have been so much fun growing up on Cecil Street. 99

—*Washington Post*

Mood Music
While Reading
Leaving Cecil Street

Carmen McCrae and Cal Tjader/*Heat Wave*

Sarah Vaughan/*The Quintessence*

Miles Davis/*Sketches of Spain*

Taj Mahal/*Mo' Roots*

Dianne Reeves/ "My Funny Valentine"

John Coltrane/*A Love Supreme*

Louis Armstrong/*The Best of the Decca Years*

Lou Rawls/*Lou Rawls Live*

Don't miss the next book by your favorite author. Sign up now for AuthorTracker by visting www.AuthorTracker.com.